WELL AND TRULY PUCKED

LAUREN BLAKELY

Happy pucking!

Lauren B

XOXO

Dear Marah,

Happy packing!

Jennel

xoxo

COPYRIGHT

ABOUT THE BOOK

I swear I only asked *one* hot hockey-playing friend to give me romance lessons for the week, but *three* hockey stars volunteered...

The post breakup plan was simple – escape from my toxic ex to a vacation rental and stay far away from men.

But thanks to a booking snafu I'm accidentally sharing it with three hot hockey players. **One's flirty, one's broody, one's a cheeky Brit,** and they're all the most attentive men I've ever met.

After a couple of glasses of champagne, I'm telling them about the contest my ex is running on his dating advice web site. The topic? What makes a great boyfriend, and I want to submit a column.

All three offer to show me *every single thing* I've been missing in and out of bed.

We make a deal for one week only. It's only for revenge, of course. I work for the other hockey team in the city so it'd be a big mistake to truly get involved with a rival, let alone *three.*

Even though I **melt** under their touch. They show me what it means to be adored, cherished and *romanced.*

But as the week ticks on, what started as revenge fast turns into me giving my heart to three men I can't have. Looks like I'm **well and truly pucked.**

For Sharon, the hockey goddess. You were right. It's the best game.

DID YOU KNOW?

To be the first to find out when all of my upcoming books go live click here!

PRO TIP: Add lauren@laurenblakely.com to your contacts before signing up to make sure the emails go to your inbox!

Did you know this book is also available in audio and paperback on all major retailers? Go to my website for links!

For content warnings for this title, go to my site.

WELL AND TRULY PUCKED

By Lauren Blakey
My Hockey Romance Book #4
A Why Choose Friends-to-Lovers Spicy Hockey Rom-
Com

1

HE STOLE MY CAT

Briar

"I can't believe you told your new girlfriend she can have *my* cat!" I'm still seeing red but try to dodge past my newly minted ex-boyfriend and slide into that sliver of space where the door's still open, but the jerk slams the door shut before I can answer the call of the meow.

"Madison really bonded with her, and she's always loved silver tabbies," Steven the Cat Burglar says, unrepentant in his thievery.

"Oh well, since Madison likes her, it's just *fine!*"

My sarcasm is lost on him since he says, "Yeah, Madison's great. It's so cute how they love on each other. Madison said to tell you she'll take great care of the kitty."

Like *his* word means anything while I'm standing outside my apartment—correction: my former apartment—with all my things stuffed into garbage bags.

Except my dog, Donut, who's at my feet, side-eyeing Steven.

"You can't just take my cat when you kick me out for no reason," I say, livid and exasperated. I've been trying to reason with him since I returned from a trip thirty minutes ago to the biggest surprise of my twenty-six years of life.

Donut barks, backing me up.

But Steven tilts his head, his perfectly gelled black hair not moving an inch, a placating smile on his I-know-best face. "I explained what happened. It wasn't really *no* reason."

I hold up a hand, my jaw ticking. "I don't need to hear it again."

"I understand you're hurt. It'll take some time," he says, all smooth and calm, like I'm just some irate advertiser with his man's man dating advice website rather than the girlfriend he kicked out because he fell into a whirlwind romance in one freaking week while I was out of town. "But someday you'll understand that you'll do just about anything for love."

"Including stealing," I sputter, then gesture wildly to all my things. "It's bad enough you threw all my things out like garbage to move her in while I was at a conference."

"Briar, calm down. Those are *lawn and leaf* bags, and I bought the extra-strength ones just for this."

"Well, that makes *all* the difference," I say, rolling my eyes.

He pats my shoulder. I jerk away, Donut moving

with me. She never liked him. I should have trusted her. Dogs always know best.

"Maybe you need to *do* more downward dog rather than trying to make a business from your little hobby," he says.

That's it. Red billows from my eyes. *This guy.* What did I ever see in him?

"It's not a hobby. It's my business," I say as I tie up the ends of one of the bags.

"Sure, sure. I bet your little yoga fitness app will go big and then you'll be able to get another cat," he says with a slick smile, and glances at his watch, then to the bags littering the hall in his apartment building in Russian Hill. The one he moved me into four months ago when he fell into a whirlwind romance with *me*. When he told me I was special. When he said he'd never felt this way before. Now, those bags are filled with my underwear, leggings, and books.

It's official. I have the worst taste in men in the history of the world.

While I knot the final garbage bag, I race through options to get the cat myself. Maybe I can pick the lock since he told me he's already changed them.

He clears his throat. "Do you need my help to get them in your car before I pick Madison up from her life coaching session?"

Seriously? He met someone else, screwed her, moved her in while I was gone, kicked me out, and thinks I want his help?

I tie the knot tighter and shoot death rays at him

from my eyes. "There is absolutely nothing I need from you. Except MY CAT!"

Adjusting the cuffs on his purple paisley dress shirt, he nods toward the door to my former home. "Let's go before you make a scene, Bri."

Maybe that's the trick. He always did hate scenes. I could shout and let the neighbors know what he did when I remember...*the balcony.*

My lips threaten to curve up in a grin. But I fight off my evil genius-ery.

He's leaving, and Madison's not here, which means the apartment is empty except for...my cat.

"Of course," I say, doing a one-eighty and flashing a grin. I wind Donut's leash around my wrist, hoist two bags on one shoulder, and drag the other down the hall.

Bump, bump, bump.

Then the steps.

To the front door while Steven holds it open for me. Like that's gentlemanly. "There. Told you I'd help."

"You're so generous," I lie, faking a smile as he heads to his sleek SUV parked at the curb. He hops in, waving goodbye.

My smile burns off.

And I hustle. With Donut trotting on her tiny Dachshund legs, we race to my little car in the parking lot. I load the garbage bags into the backseat and set Donut in the front. "Be a good girl," I tell my rescue pup as I crack the window a little for her.

She barks back a yes. I grab my backpack from the floor of the car and dump the contents of it on the seat, assessing the inside of it. "This'll fit a cat," I say, determination powering me on as I slide the pack onto my shoulders.

I shut the passenger door, rush over to the side of the building, and crane my neck. Steven's on the second floor. That balcony is about ten feet high. There's a cat door right over there. I'm limber. I can wiggle into it and rescue my girl.

There's no time to waste. I jump.

Um, was that a one-foot jump?

I squat, then push off again, blasting up...a foot and a half.

Why didn't I pursue gymnastics?

But all I have to do is get a good boost. I pace around the parking lot, hunting for anything. A chair. A table. A suitcase.

Yes, a suitcase!

I rush back to my car, pop the trunk, and grab my carry-on, hauling it back to beneath the balcony. I step up on it and try again.

And I'm still a foot away.

I hunt through the lot, spotting a...garden gnome by a storage shed.

Desperate times...I grab the red and green dude that's about a foot wide and rush back. I set it on its side on the suitcase and climb my makeshift step stool under the balcony.

I jump again. My arm gets maybe a foot away from my goal.

Okay, almost there. That's half a foot. I need a bit more boost.

Books!

Back to the car. I yank open the backseat door, grab several paperbacks my book club friends gave me, and run.

"It's for a good cause," I tell the books, then I spread them on top of the suitcase, set the gnome on its side on the books, and step onto its red concrete ass.

I give it everything I've got.

And a few seconds later, I'm dangling from the balcony by one arm.

2

SAVE THE CAT

Rhys

I almost want to lose a hockey game so the three of us can stop eating sushi.

Almost.

I've had raw fish far too much over the last two weeks of wins, and Gavin's superstitions are just about killing my love of dragon rolls.

"I'm just saying, I don't reckon it would ruin our streak if we ate curry. Or Thai. Or a fucking sandwich now and then," I point out as we walk through Russian Hill with—surprise, surprise—sushi leftovers in a small paper bag. The regular crew went to the same sushi place tonight following an afternoon victory. Gavin, Hollis, and me. *Again.*

"Don't mess with a streak, man," Gavin says, implacable in his superstitions.

"But you change your socks, right?" Hollis asks with genuine curiosity.

"I'm not a savage," Gavin answers, but the question gives me an idea—a new tactic I mull briefly as we turn onto Polk Street, since we're going to do a walk-by of a building we're thinking of buying some rental property in.

I turn to Gavin, meeting his stoic gaze. "That's a fair point. Do you truly think the thing we eat *after* a win contributes to the streak?"

Before Gavin can even speak, Hollis brings a hand to his forehead, like I've blown his mind. Good. We don't call Hollis the *Magician* for nothing. He can work his magic on our broody teammate with his charm.

"Rhys has got you there," Hollis says, revving himself up apparently as he makes the case. "Now, if we were eating sushi *before* a game, maybe that'd be what caused the streak." He snaps his fingers. "Hey, idea. And this is borderline brilliant. But what if we tested the Viscount's theory by getting fish tacos *before* the next home game?"

Hollis has been calling me that since I joined the team. He decided I'm secretly royal on account of being from London, and I don't dispel him of that notion. As for his proposal, that's still a lot of seafood, but tacos are tacos, and at least it *might* set Gavin free of his streak superstitions.

"I'd be amenable," I put in, like I wasn't trying to architect this in the first place.

But Gavin scowls, his motorcycle boots clomping

against the sidewalk. He's as good at scowling as he is at blocking shots. "Too risky."

Of course it wouldn't be that easy to move a brick wall. "So is too much of a good thing," I add as we near the building we're meaning to check out.

"Like winning?" Gavin retorts, but the question dies when we reach the parking lot, his gaze snapping instantly to the far end. "Is that woman doing parkour off her balcony or is she trying to break into an apartment?"

At the end of the second-story row of apartments, a blonde woman is gripping the bars of the railing and trying, but failing, to hoist herself *American Ninja Warrior* style onto the balcony.

She's wearing pink yoga pants, bright white sneakers, and a mint green cropped hoodie. Her long, sleek ponytail is poised high on her head, and a purple backpack is looped over her shoulders. Granted, I don't keep up on the latest fashion trends among robbers, but I'd have figured head-to-toe black and perhaps a beanie in the same shade would be suitable if she were nicking something.

"Maybe she was locked out of her place," I posit.

As she tries to swing her other foot up onto the ledge, scrabbling for purchase, something about her form feels familiar. Like I've seen that ass before. Where though?

"We should stop her...or help," Gavin adds.

It clicks. She's not a random woman. She's someone we all know. "That's Briar."

The bright, upbeat, confident yoga teacher whose

classes I go to as religiously as a man can. Well, it feels pretty fucking religious the way she downward dogs.

Hollis smacks my arm, recognition clearly dawning for him too. "Dude, you're right," he says, since he's friendly with her as well. She used to teach classes for our team before the rival Sea Dogs lured her away.

I don't know who takes off first, but in no time, the three of us are jogging across the lot, heading straight for her.

"New workout, Briar? Or are you trying to break into your boyfriend's place?" Hollis asks.

Boyfriend's place? I guess he knows a little more about her than I'd realized, but he's been with the team longer. He's also the most social cat I know.

"Ex," she huffs out, hanging in a U like a monkey, but her hands look dangerously close to slipping.

Without a second thought, I step under her, reach for her waist. "Let go. I'll catch you."

With an aggrieved sigh, she drops into my arms for a quick second before I set her down on her feet right next to a suitcase loaded with several pink, pastel blue, and ruby red paperbacks, as well as a dastardly looking gnome. There's a story here, all right.

"What the hell is going on, Pretzel?" Hollis asks with friendly concern. And they're even close enough for a nickname.

She smooths a hand down her front, sighing again. "The world's worst boyfriend met another woman while I was away for a week. Moved her in, tossed me out, and stole my cat. Now I need to steal her back. But the only way I can get her is to go through that pet door, and they could be back any minute," she says, then points to the balcony. "And I've been trying for twenty minutes to climb up there. I'm totally desperate."

I step back, surveying the wooden balcony with an Adirondack chair and a grill. For fuck's sake, that barbecue is against the fire code. The scofflaw.

But that's not why I say the next thing.

I say the next thing because she's Briar, I'm a little into her, and I'm very good at fixing things.

"We'll help save your cat."

3

THE PLAN

Gavin

Of course Rhys has a plan. He's a center on the second line for the Golden State Foxes, so he's a key playmaker.

With dark, assessing eyes he scans the deck, the parking lot, then the three of us, before saying decisively, "We need a lookout, a boost, and a bodyguard who's ideally an acrobat."

Tapping his sternum, Hollis wastes no time taking on the second-in-command role. The tallest of the three of us, and the most agile, he pats his chest. "I'm like a motherfucking cat." Also the cockiest. Hollis swivels to me, pointing. "You're the boost." Then he turns to Rhys. "And you're the lookout. You can sweet talk that jackass if he shows up. Or the neighbors. Or the cops for that matter. Your accent fools anyone."

"Yes, that's why I got the accent. For trickery," Rhys deadpans.

"Let's put it to good use," Briar says urgently, clearly ready to get on with it, then sweetly to him and Hollis, she adds, "And thank you."

Admittedly, it was damn impressive the way Rhys and Hollis delivered that one-two punch. But that's how they play the game too, the laidback California surfer guy and the quick-witted guy from London trading off the puck most nights.

And I know how to spot opportunities as well. That's my role on the team and I take it very seriously —on and off the ice. I lift the bag of leftovers, brandishing the remains of the superstitious sushi, complete with tuna. "Might need a little something to lure the cat to the door."

Briar beams, those big blue eyes sparkling my way like I've given her the sun. "You're brilliant," she says, and for a hot second, I think she's going to come in for an adrenaline-fueled pre-heist kiss.

And I wouldn't mind if she did.

But that's a crazy thought.

I brush it off, then hand her the smaller of two takeout boxes. She drops it into her pack as Rhys recaps the plan. When he's done, he points to my bag. "And give me that."

I smirk. "You want my sushi now?"

"It's just for show. A decoy."

"Yeah. Sushi's your costume, Viscount. Keep telling yourself that," I say, then hand him the bag with the bigger box.

Rhys jogs through the lot to the street, scans the sidewalk, then lifts his free arm, giving a go sign.

Like he's doing a how-to video on Spider-Man moves, Hollis hops up on the gnarly gnome, then jumps, grabbing the edge of the balcony with sure hands.

"You're a fucking monkey," I say with a low whistle, and his height helps but so does his bendiness. In seconds, he's clambering over the railing and standing on the balcony.

"That's...impressive," Briar says, and I want to impress her too.

Here goes. I squat, pat my right thigh. "Hop on," I tell her. "And hold my hands."

I lift my hands above my head.

"Got it," she says, moving quickly behind me, curling her fingers around mine. Then with the limberness of a, well, a yoga teacher, she sets one sneakered foot on my right thigh while the other scales my back, then lands on my left shoulder. She shifts the foot from my right thigh to my right shoulder and stands up like a cheerleader on the pyramid of me.

She's eye-level with the balcony now. She could probably execute the rest of the operation herself, but she'll need help getting down with a cat on her back. She climbs over the railing on her own, but Hollis offers a hand just in case.

I turn in the direction of Rhys to take the temperature. He's fifty feet away and...aw shit.

He's chatting with someone. A guy in a...mesh trucker hat and a flannel shirt. That's no good. Never leave a teammate hanging.

Or a woman whose ex treated her like this. That

guy is just unacceptable and deserves a lifetime of fire ants in his pants for how he's treated this woman.

"Hurry, guys," I say, only loud enough for Hollis and Briar.

"On it," Hollis mutters.

When I look up, Briar is lying flat on the balcony and calling through the cat door, "Frances Furbottom..."

4

HER PRAISE KINK

Hollis

I'm trying. I swear, I'm trying not to laugh. But seriously?

"Who names a cat Frances Furbottom?" I ask, but the question's for the universe since Briar has already wriggled halfway through the pet door. "Who's a pretty girl?" she coos, her voice a little muffled. "Such a pretty girl with such a pretty tail."

Well, someone has a praise kink.

I kneel next to Briar, gripping her backpack, ready to execute the hand-off back to Gav the second our gal grabs the quarry. Ready, too, in case anything goes wrong. I'm inches away from her and here to help, no matter what she needs. Cover, a lift, a pep talk—anything.

Briar slithers in even more, and now it's just her pink legs sticking out. "It's the fluffiest tail I've ever seen. And yes, good girls get tuna. That's right, Mrs. Frances Furbottom. I have a special treat for you."

A pause.

A *too fucking long* pause.

"Is she even coming to you?" I whisper, eager to help my friend score this feline. Eager to do it quickly since Gavin is rolling his hands, indicating we need to speed it up, so I've got to get her off the balcony ASAP.

"Almost here," Briar says in her normal voice, then returns to her sweet talking. "Such a good, pretty girl. No one in the whole world is prettier. And tuna makes you even lovelier."

Another stretched out silence, like the second before the puck drops. I sense the capture is about to happen before paws scrabble, then Briar declares, "Gotcha."

Victory! But the sound that rips through the air rends a hole in the fabric of the universe. "Meow!"

I shudder at the thunderous cat cry. It's a demon summoned from the depths of the underworld. "Is she killing you, Pretzel?"

"She's"—Briar wriggles her ass out to the tune of an unholy wail—"not"—she shimmies her waist back through the door. The creature howls—"happy."

Yeah, that's clear.

Gavin hums the *Jeopardy!* theme song.

That's clear too. I gotta move this along. "Gonna pull you out, 'kay?"

"'Kay."

"Hold on tight to Frances Hellcat Furbottom."

"Yup."

I grab Briar's hips, nice and firm, and yank her the rest of the way then jump out of the line of cat fire when Briar's free. Good thing since the silvery fluffball in her arms is gnashing her teeth and spinning her head in a cat exorcism. In a flash, I shove the open bag at Briar, and she performs the most impressive yoga move of all time—stuffing the devil beast into it, zipping it up, then swinging it onto her shoulders in seconds flat.

"C'mon, guys. Let's go," Gavin whispers urgently.

I give Briar a boost over the railing, where she drops down into Gavin's waiting arms, and I'm the last one out. I climb over too, catching a fleeting glimpse of Rhys handing something to a dude in a mesh hat.

Pretty sure there's a clause somewhere in my contract that second-story cat rescues are verboten so I pray to the hockey gods that I can keep living an injury-free life as I jump down seconds after Briar, who's telling Gavin he can leave the gnome behind.

Gavin must have put the books away while we were up there, since he's already got the suitcase in his hand as he sets the gnome down. The three of us race across the lot toward a faded blue Honda, old but well-kept, as the cat thrashes and roars.

Grabbing the key fob from her pocket, Briar points it and unlocks the car while running, which might be one of the hottest things I've ever seen, and maybe that's what's fueling my attraction to her right now—because I lusted after action heroines when I was a kid. Though, in all fairness, I've pretty much thought Briar was hot every time she played pool or Ping-Pong with our friend group over the last couple years. She slides in and drops the cat bag onto the floor of the passenger seat next to the world's cutest wiener dog right as I climb in shotgun. The pooch barks a surprised but enthusiastic hello, then scampers into my lap to lick my face.

"Hey, long dog." I hold the pup while I locate the buckle.

Gavin piles into the backseat with the suitcase, shoving aside a couple garbage bags with clothes peeking through the top. Jesus. Briar's ex is a piece of work.

Briar cranks on the engine and peels out of the spot like she's a Hollywood racer. "You're the grease woman *and* the getaway driver," I say, impressed.

"I can handle more than one task at a time," she says dryly, flashing a smile as she cruises over to Rhys, who's waving goodbye to the guy in the hat, then calling out a chipper "cheers" to him. She stops for our friend as a gleaming black SUV pulls up to the curb twenty feet down the road.

My teammate grabs the door handle and gets in behind Briar onto the backseat, hauling the trash bag next to him onto his lap. I'm dying to know what went down with the hat dude, but I'm a little worried about our driver. Her trace of a smile has vanished. Her fingers grip the wheel tighter as she flicks the right-turn signal, checking traffic anxiously.

"That's my ex," she says tightly, nodding to the SUV where a guy in a paisley shirt now offers a hand to a leggy brunette stepping out of the passenger side, dangling a pink rhinestone-studded cat collar in her hand.

Spotting an opening, Briar pulls onto the road, exhaling. As we drive past them, the cat caterwauls once more.

"And I believe that was *fuck you* in feline," I say.

"Yes. Yes, it was," Briar says, giving me a faint smile that makes me feel like we made her shitty day a little bit better, and that's even better than winning our game.

She hits the gas, and I don't know where we're going. I'm not sure where runaway cats and sexy action heroine yoga instructors go when the chips are down, but I know one thing for sure—I'm comin' with her.

5

I OWE YOU

Briar

My pulse is still pounding several blocks later. Is this what it's like to pull off a heist? My dad loves those kinds of movies so he made me watch all his old faves countless times when I was growing up.

Now, as I slow to a stop at a red light on the edge of Russian Hill, finally feeling like I'm far enough away from Madison and Steven the Cat Burglar that they aren't going to hop a trolley, catch up, and pound on the window of my car, I turn to the guy next to me.

Hollis, with his floppy hair that falls just past his ears, eternal laidback smile, and light, glowy skin, has given Donut to Gavin and is holding my backpack in his lap. Mrs. Frances Furbottom is still in the backpack, but she's settled into her rescuer and is now showing off her purring skills. As the adrenaline starts to wear off, I catch my breath. I'm a little curious about my three heroes.

I peer in the rearview mirror into the dark brown eyes of the Brit. "What happened with that guy in the hat? The one on the street talking to you?"

"Yeah, and where's the sushi?" Gavin asks from the backseat.

"Is that really the priority? Your fucking fish?" Hollis raises his eyebrows in his teammate's direction.

"No. It's the point," Gavin says firmly.

Rhys ignores them, answering with, "He thought I was the delivery guy from the other night. And he felt terrible that he'd forgotten to tip me. So he was apologizing."

Hollis barks out a laugh. "Apologizing?"

"And he tipped me a twenty," Rhys says, seeming amused.

"Did you keep it?" Gavin asks.

"He was insistent," Rhys says with a shrug.

Hollis shakes his head next to me. "Dude, that would only happen to you."

"Why would that only happen to him?" I ask as the light turns green and I go. I'm not even sure where we're headed—just away from the scene of my awful mistake of falling for a very bad man.

"His accent," Hollis says confidently. "Charms anyone. Probably even demonic cats."

I glance down at the pack in his lap. Hollis is scratching Frances's head through the fabric. "Seems you've got that skill too."

"Just a little hobby. I don't like to brag."

"Humble brag," Gavin coughs under his breath. Then he clears his throat. "But where's the sushi?"

"Gave it to the guy as a thanks," Rhys says.

Gavin's hazel eyes twinkle with mischief. I steal a glance at him in the rearview mirror. His wavy brown hair looks soft in the streetlights whooshing by and his cheekbones are sharp. Stubble lines his jaw.

"Told you sushi brought us good luck," he says, smug.

"You were right," Rhys grumbles, and as much as I'm amused by their camaraderie, I should figure out what's next in the night. Then, in my capsized life.

Like, say, where I'm going to live with my two rescue pets so I can manage my teaching gig with the Sea Dogs, the rival hockey team in the city, my classes at various fitness studios, and the app I want to launch.

But first things first. My father always taught me my manners.

"I can't thank you guys enough. You may be my rivals but tonight you're knights in shining armor. Can I give you a ride home or something?" I ask as I head toward the bay, the water sparkling in the starlight.

Gavin clears his throat, then asks with gentle concern, "I think the bigger question is—can we give you a place to stay?"

Embarrassment crawls up my chest. They saved my cat tonight, and now they're offering to put me up? Tempting as that is, they've done more than enough. While we're all friendly-ish—though I know Hollis the best since he's close with my friends' hockey-playing husbands—I don't want to take advantage of their kindness. I catch a quick glimpse of Gavin in the mirror. His eyes are earnest. Caring.

"I'm good. I'm staying with a friend," I say, lying, but I'll figure something out. "Besides, in a week I'm going to be at the Sunburst Summit Festival in Lucky Falls during All-Star Break. I have a booth-slash-tent thingy and I'm doing some classes."

"Nice. We'll be there too," Hollis offers.

"You will?"

Hollis gestures to the three of them. "We're hosting the obstacle course for our energy drink sponsor," he says.

"So tonight was training?" I ask.

"A dry run," Gavin says, as dry as the words.

"How'd we do?" Rhys asks.

"Ten out of ten," I say, then hum. "Though it was more like one million. You guys were amazing. You were heroes. Above and beyond."

At the light, I can tell Rhys's smile is crooked and pleased, then it's as if he tries to fight it off. Going a little stern, he says, "We'll get out at the corner. Let you get on with your night."

I almost don't want to say goodnight, but it's clearly time. I pull over and cut the engine.

"Listen, if you ever need a cat rescued, just call us," Rhys says, curling a hand over the seat I'm in, almost touching the back of my shoulder. "Little known service we provide."

"May I never need the three hockey stars to rescue another cat of mine from a terrible ex."

"But before we go, I need to know why she's named Frances Furbottom," Hollis says, unzipping the top of the bag and stroking the now tamed beast. Frances purrs loudly, offering her pretty chin for scratching. "There's gotta be a wild story behind that. Is Frances your grandma? Or was Frances a little old lady's cat? Oh wait. I bet a little old lady who made doilies had her first."

"Do you even know what a doily is?" Gavin barks from the backseat.

"Do you?" Hollis counters.

"Something little old ladies have," Gavin grumbles.

Hollis lifts a finger to make a point. "A small napkin. Or a decorative little mat, often made of lace."

"What are you—the dictionary?" Rhys asks, laughing.

"He did sound just like one," I say, smiling too. It feels good to smile after the drama of the last hour. And the drama to come when I try to get my life back in order.

May no one who watches my yoga videos ever know what a hot mess I am.

While petting the cat, Hollis turns back to me. "So did Frances Furbottom belong to a doily-making old lady?"

He seems so delighted by this story he's concocting that I almost hate to burst his bubble with the truth. But I blow out a breath and tell him anyway. "No," I say. "She just has a really furry butt."

The car is silent for several seconds. Then, the guys laugh and one by one make their way out of the car, with Gavin carefully setting Donut into a dog car seat he's somehow unearthed amidst the rubble of my garbage bag life. They stand by the passenger window, my three tall, strapping hockey rescue hunks who rose to the occasion.

They look good in the soft lamplight of the January evening. Rhys, who's tall and lean for a hockey guy, with dark hair that's nearly black and a trim beard the same shade. A slice of white skin splits his right eyebrow—probably one of many scars.

Gavin is the broadest of the bunch with a thick slab of a chest, barrels for arms, and a dusting of light brown stubble across the fair skin of his jawline.

Hollis is all California sunshine and muscles. Light freckles and dark blond hair, surfer style, like the ocean breeze always blows through it.

I know him the best of the three. But I think he also makes himself the most known. The others probably know me more as a rival since I work for the opposing team.

And now they've seen me at my worst.

My most helpless.

And frustrated.

And hurt.

I squirm a little under the spotlight. I really need to go. "Thanks again for the help." Donut barks in solidarity from the backseat. "I owe you guys one."

Hollis flashes the biggest smile of all and taps the open window. "Can't wait to call that one in."

They leave, walking the other way, and I drive into the night, desperately needing someplace to stay.

I fumble for my phone and hit the first number I find. "Any chance I could get into that rental a week early?"

6

I NEVER LIKED HIM ANYWAY

Briar

Aubrey waggles a bottle of champagne at me. "Breakup champagne. You need it. I've got it."

I'm not turning bubbly down. Or friendship. Twenty minutes after saying goodbye to the guys, I sink onto the cushy stool in the state-of-the-art kitchen at her palatial home in Pacific Heights—the one she shares with her two hockey boyfriends.

I glance at the label on the bottle. *I Never Liked Him Anyway.* "How fitting," I say as she pours. "A prototype of yours?"

"Yup. I'm thinking of making a line of breakup champagne with my friend Juliet. She's a party planner. So we made a few types to test."

"I'm the perfect guinea pig," I say with a frown.

She hands me a flute and gives me a sympathetic smile. "Been there."

"I know," I say, heavily.

After I called Kailani, who's handling logistics for the festival, about getting into the rental in Lucky Falls early, I rang Aubrey to see if I could crash at her place for the night. If anyone understands my situation it's Aubrey. Her story's not identical to mine, but her line of breakup champagne is inspired by her own failed love story. Her groom ditched her at the altar ten minutes before their wedding. Now, more than a year later, Aubrey is living her very best life, happily in love with two men who adore her. One is the goalie for the Golden State Foxes and the other is the recently retired forward from the Sea Dogs.

Their dog, Puck Fitzgibbons, is here too. He and Donut are tussling over a couple stuffed armadillos in the spacious living room, their happy barks and playful growls telling me they're getting along. Frances Furbottom is already lounging in the guest room.

Take that, Madison, and your stupid rhinestone collar.

But even though I have a place for the night and, thankfully, my pets, I still feel so stupid. It's not like I was in love with the guy, but I liked him enough to live with him. I liked him enough to think we could have a future.

I knock back some of the delicious bubbly then set it down. "How did I miss the signs, Aubrey? Why can't I just pick a decent guy?"

She smiles gently. "It's hard to know who to trust," she says. "And it's really hard to be out there dating."

"He seemed so...into me. Calling, and texting, and taking me out. He was attentive. He took me to his networking events, and his dinners with advertisers, and his cocktail parties with sponsors, and he bought me these dresses to wear—" I stop as a sharp realization hits me like a slap to the face. "I was his advertiser candy! For that stupid site he runs. He needed to look involved so he could pitch advertisers on the articles and advice columns he runs on his man's man dating advice site. That's why he went all in on me," I say, shaking my head, disgusted with him and with the way I fell for him. "How did I miss it?"

Aubrey tucks a finger under my chin and makes me meet her brown-eyed gaze. Waves upon waves of lush red hair frame her face. Freckles dance across her pale skin. "Because people wear masks, and it's really hard to get them to take them off."

"I guess Steven's was like one of those sexy Venetian masks you wear to a masquerade. But underneath he was a chameleon."

Like my mother. Always changing her mind about what she wanted—to eat for dinner, to watch on TV, to do a job. Then, whether she wanted a family or not. She'd promised to be there for us. Then one day she just...left.

She laughs. "He was. And listen," she says, her laugh fading away as she sets a hand on my knee. "We've all trusted the wrong person. Given our hearts to the wrong guy. Gotten hurt."

"We should have a club."

"We'll call it the Karma Club," she says, then shrugs a playful shoulder, letting her gaze purposefully drift toward the hall and the game room beyond. Her guys are here tonight—Dev had a hockey game this after-noon, the same one my cat rescuers played in. Ledger worked in his plant shop all day and now the two of them are playing poker. Probably betting on who gets to please Aubrey first. Karma, indeed. "It's when you upgrade to two hot guys," Aubrey adds, twirling a strand of her hair. "You did say some Foxes helped you save the cat. Including Ledger's cousin..."

I scoff, nipping her idea in the bud. Hollis Bouchard, Gavin Worthy, and Rhys Corbyn are friends. That is all. "The last thing I need in my life is another man. Let alone three. All I need is a place to stay. So thank you for letting me stay here."

"Anytime, bestie."

We finish our champagne, then I head to bed, crashing in a soft guest bed bookended by my cat and dog.

* * *

In the morning, I'm up early. I have to teach two yoga classes—one to the Sea Dogs, then one at a studio. After I shower and get dressed, I whiz through the kitchen, making coffee with Donut and Puck at my feet, when a text from Kailani blinks up at me.

Bad news, babe. No cats are allowed here at the rental. I can try to find you another one that permits cats though.

I wince as Aubrey strolls in, Ledger by her side. They're both dressed for work—Aubrey's heading to her salon, Ledger to the plant shop. Dev's probably at a morning skate.

"What's wrong, Briar?" Ledger asks, as I hand him a cup.

I read the text out loud to them.

Aubrey rolls her eyes. "We'll watch your cat as long as you need us to, right, babe?"

Ledger nods. "We like cats. We do have one, you know."

My brow knits. "But I thought your cat hated cats and, well, everyone?"

Ledger shrugs casually. "Jack did. But Hollis has a way about him. He comes over and trains him. My cousin has the Midas touch." Ledger takes a swig of his coffee, then sets down the mug, and checks his watch. "I'm meeting him later today to work out. But last night I mentioned to him you were here."

The memory of Hollis's easy grin—which is also easily panty-melting—warms me up. So does the memory of his touch. The way he wrapped his hands around my hips last night and tugged me out of the cat door, I couldn't help but notice how big and strong they were. How solid his grip was. How sure.

Like Gavin's, too, when he boosted me up. He had the confidence of a man who knows what he's doing with his hands. And his whole damn body.

But given my garbage bag life, it's best to shake off those thoughts of the two of them.

After Steven's insults about my little yoga app, I'm more determined than ever to launch Flow and Flex Fitness. I've been making videos online for over a year that focus on how yoga can help people of all ages and body types, from seniors to athletes, with flexibility and balance.

I've raised my profile teaching yoga first for the Golden State Foxes and now for the Sea Dogs. I've made great relationships with both teams. When the Foxes wanted to hire someone full time to work for the team and its minor league affiliates—a job I didn't want since I wouldn't have been able to do my own thing too —the strength and conditioning coach with the Foxes recommended me to her counterpart at the Sea Dogs, Nova. And I have a great relationship with Nova, who's been supportive too of my goal. It's time for me to get my new business up and running. To rely only on myself like my dad has always taught me. To live alone and without the help of a man.

That is my new goal.

I clean the kitchen, then as I'm leashing Donut to drop her off at doggie daycare, Aubrey pops back in, saying, "By the way, something came for you this morning."

She gestures to a gift in the front hall.

A very large gift. Two, actually.

7

I'M JUST HERE FOR THE BALANCE

Rhys

I take a quick wrist shot, the puck whizzing past our goalie's glove and into the net. Dev grumbles from behind his mask, "I let that in."

"Are you sure about that?" I tease as I skate by our fiercely competitive goalie, sending a spray of ice in his direction.

Hollis takes his turn next, sprinting toward the net with determination. But Dev easily blocks Hollis's shot with his leg pad.

It's morning skate and it's optional, especially since we had a game yesterday afternoon. But I've always taken the option since I've been with the Golden State Foxes.

We're almost halfway into a long season, but it's been a good season so far. I'm grateful to be on this team after being traded from New York a year and a half ago. My old team was going nowhere, and my personal life wasn't much better. The two seem to move in tandem.

I shake off the memory of Samantha and her tricky ways, her multiple profiles, her stacks of lies. Here on the ice, all thoughts of that shitty year disappear. It's just me and the game and the challenge as we move into passing drills. Gavin slides the puck to me, then I wing it over to him as we attack the net. He shuffles it back, and I take aim and slap one past Dev in the net once more.

"Just don't forget to do that in a game," Dev calls out.

Which, *ouch*.

Yes, I'd like to score more points when it matters. Who wouldn't, really? But I'm acutely aware that I'm surrounded by great players here on this team. I'm not one of those great players. I'd like my stats to be better, my contributions stronger, my game time just... more.

We move through power-play practice, then deflections, then the clock unwinds, and we head to the tunnel. Hollis is right behind me, and Gavin too.

"Gonna hit the weights," Gavin says, which is Gavin-speak for *who's in*.

I'll go later at my building. "Can't," I say, and they know why. But it feels...strange, maybe, to admit that after last night.

"Because you have yoga class," Hollis singsongs.

That's the problem with sticking to a regular schedule. Your mates know your whereabouts too well.

"Yeah, I do," I say, like saying it casually will make my attendance seem...casual.

"Well, you wouldn't want to mess with a streak," Gavin deadpans when we reach the hallway leading to the locker room.

And...touché.

"Exactly. My devotion to yoga is why we're winning," I say.

"Then, better not miss a class. Say hi to Briar for all of us," Gavin adds.

"Give her our love," Hollis says, batting his lashes.

My friends are such assholes. It was Gavin's fucking idea to get her the gift. "Absolutely. I'm definitely going to talk to her about the two of you."

"Knew it," Gavin says, then tips his chin at Hollis. "Weight room?"

"And then fish tacos."

"It's not a game day," Gavin points out, and the two of them argue about fish tacos and rituals the rest of the way.

When I'm out of my gear and into joggers and trainers, I take off. Yes, I am religious about weights, exercise, yoga, and practice. I'm religious about making the most of my opportunity to play. I can't squander it. Not when it's something others in my family don't have. I'll do what it takes to have a body that works, that can play at the highest level. A private trainer I hired this year recommended adding yoga to my routine. "You can pivot better. Have more explosive crossovers. It can give you an edge," he'd said.

In this sport, an edge can make all the difference

between a good year and a great one. *An edge* makes you better than the next guy they'll trade you for.

When I leave the rink, I head over to Fillmore Street, to the studio where Briar teaches.

As I near the red-brick facade of Peak Performance Yoga, my skin buzzes like it usually does when I know I'm going to see her. But the charge is even more electric after last night.

Which is utterly fucking ridiculous.

I mean, it's not like I'm going to ask her out—not after what her wanker of an ex did to her *less than twenty-four hours ago*. I'm off romance altogether, too, after Samantha.

This buzzing in my cells is just...because I like her style of exercise.

Yeah right.

After I check in I head to the class, but she's not here greeting students, setting out mats, or offering individual tips. She's usually here early. Ten minutes early. Like I normally am.

I'm not bothered. I'm really not bothered.

I grab a spot, roll out my mat, and take a drink from my water bottle. The class filters in. I check the time.

Class should start in three minutes.

A bright voice carries confidently across the studio. "Good morning, friends. Are you ready to flow and flex today?"

Stupid fucking grin.

I fight it off over her usual greeting as she strides to the front of the class on agile bare feet, dressed in sky-blue leggings with crisscross cutouts along the side revealing her creamy flesh.

After she sets down her mat, her blue eyes linger on me a little longer than they do everyone else. They curve up in a hint of a grin, a private acknowledgement of last night.

At least, I hope.

Which is a stupid hope.

Dismissing it, I laser in on balance.

I'm just here for the balance. That edge.

That is all.

* * *

An hour later I roll up my mat, lingering behind as Briar says goodbye to other students. When everyone's gone, I head over. It'd be weird not to, I reckon. "And how is Frances Furbottom?"

"Very, very furry still. And, Rhys," she says, my name sounding like it tastes good on her lips, "thank you again for the gift. It was really incredible. I was going to send you guys a thank you this afternoon. I was just waiting for Ledger to send me your numbers."

Shit. I don't want her to think I'm in class today because I'm shilling for a thanks. "No worries. I'm just here to work on my balance," I say and wow, that doesn't sound like I'm trying to cover up a massive fucking crush. I try to inject some chill in my voice. "Anyway, I'm glad you got them."

Last night after she dropped us off, we didn't go back to check out Steven's building after all. We grabbed a beer and decided we couldn't just let a woman who'd been kicked out have to haul her clothes around in rubbish bags. We ordered some luggage online and since Hollis heard that she was staying with his cousin, we arranged for our group gift to arrive there this morning.

"I was just going to borrow some suitcases from Aubrey, but now I have my own. In pink and purple," Briar says, and she sounds delighted to have the luggage.

"We had a feeling you liked the colors," I say.

"Well, you felt right." She doesn't seem to realize the double entendre at first, then she does, dipping her face. "I mean..."

"Hopefully it feels good. You shouldn't hesitate to feel up luggage."

"Then I'll have my hands all over it later."

I might regret *this* later. I probably will. But I say it anyway. "Lucky luggage."

Her smile lingers, and for a long beat, the air sparks hotter between us, charged with this electricity. "And it'll go to good use. I'm going to Lucky Falls later today."

"Oh, really?" That's where the festival is. But it doesn't start for a week.

"I got into my rental early—break out the champagne—so at least I've got a place for a couple weeks. Which also gives me time to find a place in the city."

"You won't be teaching then? For the next week?" Ah fuck. I hope that doesn't sound like I'll be a sad sack, kicking a can around the fitness studio forlornly.

"I will. I'll drive back and forth from Lucky Falls each day."

That's an hour each way. I hate her ex even more than I did last night for this massive inconvenience. "We'll have to get you a gift of petrol next time," I say.

"You guys are already too good to me. Do you mind giving me Hollis's and Gavin's numbers?"

"No problem," I say, and we quickly exchange all the digits.

Then she reaches out and squeezes my bicep. "Thanks again for last night."

She holds my arm for a bit longer than I'd expect, which is fine by me. For a second, it looks like she's going to say something else. Maybe even lean in and give me a thank you kiss on the cheek.

But that's wishful thinking. Of course she doesn't do that. I've been burned by romance in the last year or so, but she was burned by it just last night.

Best if I keep this obsession exactly where it should stay—in a tiny purple and pink suitcase in the corner of my mind. Fact is, I should avoid her in Wine Country next week too.

It's a big festival. I probably won't even see her. "I hope you have a good time at the festival," she says.

"You too. I'll get you that champagne when you snag a new place."

"Champagne's my favorite," she says, and I file that away for safekeeping.

When I leave, my agent's name and number flashes across the phone and I tense.

This could be the news I've been dreading.

8

SPECIAL PROTECTION

Briar

I didn't plan to send them a photo, but Donut is making it impossible not to. My tiny rust-colored Dachshund has burrowed into my clothes in the pink suitcase in Aubrey's guest room, wiggled her way through leggings and bras, and is stretched out across nearly the whole length of the luggage, her little head poking out of a lavender sports bra, her tail twined around a white hoodie. I add a sticker saying *thank you* then hit send on a group message.

> Briar: Apparently, it's a dog case too.
> And it's Donut approved.
>
> > Hollis: She's making sure she's never
> > left behind.

Briar: Her MO. Also, thank you. That was unexpected and awesome. Also fortuitous since I'm heading up to Lucky Falls today with Donut, and Frances Furbottom will stay with her grandad. I got into my rental early, in case Rhys didn't mention it.

Gavin: Oh. You mean Rhys went to your yoga class? What a surprise.

Hollis: I had no idea he went to your class.

Gavin: Does he go every other day?

Hollis: Right after morning skate?

Rhys: I'm like literally in this chat, wankers.

Briar: He went, and he's an excellent student. Such a shame I didn't see you guys there. But maybe someday you can be as flexible as Rhys is.

Rhys: Not likely. But it's nice of you to try to prop them up, Bri.

Hollis: Let's not forget you're the rival, Pretzel. We've got to be careful who we consort with.

Gavin: Is that another dictionary word of yours?

Hollis: Like doily?

Gavin: Yes. Like doily.

Hollis: Do you even know what consort means?

Gavin: I know what consort means. It means...associate, as in a verb.

Hollis: Are you sure?

Hollis is bluffing. That's clear. How Gavin will handle his bluff is anyone's guess. Especially mine. But I can't look away from their text tennis match. Three dots appear and Gavin replies with...

Gavin: Indubitably.

I crack up as I write back.

Briar: And that round goes to Gavin.

Then, I tug Donut from my clothes, zip up the suitcase, and pop Frances into her newly purchased carrier. She yowls at me.

"But you look so pretty in your new bag," I say, and before I close it, I toss her a stuffed catnip alligator and that hits the spot for her. In spite of Aubrey and Ledger's offer to look after her, my dad called dibs when I mentioned I needed a place for her, though I haven't told him why yet. He'll be pissed on my behalf. Since Aubrey's at work, I let myself out and head to my car, Donut by my side. I set the pets safely in the car. After I drop the suitcase into the trunk where the other one's already stowed, I check the chat again.

> Hollis: Damn. It fucking does. I need to step up my game. Speaking of stepping up our game...I take it the cat is staying with your dad?

> Briar: She is. He's a cat man, even though he's a Sea Dogs fan.

> Hollis: I'll pretend you didn't say that last part. But if Mrs. Furry Butt needs any special protection while you're gone, you know where to find us.

> Briar: I do.

I don't know exactly how I wound up with a crew of three hockey protectors but somehow I have one.

Serendipity, I suppose.

I close the thread, turning on my girl power playlist. I need an epic breakup tune, something to signify I don't need anyone. I find the Amelia Stone tune—Better Off—blast it, and hit the road, leaving the hockey guys behind me, and the next phase in my life ahead.

9

BIG RED FLAG

Briar

I pull into my dad's garage in Petaluma about an hour later. The sign reads Henry's Garage, but everyone calls it Big Daddy's Garage. Everyone but me.

Dust kicks up from the ground and the smell of motor oil tickles my nostrils. My dad's working on a Dodge Charger, black with a bolt of lightning painted on the side. When he sees my car—one a customer gave him years ago that wasn't worth fixing, but Dad fixed it anyway—he sets down his tools and heads my way.

"Hi, Dad," I say, hopping out of the car, grabbing a little gift I picked up at a roadside candy and fruit shop, and bracing myself for the inevitable *romance is the worst* sigh that's coming my way in about thirty seconds.

I'm no good at keeping my life from him. Ever since

I cried buckets when my prom date who I'd thought would love me forever dumped me, I've been a see-through daughter with him. But then again, it's not like I hid my emotions from him when Mom left either when I was ten, returning to her hometown of Sydney with barely a word and the even rarer visit. I was devastated then. He was too. But he shoved aside his own hurt to handle my brother and me. This is why I share my life with him. Because he shared his life with us.

Dad scrubs a hand across his bushy beard, his brow crinkled, a dirty rag in his hand but a smile teasing at his lips. Donut hops up and down in her car seat, attempting what she believes is a fail-safe method for opening any door—jumping. The window is cracked open, a boisterous *arf* coming through the sliver as she pogos.

"Hey, kiddo. What are you doing in these parts?" Dad asks, his standard greeting, even though he's been expecting Frances and me.

But I also don't want to spend too much time on why my life is a mess. Don't want to worry him.

I waggle the bag, hoping the distraction ploy helps. "First of all, I stopped and got your favorite gummi bears."

He studies the bag skeptically but takes it. "I like these."

"I know. Second, my tire pressure is low, so I figured I'd check it on my way to Lucky Falls." I head for the tire pressure machine, figuring this is the moment to drop the news. I say breezily, "Also, you were right.

Steven was an oily businessman who I can't trust. 'Kay? Can you drop a coin in there for me?"

A pause. A grumble. "So that's why I'm watching the cat for the next couple weeks."

"Well, that and you love her."

He turns to the car, a small smile for Frances tipping his lips. "She's good people," he says, then looks back at me, muttering, "But your ex? He's a jerk. Love is the worst. And so are men today."

"You do have a son."

"And Griffin knows better than to treat anyone like that," he says, moving me aside and swiping a card on a key ring into the tire pressure machine. "I'll do it."

"I can do it."

"But I want to."

As he fills the tires with air, he reminds me that his tow truck business never once abandoned him like Mom did us, returning only twice—once for a summer vacation when I was twelve and probably needed her most, but she was mostly busy taking painting classes in the city that week anyway, then again a few years later when she was *just stopping by in the area while on her travels*—whatever that meant. He reminds me that the garage is faithful. That his business is reliable.

"You hear me, kiddo?"

"Loud and clear," I say.

"Good. Now gimme my grandcat. I bought her some tuna and a new feather toy," he says.

I grab the carrier, scratch her chin through the grates, then thank him and head on my way.

* * *

Damn, I could kiss Kailani. As I wend my little car down the long gravel driveway toward the cottage in nearby Lucky Falls, I open the window, inhaling the heady smell of vanilla.

"This is the real karma, Donut," I tell my girl.

She peers out the backseat window at the yard. It's late January in Napa Valley, so it's peak mustard flower season, and the yard is a carpet of bright yellow blooms that smell a little like heaven.

In addition to the main cottage, there's a tiny house on the property, and a cute little garage with a basketball net hanging over it. I press the button to open the door, drive the car inside and cut the engine, then I free my pup before she jumps too many times. Her long snout must go haywire because, in seconds, she's tugging on the leash to check out the flowers. "Let's go inside first," I tell her.

She whimpers her displeasure and since I'm a sucker for her, I let her explore the yard and turn flowers into fire hydrants.

I take a few more unhurried minutes to wander with her, before we head into the white cottage. As I step inside, the warm embrace of the cozy space envelops me. A line of tall, arched windows extends across the back wall, showing off the soft rolling hills of the Wine Country town.

The sun streams in through the panes, painting the room in golden late-afternoon hues, and I let out a contented sigh. The scent of lilac from the dish towels

—must be the laundry detergent—mingles with the heady smell from the mustard flowers floating inside.

The open floor plan of the cottage is perfect for my temporary two-week home, with the living room, kitchen, and dining area all sprawled across the main level. A plush blue velvet sofa faces a fireplace I won't need.

Down the hall, I find two bedrooms and above me is a small open loft with a futon. "Hey, you get your own room," I say to Donut, showing her the bedrooms. "Just kidding. You can sleep with me."

She trots gamely by my feet as we return to the kitchen where I slide open glass doors to a wraparound deck. Well, that's nice. Kailani didn't tell me there was a hot tub here, but I'm not complaining.

Another reason I'm not complaining?

I can wake up early, shoot some Flow and Flex videos on the deck at sunrise, and create my new series of Seven Days at Sunrise to Lower Your Stress for the app. I've got some other video classes planned too. Balance for a Bad Day, Stretching for When Work Sucks, Pilates for When Everyone Pisses You Off.

Heck, maybe I'll even do yoga for better sex, for intimacy, for romance.

That's something Steven thought was a terrible idea. *People would rather have sex than do yoga for sex. Now c'mon, babe, lemme show you how my cock can do the tree pose.*

But what did he know? He'd sooner find Cleopatra's tomb than the female orgasm. I almost feel sorry for Madison.

Almost.

* * *

About a week later, I'm somehow both exhausted and rejuvenated. I've been driving up and down to the city daily, with Donut coming to most classes with me at the Sea Dogs. The strength and conditioning coach is a dog lover, so I'm lucky that Nova lets Donut join me at the arena.

Donut has proven herself though. When I adopted her at Little Friends a couple years ago, I did the rescue's therapy dog training program so I could bring her to visit the assisted living home where I do gentle stretching on a volunteer basis for the residents. With the hockey players, though, she mostly just shows off how much better she is at downward dog than anyone else there.

In between classes, I hunt for apartments. My friend Ivy has a lead on a place in her old building but nothing's solid yet. The rest of the time I'm shooting videos and working with my tech wizard younger brother to fine-tune my app.

But the festival starts tomorrow, so I'm going to focus on that. As Griffin and I finish our latest Zoom on the back deck, discussing what he thinks it'll take to get the app up and running—translation: marketing money—he takes off his glasses, then adds, "And listen, don't look but your POS ex is running a piece on his site on Five Ways to Know You're In a Relationship Going Nowhere."

I seethe. "Are you kidding me?"

"I wish," he says. "That guy is such a tool. Like he's a fucking relationship expert."

"That's how he positions himself."

"He really does."

My jaw ticks with anger. But my gut churns with worry. Did he say something nasty about me in it? "Do I want to look at it, Griff? Is he talking about me somehow?"

"No. It's just generic toxic-ex stuff."

"I'm the toxic ex?"

"This is why I visit his site," he says gently. "So you don't have to."

But the thing is, as I cook dinner, as I walk Donut, as I prep for the festival, my laptop is a siren calling to me. I can't help it. I've got to know what he's said.

I sink onto the couch, flip open my computer, and pop over to his dating advice site. I grip the edge of the machine as I read.

Is he for real?

I want to fling this computer at the wall. Maybe I need Yoga for a Toxic Ex.

Because I can't believe he wrote this: *I never felt an ounce of chemistry when I kissed my most recent ex-girlfriend and that should have been a big red flag, boys.*

I uncork a bottle of wine, pour a glass of Chablis all the way to the top, put on a bikini, and turn on the hot tub.

Time to detox.

10

MY SUIT

Hollis

Down by one.

The clock is ticking. Nine minutes left in the third period.

The Vegas team's defenders are a wall around their net here in our arena. But I have a plan.

I flip the puck to Rhys, or so they think. My guy, Fisher, sneaks up and takes the puck from me instead, swiftly maneuvering it through the chaos of sticks and skates. While Rhys lures the defenders toward him as Gavin fends them off, Fisher slaps that little black disc through the five-hole. A clean, see-you-later-sucker shot.

The lamp lights and the score is tied. The sound of the horn blares as the crowd erupts in cheers, our hometown audience going wild.

"Yes! Fuck yes," I shout as Rhys speeds past me, giving a congratulatory shoulder bump.

"That's how we do it." He grins, and I can't argue with him there.

"You know it, bro."

He shakes his head, laughing as I call him that.

"C'mon, bro! Say it!" I goad.

Another shake.

Rhys has adapted so many Americanisms after playing here for so long. But he's never picked up *bro*. Maybe someday. I am nothing if not optimistic.

I jump over the boards, snatching my water bottle from the bench, and take a quick swig during the line shift.

The sound of skates scraping against the ice fills my ears as guys like our captain and star winger handle the puck now. We're always in good hands when they're leading the charge. We lost our last game. Gavin blamed the fish tacos. But we had banh mi for lunch today since I insisted we just needed to mix it up.

A couple minutes later, I'm back out there. And a few minutes after that, I'm delivering another assist.

Yes!

We hold them off and end the night with our fox mascot hitting the ice for a victory lap as a W flashes across the scoreboard.

"And now, more than a week off," I say to Gavin and Rhys as we reach the tunnel. It's Wednesday night and I'm not even annoyed I wasn't selected for the All-Star game this weekend. I have the stats—but our team is stacked and we're already sending a guy better known than I am and one with a more storied career, our captain, Stefan Christensen. Our goalie, Dev Ryland, is a star too and he got the fan vote.

My time will come. It'll absolutely fucking come.

For now, I've got sore muscles and a date with my favorite pillow, my sleeping mask, and some smooth waves on my sleepy time app. I fucking love sleep. I can't wait to crash.

At the end of the tunnel, I say, "Banh mi. Was I right or was I right?"

Rolling his eyes, Gavin says, "You were right."

"What did you say?"

"You were right," he repeats louder.

I cup my ear with my glove on. "Can't hear you."

"Your ego requires so much stroking, Bouchard," Rhys says, shaking his head.

I wiggle my brows. "That's not the only thing that requires stroking."

"Ah, fuck off," Rhys says with a laugh.

Gavin tips his chin toward me. "And I guess now we've got a new streak, so we'll be eating banh mi every night after the All-Star break."

Rhys groans but even Gavin's superstitions can't get me down. I am going to enjoy the fuck out of several days off.

Twenty minutes later, I'm showered and suited up. I pass the guys at their stalls, clapping each of them on the shoulder. "Catch up with you tomorrow. I'm heading up to Lucky Falls tonight."

"See you then," Rhys says.

"Good luck with the meeting," I say, just to him.

Rhys gives a quick nod. His expression is mostly stoic, but the dude's been stressed for the last week. The rumor mill is working overtime, speculating he'll be part of a trade, so he's seeing his agent tomorrow morning to strategize about whatever might come next.

I'm too young to have a no-trade clause, but I don't worry about that stuff. I can't control *where* I play. I can control *how* I play. My goals here are simple—make the coach and the owner happy and cause zero trouble.

Had enough of that growing up. Don't need it now.

Once outside, I hop in my matte black electric ride, toss my suit jacket on the seat, and loosen my perfunctory tie.

I turn on the car and beat the rush out of the players' lot. As I weave through city traffic, I call my mom. She answers right away and I launch right into the postgame recap like we do after almost every game. "How'd I do?"

"Love a good fake out," she says proudly. "I taught you well."

"Yeah, you did."

She used to play hockey in college and she taught me pretty much everything I know. But there wasn't a feasible career path for her in the sport, so she became a nail technician, then worked her way up and bought into a nail salon in a strip mall with a couple other ladies.

After we talk shop, we catch up on my little sisters and their upcoming college tours. The twins are applying to school in the fall and it's pretty much all-consuming at home. "I just want them to get into decent schools, so we need to see a lot," she says.

"We'll get them in someplace good, Mom," I try to reassure her.

"I hope so," she says, but I can hear the nerves in her voice. Since that's not her real worry.

The cost is.

But I've told her a million times, I've got it covered.

She raised three kids on her own. Least I can do is handle the big bills for her now that I can. But sometimes it helps to take other worries off her plate too. "Can I send you dinner, Mom? I know you like that Thai place in the city and it delivers late."

"It's late, Hollis. And I already ate. But thank you."

"Then lunch it is tomorrow."

She laughs. "You're relentless."

"Did you say I'm wonderful?"

"Same thing."

We say goodbye, and I ask my phone to set a reminder to deliver Mom some lunch tomorrow. Before I know it, I've reached the rental cottage the festival organizer set us up with. It's dark out since it's nearly eleven, but all the lights on the wraparound porch are on.

Nice.

I appreciate that touch from the property manager.

After I turn off the car in the driveway and park just outside the garage, I grab my duffel from the backseat and toss it over my shoulder, stretching my neck as I go, trudging up the steps. Everything in me aches. Back is sore too. Shoulders are cranky.

I don't even bother to go in the front door because the hot tub advertised in the property listing has been calling my name since my shoulder sent the *I'm fucking sore* alert.

I walk across the porch around the side of the cottage, so I can turn on the hot tub before I even go inside.

Why get distracted by anything else?

And damn...

That's some courtesy for you. The tub is already bubbling, with steam rising into the early February night. It's like a goddamn invitation. The service here is immaculate.

"I approve," I say to no one in particular but my beat-up body. I'm always this way after a game. That's just how it goes with pro sports. You take a pounding every night.

I drop my duffle on the back deck, toe off my shoes, undo my shirt, and peel off my suit pants, socks, and boxer briefs.

As I stride over to the steps leading into the hot tub, the back door swings open. Out of nowhere, a long dog shoots like a bullet across the deck, barking hello.

Wait.

Why is there a dog here? A dog I know.

I snap my gaze up, and I'm staring at an absolutely gorgeous blonde who is staring back at me in my birthday suit.

11

STRATEGIC DACHSHUND

Hollis

Modesty is not in my nature.

But manners are and when a lady is covering her eyes with her hand, white wine splashing out of the glass in her other hand, and chanting, *"I'm so sorry. I'm so sorry, I'm so sorry,"* it's time to do the gentlemanly thing and cover up the goods.

Trouble is my clothes are on the other side of the porch, and there's no towel nearby. Improvising, I scoop up the barking beast and use the dog as my fig leaf.

"I had no idea someone was here," I sputter as Donut stands guard in front of my dick, squirming in my hands, while some kind of pop anthem plays low in the background.

Blinking, Briar lowers her head, peering cautiously through her fingers. "Are you using my dog as a censorship tail?"

Well, yeah. And even though it's asked more with curiosity than accusation, I don't want to sully her dog's innocence. "I can put her down."

"No, it's fine," Briar says, waving that off. "She's not weirded out by nudity."

"Good to know."

"I'm not either."

That's also good to know. But I'm a little afraid to move.

Briar and I are definitely friends. We got along well when she worked for the Golden State Foxes last year. We hung out often as part of a bigger group. We partnered up in Ping-Pong some nights with the crew at Sticks and Stones. Played pool there, too, with our friends. But I haven't seen much of her since she was hired away to the rival team and then started dating that cactus of a man.

So I'm just not sure what my next move is. Set down the dog censor and pull up a chair? Or pull up a chair and put down the pup?

"I just wasn't expecting anyone," she adds.

"I wasn't either."

"I gathered as much."

The silence extends awkwardly for a few beats as the stars wink in the sky, the hot tub bubbles, and the wiggly little dog in my hands stares curiously up at me as if she's asking, *"How long are we really going to do this?"*

Briar breaks the awkward moment, asking, "Would you like to wear something besides my dog?"

I laugh awkwardly, then look down at the strategically placed Dachshund. "Probably a good idea."

But I'm not about to ask her to riffle through my bag for my swim shorts. Only, I don't have to since Briar's a problem solver, crossing the deck to the lounge chair, grabbing a towel, then advancing toward me, eyes up the entire time. She's staring straight at my face, like she's walking a tightrope and my nose is the spot on the wall she uses for balance.

Damn, that's cute the way she's trying to make sure she doesn't inadvertently check out my dick. Something about her consideration warms my heart. I feel bad that I accosted my friend with accidental nudity, but I also seriously appreciate that she's giving me the same respect I'd give her. That's just...unexpectedly hot.

Even though I probably shouldn't think of her that way. She works for our rivals.

It was one thing to flirt when she was on the same team as me last year. But now that she's on board with the enemy? That might not sit well with fans.

When she reaches me, her lips curve up and she holds the towel high, letting it dangle between us like a declaration that says *see? I'm a lady.* "And how would you like to do the trade-off?" she asks, still staring pinpoint straight at me, lips twitching, fighting off a grin.

That's more like it. I'm on familiar terrain now—teasing territory. "You want to close your eyes on a count of three?"

"I swear I won't peek," she says, then closes her eyes, almost defiantly, jutting out her chin, comically squeezing them shut, and waving the towel blindly at me.

"If you insist on decorum," I say, setting down the helpful dog with a pat on the head and a *good girl*.

I take the terry cloth, hook it around my waist, and stage whisper, "I'm decent now."

Briar opens her eyes, stares me up and down, and gives a crisp nod. "A little more than decent."

Did someone just compliment my abs? My chest? My arms? Well, thank you very much. But there's no time to revel in it since Donut is shouting at me. It's sort of half dog greeting, half canine question, and the question is *what the fuck are you doing here?* I kneel and stroke her head. "How are you doing, cutie? You were very helpful."

She's bouncing on her back legs now, tongue lolling, saying a hearty hello with no more questions. "I guess she's not annoyed I used her as a shield."

"Well, she *is* a wiener dog."

I snort-laugh.

Briar smiles, then takes a deep breath of the cooling night air. Her smile vanishes as she says, "Want to tell me why you're standing naked at my hot tub of contemplation?"

I glance down at the glass of wine in her hand. "Does that mean you were drinking a cup of regret?"

"You could say that."

That's no good. "Regret is best not drunk alone."

"True, but..."

She's waiting for a real answer. She deserves one. But I have no idea why she's here either.

I point to the tempting tub that I really want to be in right now. But I feel a little like a schmuck when I take a good look around at the open bottle of wine, the phone on the table, the towels on chairs, the wet purple bikini on her. Seems she's been staying here, and I do not want to be the kind of guy that just horns in on a woman's place. "Because I'm pretty sure your hot tub of contemplation is...is my hot tub of relaxation." With an apologetic sigh, I add, "The festival organizer sent me the info for this rental. They're the ones who booked it."

Her expression looks pained at first, then she shutters that down, like she's putting on armor. "No, this is the rental I booked," she says, tough, like she needs to protect herself.

From shitty men, probably. I do not want to be one of them.

"I could have the info wrong," I say and then pad to the pile of pants I shed minutes ago, fish out my phone from the pocket, and click over to my email, showing her one from Kailani that has the address. It matches this home. "Pretty sure this is 303 Dogwood Lane."

Briar's jaw tightens and ticks as she reads. A hard, frustrated breath comes next, then she spins around, grabs her phone and swipes across the screen.

I try not to stare at the trim, toned muscles in her legs and arms. But she's strong and athletic, a woman who uses her body for work, and that's hard to look away from. She reads out loud from her screen. *"I can get you into another rental a week early. 303 Dogwood Lane."* Briar drops her head, groans, and lets out a terrible sigh. She looks up and meets my face. "She must have accidentally booked me into your rental a week early, not realizing it was booked for *this* week too. I'll just check with her tomorrow and see if she has another one for the week." Stoic, chin raised, she adds, "I'll grab my things."

Hold on. "It's past eleven. Where would you even go?" I ask, a little shocked.

There's a crease in her brow and sadness in her shoulders. But she seems to shake it all off. This is a woman who doesn't let shit get her down. "My dad's not far away. He's about a half hour from here. I'll just go there. It's not a big deal."

That is not okay. "No."

"What?"

"Just no," I say decisively, my tone brooking no argument.

"What do you mean *just no*?"

"You don't need to leave. It was a mistake. That doesn't make it more mine than yours. I can get a hotel."

She scoffs. "There aren't going to be any available, Hollis. Everything is booked."

She has a good point there.

Scratching my head, I stare at the hot tub for a few beats. Tendrils of steam wrap around me. That bottle of wine looks good too. It's late, and we're both adults. "Let's sort it out tomorrow. For tonight, wanna share?"

12

MAY I?

Briar

Tonight I've only had one glass, so I can't blame the wine for the way I feel right now.

Flirty. Curious. Hungry.

I can't blame my MO either, since flirty isn't my usual speed. When I go out with friends, I'm usually the designated driver. The mom of the group. My dad's constant warnings about being reliable and dependable above all stuck with me.

But I'm just so ready to say *screw it* for the rest of the night.

As Hollis's question lingers in the hazy night—*wanna share*—I shrug and let my *fuck it* playlist be my guide. "Well, I do owe you one," I say as the song grows louder.

His lips curve up in a thoroughly kissable grin as he

recalls the favor I promised him the night he saved my cat with his friends. His eyes stray to the bubbling jacuzzi in front of us, steam wafting up in invitation. "Then I'll cash in that favor for a hot tub."

Company in the form of a kind and very easy-on-the-eyes man works for me. I've been so tightly wound since the breakup, trying to keep it together as I tried to balance searching for an apartment, launching the app, and prepping for the festival. But reading that awful article tonight tipped my stress right over. I want to forget how it felt to read Steven's cutting words.

Perhaps Hollis can help. Hollis, with his easy smile. His surprisingly thoughtful attitude. His humor.

And, as I look at him a beat longer, his sea-blue eyes, his muscles for days, and that constellation of blue ink-spot bruises that travel across the fair skin of his shoulders and abs.

I want to touch them gently, ask if they hurt.

Yes, he's a very nice distraction from my shitty night. Even Donut thinks so. She hasn't let him out of her eyesight. She's stretched on the wooden planks of the deck, watching his every move as he heads to his duffel wearing nothing but that low-slung towel. He grabs the bag and slings it on his shoulder. "Be right back."

I didn't stare before, wanting to respect his privacy, but I peek now, cataloging the breadth of his chest, the strength of his legs, and most of all, the crook in his grin as he heads inside, leaving me with a wink and a fizzy feeling in my chest that I can't entirely blame on the Chablis.

The guy is lightning fast. I barely have a few seconds to catch my breath, since he's striding right back out onto the deck wearing yellow board shorts and holding a mug. I look him up and down appraisingly. "You're speedy."

"I'm fast at some things. Not others."

Well, that's an invitation, and I take it. "What are you fast at?"

Setting the mug on the wood planks of the deck, he dips a toe in the water. "Skating. Talking. Listening to a woman."

"And what do you take slowly?"

He steps into the hot tub, releasing a slow and satisfied breath as the water caresses his legs. "Getting into a hot tub. Enjoying a meal. Making sure everyone is satisfied," he says, letting that last one float temptingly over to me.

He sinks down, sighing appreciatively as he disappears into the water. I join him, sitting across from him on the other side as my pop playlist cycles to the next tune—an upbeat number on moving on, full of brassy vocals and power chords.

Hollis dips his head back in the water then slides his hands through his hair and groans. Watching him enter a hot tub is one of the sexiest things I've ever seen. It's exciting to watch a man enjoy something so unabashedly. So often men seem to hold back, unless they're watching or playing sports. They rarely, or so I suspect, show their true selves. But there's something refreshingly honest about his visceral enjoyment, then the words, "Fuck me. This is niiiiice."

"Would you like a minute alone with the hot tub?"

Laughing, he shakes his head. "Nope. Hot tubs are like singing and showers. Best enjoyed together."

"I look forward to your morning shower serenade then," I say.

"You've been warned, Briar." He stretches his arms across the back of the tub. "Thanks for sharing. I needed this."

"Rough game?"

"Definitely."

"You should be doing more yoga," I tease.

"You're not wrong."

"It definitely helps with muscle stiffness," I say.

He smirks, perhaps thinking of other stiff things. Or maybe that's just my mind jumping ahead.

He looks around the deck, craning his neck at the stars, then the rolling hills, then the house and finally me. He gestures to my glass. "Now tell me. Why are you drinking regret?"

I grab the nearby bottle, waggling it. "Want to try some? It's a good vintage. A crisp white regret."

"Sounds perfect post-game."

He reaches for his mug and hands it to me. I pour some Chablis, then give it back to him. After a drink, he whistles in approval but then asks again, his expression serious now. "What's going on? Why is this a hot tub of contemplation?"

"It's nothing. I don't want to ruin the vibe," I say, dismissing my earlier comment.

He wiggles his fingers. "Come on. You can't ruin the vibe."

"Oh, I bet I could."

He studies me, arches a brow. "Let's see. You're contemplating life choices in a hot tub. Is it the ex-hole again?"

I grimace, and that's answer enough.

He growls. "You didn't get back together with him, did you?"

I scoff. If I'd been drinking, I would've done a spit-take all over the hot tub. "Do I look stupid?"

"No, you look smart, and smart is hot."

I freeze for a second, letting that compliment sink in. I haven't gotten one like that before, but I like it. "He wrote an article for his website about signs a relationship is in trouble, and he was clearly referencing me without naming me."

Hollis growls, low and menacing. "That guy is the worst."

I'm not usually a blurter. I'm more measured. I keep things inside. But that article unlocked something in me. Something fiery, something angry, so I let it all out. "He said we had no chemistry," I continue, surprised at how easily the details, embarrassing and insulting as they are, spill out. "His top ten list of red flags was about me. A lack of chemistry. A lack of desire. Claiming I didn't know how to kiss."

Hollis blinks, then blinks again, like I can't actually have said that. "Okay, so this guy steals your cat. And for the record, if someone stole my cat, I would have them arrested for a felony. Now, he's talked shit about your fucking sex life? Can I say it?"

"Say what?" I ask, curiously.

"I would like to murder him."

It's spoken nonchalantly, like the only answer for an ex-hole of this magnitude is offing him—and I like it.

"But then how would you take care of the cat in prison?" I ask.

He hums thoughtfully. "You're right. I will refrain from murder for now."

"Then I won't go into details on how he basically said he never liked kissing me," I say. Maybe I am ruining a flirty vibe. But the fact is I'm still ridiculously hurt from reading Steven's veiled but cruel words.

Hollis's eyes are fiery with rage. Maybe he would like to unalive Steven. "He really wrote that?"

"He did. I don't know why I ever trusted him, and I don't know why I didn't see this nasty side in him." Though maybe I do. Steven was all in from the start. For someone who's always sure she's being left, Steven's commitment was a drug. I knock back the rest of my wine, then sigh in admission. "But maybe he's right. I'm not sure I loved kissing him either. I don't know that I felt the chemistry either."

Hollis's smile is pleased and a little smug. "There you go," he says, slapping the water, almost triumphantly. "It wasn't you. It was him."

"I appreciate that. But doesn't it take two to kiss?"

"It does. But that's only part of what makes a kiss good," Hollis says, and his tone is rougher, a little husky.

Just like that, we're not talking about my ex

anymore. We're talking about kissing. "Well, what's the other part?"

The water bubbles around us. My playlist shifts to a romantic tune, a little sultry, a touch sexy, and I'm not entirely sure how this tune is on this playlist, but the pulsing sounds and the soft groove seem to melt into the night. "Communication. Understanding what a woman wants. Listening to her. Reading her body language. Giving her what she needs."

A hot curl of desire unfurls inside my chest, like liquid heat pouring through my body. "Like what sort of things would she need?"

His deep blue eyes hold mine, and for a few seconds, restraint seems to flicker across his irises. Maybe even a touch of concern. For me? For my recent breakup? I'm not sure. But he must let go of his questions, since he asks me instead, "Does she like it slow and sensual? Hot and passionate? Deep and possessive? A gentle caress? An exploration?"

I don't say a word for several seconds. I just *feel* his words. The possibilities. And the dangerous flutters in my chest. Then, because tonight I'm not holding back, I admit something else. "I don't know the answers," I say.

"Why's that?" he asks, like he can't let go of this train of thought either.

I could blame the hot tub. I could maybe blame the wine but I've only had two glasses in two hours. Instead, I blame my ex as I serve up the next truth. "He's the only guy I've been with for the last few years. I'm not even sure I've ever had a really great kiss. The kind that makes your knees weak. That makes your chest tingle. That feels like melting. With him or anyone."

There. It's said. It's out there. I'm the yoga girl who's supposedly in touch with her body, but I've never truly enjoyed intimacy with another person.

I've had sex. I just haven't ever loved it. I'd like to though.

Hollis is flustered for a few seconds, mouth agape, eyes wide. "But that's terrible. That's criminal. That's... just wrong." Then he shakes off his shock. He's strong, confident, the guy who scaled a balcony to rescue a cat. "Everyone should have a great kiss."

I tilt my head, offer a small and hopefully seductive smile. "Why's that?"

"Because kissing is another thing that shouldn't be rushed. It should be savored. It should be enjoyed. It should be drunk slowly like a glass of fine wine."

I don't feel like the mom of the group tonight. I don't feel like the wingwoman. I feel like my own problem solver. The girl who's had enough bad luck. "I don't know what that's like." Then I push past my nerves. "But I'd like to. Maybe this should be the real favor."

He studies me, and questions seem to flash across his eyes. Contemplation, like he's wrestling with something. I see restraint in them once more, then guilt flickers again, clear and obvious. I don't know what to make of the guilt but it passes, turning into *fuck it.* "Let me make one thing clear—this is not a favor. You don't owe me this. But I really want to kiss you, and I'd love to help you figure out how you want to be kissed."

"You do?" I ask the question not because I don't believe him, but because his voice right now is vibrating in my bones. I want to feel that buzz again.

"I really do. And I think I've got a good idea on how to start." He takes a beat. "May I?"

It's the *may I* that does me in.

13

TWO-WAY STREET

Hollis

She's never had a great kiss?

That makes me seriously sad. I can't think about the fans right now, or the rivalry between our two teams. I can't think about anything but fixing that problem ASAP.

Though, admittedly, there's one other issue on my mind. My teammate. I'm not the kind of guy who'd go after his friend's girl. But Briar's not Rhys's ex or his girlfriend. She's simply his crush.

That's fine, right? Yes, that's fine. Of course that's fine.

Besides, I've known Rhys for years. We played against each other a lot in college. We've partied together in the pros. The two of us don't have to call dibs on girls we both like.

For one simple reason—we're excellent at sharing.

But...if you're going to share you kind of need to be in the same place at the same time. And, well, he's not here and I fucking am.

Time to shove Rhys out of my mind as I wait for Briar's answer to the kiss question. When she tilts her head and gives me a playful, teasing smile, saying, "Yes. You may," I seize the chance.

I slide across the seat in the tub, moving next to her in the hot water, the bubbles caressing the swells of her breasts, the water licking her pale, creamy skin.

She bites the corner of her lips. Lifts her chin. Waits for me to make the first move. She hasn't been kissed well in a long time, she said. But also, maybe ever.

That's about to change.

And one of the best parts of kissing is the anticipation. The moment before. The prelude.

I drink in the view of her pretty face. The spray of freckles across the bridge of her straight nose, her rosy cheeks, her sky-blue eyes. She's fresh-faced, a California sunshine girl, with blonde hair full of golden streaks, piled high on her head in one of those magnificently messy buns that make no sense to most men.

Loose tendrils frame her face, sticking to her jawline and her cheek. I lift my right hand. Brush a wet curl away from her skin, tucking it over her ear. She shivers slightly.

My chest swells. She gives a tentative smile but a nervous one too.

I get that. After what she's shared—something

intensely personal—nerves are valid. I do my best to quell them with touch.

"What if we start with nice and slow? You tell me if you like it like that."

Her breath seems to coast across her lips, chased by a hint of laughter, and excitement too. "Try me."

I run my thumb along her jawline down to her chin. Then up and over her lower lip. Her breath hitches. Her eyes flash with expectation. And my bones vibrate with a longing so deep, it's like I can barely remember a time when I didn't want to kiss Briar. The desire to touch her grips me everywhere, but so does a burst of nerves.

And since I'm the guy who talked about communicating, I do a little of my own with a "Hey."

"What is it?" She sounds wary.

I lick my lips. "I'm nervous too," I admit.

Her smile is full of relief. "Yeah? Why?"

"Because all that stuff I said about chemistry? A two-way street?"

"Yes?"

It's like she's on the edge of her seat, waiting for my answer. So I give her a full dose of patent honesty. It's a bare confession: "I really fucking hope I'm not the only one who wants this so badly."

Her arms rope around my neck, her fingers twisting in my hair. "You're not alone then."

"Good. That's so damn good."

I dip my face to hers without a rush in the world, without a worry on my mind, with just this deep, powerful need to kiss the woman I'm unexpectedly sharing a hot tub and a night with.

I coast my lips over hers, tasting chlorine, white wine, and...a wish.

I can taste her vulnerability and hope too. The hope for a kiss that makes her knees weak. Her chest tingle. Her body melt.

I want to make this so damn good for her. I use my best skills. *My ears. My mind. My focus.* I pay attention to everything she does. To the soft murmurs when I kiss her slowly and languidly. To the faint sighs as I tug on her bottom lip. To the curl of her hands tighter and tighter around my neck as I kiss the corner of her mouth. Then, to the way she leans her head back, inviting more kisses.

I kiss and I listen.

I kiss and I learn. In a few short minutes I have a very good idea how Briar likes to be kissed.

Teasingly slow. Temptingly sensual. With subtle hints of kisses that twist and turn into deeper, thirstier drinks. To my lips covering hers, to our tongues skating together. It's a hazy mirage of slow and deep kissing. Nips on corners, bites on lips, then out of nowhere she's sucking on my tongue.

Hello!

That's fucking nice and hot. My cock throbs in my shorts, eager to get in on the listening act too.

But I let Briar take the lead since the woman seems to want to. She gets a little aggressive and feisty and I'm here for it, answering her tempo of hungry kiss after hungry kiss, kissing her harder now, threading a hand through damp strands of her hair.

I promised, though, to help her figure out what she likes, so I break the kiss long enough to ask another question. "You like it a little rough now?"

She nods eagerly. "Yes. Harder."

I groan. "*That word.*"

She wiggles her eyebrows, then whispers, "Harder." It's like she's testing out how it feels to make a request. To ask for it.

"What the lady wants." I curl a hand around the back of her neck then tug her onto my lap.

Water sloshes as she straddles me, sinking onto the ridge of my erection.

I'm the one groaning now—loud and rough and so fucking eager for more of her.

She slides against me, riding the outline of my cock. We kiss until we're hotter and more bothered. Until the temperature between us rises higher than the temperature in the hot tub. Until I can feel the slickness in her bikini even in the water.

Then, I feel a wet eager tongue against my cheek. I break the kiss, laughing as Donut gets in on the action, licking my face.

"She's affectionate," I say.

"I guess she's into you," Briar says, lifting a playful brow.

My lips curve into a cocky grin. I don't say what's on my mind, but maybe Briar reads it since she leans closer, tits pressed to my chest as she whispers, "She's not the only one."

I listen to that cue too. Oh hell, do I ever.

I cup her face, slide my thumb against her top lip, then shove it into the corner of her mouth, letting her suck for a few mind-bending seconds. Letting her take the lead as she kicks this up another few notches.

When she lets go, I say, "Want to take this inside?"

14

THE FIRST GUY

Briar

We sprint.

We're grabbing towels and wine and phones as Donut races with us, jumping at the door as I open it, then immediately beelining to a cushy chair in the living room and curling into a dog ball on it, since she believes all furniture is dog furniture.

Which is reasonable.

But a few steps into the kitchen, it occurs to me Hollis hasn't even seen the inside of the cottage. As I dry off quickly, I nod toward the open living room. "Want a tour?"

"Not on your fucking life," he says, dragging the towel across his broad chest, then tossing it onto a stool.

Stalking me.

Before I know it, he's grabbing me, jerking me against him, then hoisting me up on the kitchen counter, kissing me all over again. There will be time for a tour later.

As he kisses me thoroughly, all I can think is *Steven was wrong*. Or maybe he was right about our kisses.

I never felt like this with my ex. Any ex. I never felt this thrumming in my cells. This heat under my skin. This sweet, slow ache between my thighs.

I tip my face up, asking for more of his ravenous kisses, and he gives them to me, wedging himself between my legs, making himself right at home where I want him. I wrap my ankles around his ass and tug him closer.

The man kisses like he plays hockey. He goes all out. He hustles, he chases opportunities, he holds nothing back. He seems like a damn good candidate to break my streak—the zero *O*'s with another person streak.

A man who goes all out might be just what I need. When he hauls me closer, I go with it, doing my best to just...*enjoy*.

What's not to enjoy, really? His hands coast up my belly, then around to my bikini top, untying it, letting it fall to the tiled floor with a wet *thwap*. I laugh. He laughs at the sound too.

Then our laughter dies when his gaze lands on my breasts.

His smile makes me feel like I'm the birthday present he's always wanted. He looks up, his hungry eyes on me. "You are so fucking pretty everywhere," he says, then he bends and presses a hot, hungry kiss to my right breast, then my left, murmuring, praising them, kissing and sucking and...*wow*.

Maybe this can happen.

His attention feels so good my toes are curling. My skin is tingling. I'm hot, a little electric. Like a firework just lit, the end sparkling. The more he kisses, the faster the flame goes.

But then there's this nagging voice in my mind.

What if...

What if I don't like it...

What if I'm bored...

What if, what if, what if.

I try to shut off the noise, to enjoy the sensations, the pull in my belly, the throb in my core, but I can't quite escape the hum in my head. So I tug his face up and before he can even ask a question, I slide a hand over his hungry cock. It jumps under my palm. His breath hisses.

I squeeze his cock.

This I can handle. Him. His pleasure. So in a flash, I hop off the counter and get down on my knees. When I look up at him, his blue eyes register shock but excitement too. My fingers tease at the waistband of his shorts. "May I?"

He blinks.

His eyes still look hazy. Almost confused. "Yeah," he says huskily.

I peel down the shorts, his cock springing free— long, thick, and hard. I lick the head, swirling my tongue over him, savoring the salty taste. He groans.

I suck a little deeper, looking up at him, a cue for

him to stare at me the whole time. To watch his dick slide past my lips.

It's a sight most men lose control over.

I draw him in deeper. Sucking. Teasing. He ropes a hand in my hair, hips moving slowly almost of their own accord, cock easing past my wet lips. Breath harsh and ragged.

It's good like this. Watching him start to lose it. Knowing he's close. One of us should be.

He's grunting and pumping and panting and gripping my hair. Excitement builds in me. The desire to please. The thrill of an orgasm for someone at least. It won't take long.

But then he grits out a sharp, bitten-off curse. And in a flurry, he hauls me off his dick and pulls me up.

I pout. "Why'd you stop?"

He shakes his head, presses a finger to my lips. "That was so fucking good, I was too close."

"So?"

He shakes his head. "No way am I coming first. You come first," he says.

"Bossy," I tease to keep the mood light.

But maybe he can be the one to back up the demand. He's the best kisser. Maybe he can give me my first joint O.

"Okay," I say, hoping it'll be different this time.

His brow knits. Confusion passes in his eyes, but he's clearly up for whatever challenge I'm throwing his way since he lifts me, tosses me on his shoulder, and carries me to the couch.

Donut watches us, her head cocked in curiosity. I

look away from her though, trying my best to focus on the moment just like I focus on a yoga pose. I'm going deep into my body. I'm sinking into a pose.

Hollis lays me next to his naked body then shimmies off my bikini bottoms, sucking in a powerful breath as his eyes coast over me.

"So fucking gorgeous," he says. "Gorgeous everywhere."

I beam under the praise. I'm not used to it. And I do like it.

I like it, too, when he slides a big hand between my thighs, his fingers finding my slickness right away.

I gasp. Objectively, it's good. I close my eyes, savoring the glide of his fingers, the circling of his thumb, that delicious attention to my clit.

The ache between my thighs sharpens, turns insistent. I feel close, like I can grasp the possibility of a climax, hold it in my hands, clutch it and never let it go.

With more urgency, he kisses my face, my neck, the corner of my mouth while picking up the tempo with his fingers.

He draws maddeningly fantastic circles through my wetness. "You feel so fucking good," he whispers.

And so does he. I'm lifting my hips, asking for more, so impossibly close.

It'll happen. It'll happen this time. I just know it. I'm so sure that I'm panting, moaning, arching. I can feel it.

It's there, just out of reach. Right on the other side.

Almost. *Almost.*

But then, I'm so far into my head, so lost in my wish to finally, *finally* come that I simply can't.

Story of my love life.

I go into cruise control instead, chanting, "Oh god, oh god, oh god."

I curl my toes. Arch my hips. And then I smile woozily. Breathe out hard, like I'm satisfied.

Sigh contentedly.

Maybe now I can finish him off. Someone should get to come, and he deserves it for trying so hard.

But when I blink open my eyes, Hollis is staring down at me like I'm a puzzle that both impresses and intrigues him. "You just faked it."

I freeze. It's not the first time I've faked it.

But he's the first guy to notice.

15

DISTRACT ME

Rhys

"So they're not trading me?"

"Rhys. I already answered this," Amira says, then stares at me sharply, her gaze even more intense in those silver-framed cat-eye glasses. It's intimidating, the intensity of her glare. But that's why I hired her last year. I needed a change.

We're at Eggs-cellent on Thursday morning. This breakfast café in Hayes Valley is Amira's choice. The remains of her omelet—no butter, no oil, extra kale—are debris on her plate.

"But what do you hear? You know, the grapevine and all," I press.

She sets down her cup of coffee. "What have I told you a thousand times before?"

Chastened, I mutter, "You don't have a crystal ball about trades."

She's not done though. "And do I read minds?"

I look down at my empty plate that once housed scrambled eggs and rosemary potatoes. I don't answer.

"Hun," she prompts. "Did I acquire mind-reading superpowers in the last week?"

I look up, sighing. "No."

"And if I were to acquire superpowers, what would they be?"

"The ability to wear high heels while not actually arching your foot," I answer by rote.

She taps her red flats against the floor, making her point. "Exactly."

Amira called me last week after yoga to tell me she was meeting with the Golden State Foxes GM right after the All-Star break, when we head out for our next away stretch. She insists she's seeing him to discuss a renewal for me.

I'll believe that when I see the papers.

It's not that I doubt her. But I've been on edge with the trade deadline approaching in a month. The rumors are rampant about me in sports media. And rumors often become facts. Like, say, all the things I heard my parents whisper about behind closed doors when I was younger. Those whispers came true—my brother's not here anymore.

Amira pushes my empty cup toward me, drained of English Breakfast. "Let's get you some more tea. You're not drinking enough tea. Did you try the Earl Grey with bergamot I sent you last week? The shop told me it was the best," she says in her rapid-fire, mile-a-minute tone. Amira's from the Dominican Republic but was raised in New York, and while she doesn't have an accent from either place, she does speak with the speed of the East Coast.

"It was great. I'm addicted to it," I say, grateful for her little agent gifts. Admittedly, the tea was a good distraction from my incessant thoughts.

Briefly, she stares at the ceiling, tapping her chin, two chunky gold bracelets jangling up and down her dark brown skin. "But what is bergamot?"

"I think it's orange?"

She lifts her phone to her mouth. "Hey, Google, what is bergamot?"

"Would you like me to play a Rick James song?" the phone asks in a robotic voice.

I laugh.

She shakes her head. "This is why AI has a ways to go." Then concern flickers across her shrewd eyes. "Wait. I'm all wrong. Robots are smart. This is subliminal stuff. I wouldn't mind hearing some Rick James later."

I laugh more, and for the first time since we sat down, I feel a bit less tense. It's nice *not* to talk shop for a moment.

"Bergamot aside," she says, gentling her tone, "you need to try to stop worrying. What have I told you? You can't control trades or the trade rumor mill."

"But have you met my anxiety?" It's said self-deprecatingly, though Amira knows it's true.

She pats my hand in a maternal sort of way. "I know. But have you met me? Let me handle the trade worries, contracts, and sponsorships. You handle the stick."

"I will but…" I drag my hands through my hair, messing it up, tension seeping back into my bones as I think about the future. It's a gift to be able to play at the highest level. Hell, it's a gift to be able to use your body at all. "I want to have a great year. Last year I was out for nearly a month with an injury. The year before with my old team went to the dogs. I can't let any of that happen again."

"I know. Your old team. The ankle. Your ex. But you just keep playing the best you can."

"That's always the goal."

"And you are terrifically obsessive about it," she says, knowing me too well.

"So don't get distracted by romance?" I add because that guideline has helped this season. I've stayed far away from the scourge known as love.

She arches a brow, then gently chides me with, "I didn't say that. But your ex sure did a number on you."

"Maintaining multiple profiles on a dating site and shagging other men had an impact," I say dryly.

"Yes, but you're also hard on yourself. Maybe you want to do something about that? Meditation, mindfulness—maybe see a therapist about anxiety. There are some great psychologists who specialize in sports. The team has one."

I shudder.

"What's that for?"

I lean closer, like that'll drive my point home. "I want to stay with the team. I don't want to let on I'm a fucking mess about staying with them."

She smiles sympathetically. "Seeing the team

psychologist is not some kind of negative mark. But be that as it may, do you want me to find a therapist that specializes in sports and athletes for you outside of your stadium?"

Yes. No. I don't know. "You do enough, Amira."

"My job is to do more than enough. And listen, I know you stress. I get it. You like the team and want to stay. But no amount of wanting will change the fact that you don't have a no-trade clause. So maybe it would help to talk to someone? Or, you know, do more yoga," she says, then knocks back the rest of her coffee.

But maybe even yoga isn't safe. Not if I keep having these dirty thoughts about my instructor. I blow out a breath, scrubbing a hand across my jawline. Am I really this tightly wound?

Truth is, I've been tightly wound for a while. I've seen plenty of shrinks, too, since my brother died a decade ago when I was sixteen and he was twenty. Fact is, this is just who I am now.

"Maybe I'll try to relax in Lucky Falls," I say, then we shoot the breeze about the latest TV shows we've been watching and the conversation change eases some of the tension in me. From the tea talk to the TV talk, I'm finding a distraction definitely helps.

By the time we're done, I feel marginally better about the incessant trade rumors. I feel better, too, that I have an agent who understands me.

And friends.

Like Gavin, who's waiting at the curb in his car when my meeting is done. I hop inside and announce, "I need a distraction."

16

MORE TO COME

Gavin

He came to the right guy then. When a friend needs something, I make it happen. First, though, I give Rhys a little hell. Just to keep him on his toes.

I tap the gas and head up Divisadero, sunglasses on, rock music pumping through the car. "Why do you need a distraction? They're getting rid of your sorry ass?"

"You'd miss me. You pretend you wouldn't, but you would."

I scoff. Like I'd let on I'd miss him fiercely. Also, he fucking knows I'm joking. "Doubtful."

"You'd cry like a baby every day."

"I'd never shed a tear."

"You'd be a right blubbering mess."

"I'd celebrate every day. And I'd be more determined than ever to be part of the team that mows you down."

"Revenge, eh?"

"It's fucking motivating, isn't it?" Hell, it's kept me going for a damn long time.

Well, not revenge. More like...vindication. There's little quite as satisfying as proving the naysayers wrong. Not only did my aunt and uncle who raised me say I'd never be a pro hockey player, but my uncle said I'd never amount to much of anything. That it was a burden for him and Mom's sister to raise me after my parents were killed.

Oh, and the snake of a man said I couldn't cook to save my life. Proved him wrong on that count too.

As I drive, Rhys seems to give my rhetorical question some real thought. "Fair point, mate. Is that why we hate the Sea Dogs so much?"

"Because they've won more cups than us."

"And we weren't even with the Foxes when they won," he says as we cruise onto the Golden Gate Bridge.

"But revenge gets passed on. And its cousins, rivalry and passion," I say.

Rhys leans back in the passenger seat, like he's relaxing into it. "You're a helluva teammate, Worthy."

I smile, a pleased feeling spreading across my chest. That's the goal. That's all I've ever wanted to be. When you grow up raised by people you can't rely on, there's nothing better than being a guy your teammates can count on. It's a fucking calling, and no matter who I play for, where I play, I won't ever be the guy to let down a teammate.

"So are you, man," I say, then I tap the dashboard as a new tune swells across the speakers. A workout song. The kind you play to get pumped up. "And listen, we're going to play our asses off the rest of the season. Focus on the prize and be the last team standing. But what kind of distraction do you want in the meantime? New car? A poker night? A rousing round of Candy Land?" I ask as we pass the Marin Headlands, cruising by the big, beautiful hills that'll take us to Wine Country. Before he answers, I offer one more. "Or maybe you need to get laid."

He rolls his eyes but then goes quiet as we wind past Sausalito, the Richardson Bay glittering to the right.

I smirk. "I'm talking your language now. See? I think you just need to blow off some steam. Maybe when we're in Lucky Falls you can get laid again and break your un-laid streak."

"You and your streaks," Rhys says, seeming amused.

"You like your un-laid streak?"

"I don't believe in superstitions," he counters.

"But I do," I say, since they aren't truly superstitions. They're a mindset. An athlete needs habits to compete at the highest level. Practice is a habit, excellence is a habit, teamwork is a habit. If you get lazy, you get sloppy, then you start missing chances on the ice and in life.

Habit is the best friend of an athlete. Ever since his ex fucked with his heart last year, Rhys has been in the habit of resistance. But it's messing with his head. "You said you need a distraction. So, yeah, break that streak with a distraction."

"And you're my wingman?"

"If that's what you need in Lucky Falls, then yes," I say.

A little later, as we exit the highway and slow to a stop at a light, a message flashes across my phone screen.

> Hollis: It appears we may have a roomie for the week

I tip my chin toward my phone in its holder. "Can you see what that's all about?"

"Course." Rhys picks up his phone. Scrunches his brow. "Hollis says, and I quote, *we might be sharing a rental with Briar. More to come.*"

I picture the tenacious blonde who went to the ends of the earth for her pet.

I remember her offer to drive us all home.

I think about her thank you texts, her picture of her dog, and the way she looked when she ran across the parking lot that night.

Then, when my pulse pounds, my brain connects all the dots at once. I'm fucking attracted to her.

All of a sudden, I'm the tense one.

17

THE AVOIDANCE POSE

Briar

I can't hide forever on the deck.

But I can make this pose last for a long time. I can backbend the hell out of this moment here on the deck on Thursday morning in the early February California sun.

Maybe Hollis will just make some coffee and leave.

Except...

I feel awful for thinking that.

It's not my style to avoid things. I still just feel so... ridiculous after last night. I don't know what else to say to this kind, funny, outgoing man who tried so hard to please me.

Except what I already said when he called me out. *It's not you—it's me.*

Then I said it was no big deal and I needed some

sleep. I immediately retreated to the bedroom and considered never coming out.

But I can't practice the avoidance pose forever. I need to meet with the Sea Dogs strength and conditioning coach before my first class at the festival.

On that to-do list note, I finish my practice, coming out of the pose, sitting cross-legged, then taking several calming breaths before I rise. Donut rises too. I pat my thigh, a cue for her to follow me, and head inside to face the first man who's learned my dirty little secret even though I have no clue what to say to him.

Good morning! I have intimacy issues. How are you?

Inside the kitchen, Hollis is shirtless and meticulously slathering avocado on a chunky piece of sourdough toast with the back of a spoon. He must have grabbed groceries this morning since that doesn't look like the loaf of bread I bought the other day.

"Who invented avocado toast?" He holds up the breakfast item like it's Simba. "Seriously. Have you thought about it? It's up there with penicillin and birth control."

That stops me in my tracks and stops me from ogling him in just those workout shorts that hug his hips. "Birth control?"

"Well, yeah. It's a great invention. It gives a woman more choice." He taps his bare chest with his free hand. "Raised by a single mom here."

My heart twists, and I feel even worse for my sex failures. My ex was right. The problem is me. I couldn't even come for a hot, sweet, flirt of a man who not only cares about women but bought his own groceries rather than snitching mine.

"It's a top invention for sure," I say brightly, glad we're not talking about last night at least. He's moved on, so I can too. I grab onto the conversational offering he just gave me as I snag a banana from the counter. "And I was raised by a single dad," I say.

One eyebrow quirks up in obvious interest. "Yeah?"

"My mom took off when I was ten."

His expression twists in irritation. "Eight for me. Damn, are we living parallel lives?"

"Maybe," I say, unpeeling the fruit, then breaking off a chunk since it's too hard to eat a banana in front of a guy any other way. It's not like I'm going to slice it with a knife. That's the worst way to eat it. Then I add lightly, "I mean, I like avocado toast and antibiotics too."

He laughs as I pop in a chunk of fruit, and his laughter has to be a sign we're both going to sweep last night under the rug and never speak of it again. Just to be sure though, I shift to practical matters as Hollis spins around and grabs the sea salt from the cupboard. "I talked to Kailani. She said she felt terrible that she put me in your rental by mistake, but she has nothing else for me this week." I fasten on a helpful smile, since I'm kind of the interloper here, and he has every right to just kick me out. "But we slept in separate bedrooms last night, so maybe it won't be weird to share this cottage?"

I really don't want to stay with my dad. I love him and all, but I want to be close to the festival. After the last week of commuting, I don't want to drive back and forth for everything.

Hollis winces, sets down the sea salt. "About that... It's not just me though. The guys are coming too."

My eyes pop. "Guys?"

"Rhys. Gavin."

This is the mother of all booking snafus. I peer into the living room, then up the steps to the loft above. We can squeeze in. We can definitely squeeze. "There's a loft and two bedrooms," I suggest, trying to make this work as I break off another small bite.

"And a couch," he says, gesturing to the scene of my fake out and my failure.

I cringe. "I'll stay with my dad."

Hollis shoots me a look that says *c'mon.* "No. You won't."

"Bossy," I say but it doesn't feel as light as it did when I said it last night.

"I'll sleep on the couch. There's also a tiny house on the property. There's plenty of room. And you don't need to deal with more shit in your life right now."

Yup, I'm definitely the problem. "You're too kind. But I can't, especially after—"

"Listen, about last night. I'm sorry—"

I can't have him think the fake *O* incident is his fault. I have to try again to fix this. I set down the phallic fruit and advance closer but not too close. "Hollis, I swear it's not you. Truly. You're hot and sexy, and your hands are amazing, and your kisses melted me." *And you look too tempting standing here in barely anything.* "So it's not you," I say, even though I hate opening up. I hate letting people in. "I just...it's a me thing. I don't really orgasm." There. That's enough. I don't want him to think it's his fault.

He blinks, horrified. "Wha-a-a-t?"

"With others," I say quickly, fidgeting with a jar of wooden spoons, like they need rearranging. "But seriously. I meant what I said last night. It's no big deal." That big spoon should go *here*. This little spoon *there*. "But we don't have to keep rehashing it and you don't have to apologize. Can we just...not talk about it again?"

He sighs. Appears to give it some thought. "On one condition."

Is he going to ask to try again? Would I mind another shot? The tingles that rush down my chest say *I wouldn't mind at all*. But then a voice in my head says, *You know what would happen? Nothing, sucker!*

"What's the condition?" I ask. I'm not sure if I want him to sex blackmail me or not. I do, and I don't. I don't, and I do.

His grin is confident, borderline cocky. Like he knows he has a winning hand. "You stay here with us."

18

BE OUR GUEST

Briar

Before I can answer him, Donut perks up from the living room floor, floppy ears lifting. She rushes to the front door and springs into the air, attempting to unlock it once again with a jump.

I snap my gaze toward my pup then peer out the window, spotting a sleek cherry-red car. I don't recognize the make or model, but it sounds electric, since, well, it's silent. But the crunchy gravel driveway is not.

Donut launches herself up again and again. Hollis looks at her curiously. "She jumps?"

Translation: how does a Dachshund spring two feet in the air when she's not even one foot tall?

"She thinks she can jump-open a door."

He seems to take that in as we stride to the door together, and it occurs to me I should answer him.

He's been polite.

Kind.

And ridiculously generous in his shirtless-ness. But three sexy hockey studs and me sharing a house that's really for three? "You don't think it'll be awkward if I stay here?"

It's already awkward this morning. There's so much weird tension. Which is understandable. But still, it's there, like the lingering scent of garlic in the kitchen long after you've cooked a stir-fry.

A line digs into his forehead. "Because of—"

Before he can say *last night,* I wave that off. "Because of the house situation."

"We're good at sharing," he says casually, advancing ahead of me toward the door while I chew on that.

We're good at sharing.

He can't mean...

Or does he?

No, he's just talking about square footage and stuff. Not other kinds of sharing.

I try to dismiss the thoughts racing through my head as Hollis swings open the door. I tell Donut to stay by my side and she complies, parking her butt on the floor.

"Thanks but we don't need any solar panels, security systems, or window washing," Hollis calls out to the guys, wasting no time diving into the taunts.

"Then you can come get our bags and carry them in," Gavin says, not missing a beat either as he steps out of the driver's side, aviator shades on, brown hair wavier than usual, stubble coming in thicker than it was last week. It's a good look on the strapping guy. He's really got the whole strong-sturdy-man-who-can-scale-mountains thing working.

Rhys gets out a second later, unfolding his body from the passenger seat. He's so handsome it's like looking at the sun. Feels like it too. I'm just warmer in his presence. There's something so *GQ* about him, but the scar on his eyebrow humanizes him. The imperfection amidst his perfection. He wears khakis and a black Henley that hugs his strong pecs. Gavin's dressed in gray joggers and a dark blue T-shirt that's nice and snug.

My gaze swings back to Hollis now, roaming up and down the hockey player next to me who's wearing nearly nothing.

The thoughts tango once more in my brain. All new possibilities. Configurations. *Yoga poses.*

That I really need to snap out of.

Gavin turns his focus to me, nodding in a cool, slightly distant hello. "Hey there," he says, voice dry, tone inscrutable.

I don't feel inscrutable though. I feel a little transfixed as Gavin whips off his shades. Our eyes lock. Or is it just me thinking they lock? Me feeling some sort of pull? A charge sparking in the air?

"Hi," I say. My pulse stutters, and I try to get a handle on these reactions I'm having.

I turn to Rhys again, like that'll cool me off. But his lips are curved in a playful grin. Has his smile always been so...sexy?

"Lovely to see you, Briar," Rhys says, and that

accent. That word. *Lovely*. It's even more delicious said by him.

"You too," I answer, and I should say something more. *How was the drive? What's going on? Great game last night.* Really I should. But I feel kind of syrupy. A little slow as I try to figure out what's happening inside me and around me as the tension between Hollis and me warps hotly into something else—something I don't entirely understand.

Hollis nods to the tiny house next to the garage. "That's yours. Enjoy."

Gavin scratches his face with his middle finger.

Rhys rolls his eyes as he grabs a duffel from the backseat. "I believe I arranged the rental with the festival organizer, so you can enjoy the little bed, Goldilocks," Rhys says to Hollis.

Hollis shakes his head defiantly. "I was here first. Shotgun."

Gavin arches a brow, then tosses out nonchalantly, "I'm happy to take you on in poker if you want to settle it that way."

Hollis blanches. Well, I guess Gavin is formidable with cards. "Fine, fine. You two can sleep on the living room floor," he says.

As Rhys strides along the stone path cutting through the mustard flower lawn, his dark eyes hold mine. "And are you our guest for the week, Briar?"

My name now sounds like *lovely*. What kind of sorcery is that English accent doing to me? A zing rushes down my chest. An answer. But am I saying yes to Hollis's demand too? Is that what a dependable, reliable, focused woman would do?

"Well, as long as I don't have to sleep on the carpet," I say, finally, *finally* finding more than a few words to say. I'm not sure they'll cut the awkward tension between Hollis and me though. Or resolve what exactly I'm saying yes to.

Hollis turns my way, flashing that generous, easy grin that melted me last night. That still...melts me. "Ladies' choice."

There's something a little naughty in those words. A little sexy, like he's undeterred by my issue last night. Did Hollis insist I stay because he's planning something for me? Does he want...another chance? A beat of arousal pulses inside me at the thought. Then, it intensifies when I look at the other men heading my way.

As they reach the steps, Donut greets each one, saying hello to Rhys, then Gavin, then Hollis again.

She's got the right idea. Sharing her affection.

Get a grip. Your dog is not sending you subliminal sex messages. She's a dog. That is all.

When we're all on the porch though, my cheeks heat. A splash of warmth rushes down my chest.

Why am I so flushed?

It's not just because they're all handsome, though objectively they are. And yes, of course I'm attracted to Hollis. I knew that last night. But now, as I stand between the three men, forming a circle around me, a new reality dawns, like the sun rising bright and clear on the horizon.

That chemistry I felt for Hollis last night? It's even

more intense with his teammates here. I feel something floaty in my chest. A warm, hazy sensation of...attraction. To all of them. All at once.

"So, you're staying with us?" Gavin asks, like he needs to confirm that. Or maybe like he's up to something too?

Rhys moves closer to me, dropping a kiss to my cheek.

Oh. Wow. That's a nice greeting. It catches me off guard, and I'm dizzy once more. For the briefest of seconds, I lift my palm to my cheek, almost like I'm catching that kiss. But then I drop my hand when I realize Hollis is watching us. His gaze is intrigued—curious even. Like he's filing that data point away.

"Hollis mentioned you might be our roomie for the week," Rhys says.

Already? We only just discussed it minutes ago. I look to Hollis again, trying to get my bearings. "You did?"

"I texted them that you were here. I wanted them to know we might have a guest."

There's that word again—*guest*.

Not roomie. But guest. Like I'm someone special staying with them.

"But I didn't say yes," I point out but I'm not sure why I'm arguing semantics. Maybe because I'm not that sure of anything right now.

"So, are we all sharing this house for the next week or what?" Gavin asks, nodding to the inside, clearly ready for a verdict.

Hollis meets my gaze once more, looking like he did

last night when he asked *May I.* Open, considerate. "It's up to you, Briar," he says, but there's a glint in his blue eyes. It's hopeful and a little naughty at the same time.

Pretty sure he does want another chance with me.

Do I want to take one? I don't know what I want anymore, especially when I feel so unmoored. And so overwhelmed.

I picture the next several days—me shacking up in a house with three hot hockey stars while I pretend I don't want to ride the guy from last night.

While his friends watch.

While his friends touch me too.

I feel like I'm wearing these new potent wishes on my face.

I try to clear my thoughts and my voice, hoping I don't sound husky as I say, "Sure." Then I adjust my ponytail, brush a hand over the side of my sports bra, and check the time. "I should, um, get over to the festival. You guys just let me know where to sleep."

I spin around and race-walk to my room, Donut following. I shut the door behind us with a loud snick, then slump against it, trying to catch my breath.

There's a whole new tension in the cottage now, but I'm not sure I can blame what happened last night...or what didn't happen.

My heart races. I've got to calm down. To focus on the day ahead of me. The classes I'm holding. The promotional opportunities for my fitness brand. The chance to get my name out there so I can launch my app.

Not these dangerous thoughts of the guys on the

rival hockey team circling me, prowling around me, touching me.

I rush to the en-suite bathroom, splashing cold water on my face over and over. I stare in the mirror at my pinkened cheeks. "It's fine. You're a pro. You worked with them before. You're not going to do anything more with Hollis. Or the others. You're not attracted to three guys all of a sudden." I look down at Donut. "Right?"

She just jumps—her answer for everything.

Shoving this inconvenient attraction out of my head, I return to the living room where I find the guys in the kitchen negotiating the two bedrooms and the loft. "I'll take the futon," Gavin says, pointing upstairs.

"Gee. Who gets the couch then?" Rhys asks, nodding toward the blue sofa.

Gavin takes a beat before answering drolly, "I wasn't saying you should take the couch."

I'm almost afraid to ask what Gavin *was* saying.

I clear my throat as I scurry over to the counter to toss the banana rind into the compost bin. "Hi! I'm taking off with Donut. Just let me know if I can get anything for the house. Groceries? Fruit? Cucumbers? Eggplants? More bananas?"

What was that? I shut the hell up immediately.

"I'll get some food and stuff. We can all have dinner tonight. I'll cook," Gavin offers. Then, he smirks. "But I was just saying maybe you and Rhys can share the king-size bed."

He says it so innocently. Too innocently.

But there's no way that's happening. Rhys lifts a finger like he's about to speak, but before any of these guys can say another word, I wave quickly in the direction of the garage. "I'll sleep in the tiny house. I'll move my things later. And I can help in the kitchen," I say, speeding right past the musical beds and into how to stay busy when sharing a small space with three sexy men I'm suddenly fantasizing about. "I like to cook."

Rhys advances closer to me, his dark eyes intense. "Briar, you're not sleeping in the tiny house," he says, an order. A firm one.

"I don't mind," I say, even though I never checked it out. I didn't need to since for the last week I've had the main bedroom and the king-size bed all to myself.

"I looked this place up online after it was booked. There's no toilet in the tiny house. No man"—he pauses, reconsiders—"no decent man is going to let a woman, let alone a woman who's *our guest,* stay there. We're also not the kind of blokes who are going to kick you out of your room. So I have a plan."

A spark ignites in my chest. This is the Rhys from the cat rescue. The Rhys who devised a strategy just like that. "Yes?"

"You stay in the main bedroom," Rhys says, like he'd never consider me leaving that room. "Hollis can stay where he is, since shotgun or whatever. Gavin will sleep upstairs. And I'll stay on the couch."

I want to protest since no one likes sleeping on couches.

But Rhys offers a cheeky smile and brooks no argument when he says, "I can sleep anywhere. I'm flexible like that." Emphasis on *flexible.* Like he's leaning into his yoga practice. He tips his forehead to Hollis and Gavin. "Those guys? They're more set in their ways."

"You're a gentleman and a trooper," I say, amused and grateful, too, for the way he's sorted this out.

"I'll go to the store," Gavin says, all business.

Hollis clears his throat. "I'll help with dinner as well." He sounds a little put in his place.

"And I'll get the champagne," Rhys adds.

Just like that we have a plan for tonight.

But it sounds like a date.

I leave with my girl on her leash, hustling toward town, texting my brother about the app and trying desperately to focus on business when my phone pings with a message that makes me want to throw it in the river.

19

THE FINE PRINT

Briar

My heart rate quickens as I open the email. It's from my ex's website announcing a contest they're running.

I thought I'd unsubscribed to Steven's *A Man's Man* emails. But, shockingly, in the midst of getting kicked out of my home while I wasn't looking, I forgot that little detail. As I pass a pink house with an antique weather vane on the roof, I brace myself. Sneakers smacking the sidewalk, I read through the details of the contest. It's a slap in the face.

I squeeze my phone like I can shake the life out of him through this mobile device. I clench my jaw, breathe hard through my nostrils. He's such a thief. The cat, my sexual dignity, and now my ideas.

This contest he's launching was my idea.

My chest burns from the kindling he constantly throws on the ex fire, but I have to let my anger go. I have to snuff these flames. I need to manifest mindfulness, positivity, and calm.

I try some affirmations the rest of the way to the town square. *I am leading the life I want.*

As I pass a bookshop with a display of chilling thrillers, Donut looks up with her trusting brown eyes. She tilts her head, as if asking what's going on with me and my funk.

My heart squeezes with affection for my pup. She was abandoned once. That's why she wound up at Little Friends and with me. I know the feeling of someone leaving all too well. I'll never do that to her.

After my mom's two visits, she sent me birthday letters, and Christmas cards, and pointless gifts, like paintings she'd made of places she'd visited, like I wanted them. I almost wish I never heard from her again.

I tell my dog what's got me in a funk. "It's an email from Steven's site and yes, you always knew best about him, you brilliant doggess," I say to Donut, since maybe voicing that will help me let go of my anger some more.

She trots along, tail wagging. A saucy little thing who never liked the jerk. Yep. I'll keep putting Steven behind me. Like Donut's done.

The streets around us bustle with the hum of a fair just beginning. While the Sunburst Summit Festival features music, wine, and outdoor activities, there are crafts and street food everywhere too. In the town square, the air is filled with the savory aroma of grilled veggies, small-batch waffles, and homemade crepes. Booths are peddling tasty treats while vendors sell handmade crafts, vintage jewelry, and chai lattes that make me thirsty.

The sound of laughter and music floats on the breeze as families and friends gather around a large free-standing stage where two women in bohemian skirts tune their guitars—a duo ready to usher in an afternoon of sunshine, wine, and song. I pass them then set up in a gazebo past the town square, laying down my mat, then setting another one next to it. "Lie down, girl," I tell Donut.

With a beleaguered sigh—oh, the frustration of a freeloading dog who must behave during class—she complies. "Good girl," I say as she shifts into her favorite pose—dog ball.

I do a few sun salutations to calm my frayed nerves, and they work. They almost always work. Devoting energy to my body helps settle my overactive mind.

Except, well, when I'm in bed.

But best not to think about bed now either as attendees filter in. I say hi to the eager students, ask about their days, find out how they're feeling.

My dad always said business was reliable. But romance? Relationships? Trust?

That stuff is best avoided.

* * *

An hour later, I walk quietly amidst the class, checking the warrior poses, the eagle arms, the triangles and offering a tweak here, a suggestion there before I lead them into a final affirmation in the warm air.

"Take a deep breath," I say in my calm voice meant to soothe. "Repeat your affirmation once more. *I am leading the life I want.*"

I repeat it in my mind. Believing it. Needing to believe it.

The twenty-five or so attendees, including Nova from the Sea Dogs, and Aubrey, smile, breathe out, and say the affirmation one more time.

My father was right. My career fulfills me. My career doesn't stab me in the back. My career doesn't steal my ideas.

"Thank you all for coming. Be sure to subscribe to my videos on YouTube," I say, and this is always the hardest part of a class—the sale. But a necessary one. "I'll be launching my app soon, and I hope you'll all check out Flow and Flex Fitness."

There are quiet *thank yous*, and *I'll be sure to check it outs* as students pack up and leave. When most are gone, Nova comes up to me. The strength and conditioning coach is strong and muscular, the picture of health, and has a body that says she works hard for it. She also seems to enjoy her body too, judging from the plethora of piercings glinting along her ears and nose, and the intricate tattoos that coast up and down her brown skin. "Good to see you here, Briar," she says. "I'm glad you got this slot."

"Thank you for helping me with the connections," I say, since she recommended me for the festival.

"Just make sure our strength and conditioning program looks the best." Her tone is light but her eyes say she means it seriously. Innovation is important for her.

"Definitely." It's a good and necessary reminder. My job here is to represent me, yes. But also the Sea Dogs. It's not to lust after not one, not two, but three players on the rival hockey team.

As she tucks her mat under her arm, she says, "I was thinking, too, of adding an afternoon yoga and stretching class for the players. For stress relief. It's something we think about a lot with our athletes. What can they do to manage stress?"

"I'd love to help. I have a whole video series on yoga for stress relief. We could tailor it to *When you stress about winning the cup,*" I say.

"I like it," she says, then tells me we'll talk more in the coming days.

When she leaves, Aubrey waves, then nods toward a picnic table in the vineyard. Time for my own stress relief—girlfriend time. Aubrey's here with Ivy and Trina, who have just joined her. They're all good friends, and I've gotten to know them better recently. They enlisted me to join Trina's book club. And we all volunteer at the dog rescue together.

We also run in the same circles with the same friends. Like Hollis, and now Gavin and Rhys. An image of the three of them surrounding me on the porch flashes before my eyes. Heat flickers down my body.

I try once more to shake off the lusty thoughts.

After I straighten up the gazebo, Donut and I join them at the picnic table. The second I sit down, I whip out my phone and show them the email. Oops, I guess I haven't put Steven's contest in the past after all.

"So yesterday he ran a piece on five ways to know your relationship is in trouble. Want to know what the ex-hole is up to now?" I ask, irritated all over again.

Aubrey winces. "I do but I don't."

Trina raises a hand enthusiastically. "I do. Tell us what Captain Prick did."

"Remember how I was encouraging him to get more input from women for his site? To seek out a woman's POV? To hire some female columnists?"

"Yes," Ivy says, and I can hear the mama growl in her voice.

"Now he's running a contest for essays from a woman on...wait for it...*what makes a great boyfriend.*"

Ivy's lips twist into a sneer and she smacks the table. "That was your idea!"

I tap my nose. "Exactly. But he said *it's not what the audience wants, but thanks so much for your input,*" I say, imitating his patronizing tone. "But now he's taken my idea. The irony. I loved to help him and share ideas so he could move beyond just being a dude-bro advice site. I suggested he hire more woman-owned firms, like marketing firms and such. Then, I suggested this contest."

"Are you kidding me?" Aubrey asks, incredulous because of course that is shocking to her. Her two men are wildly supportive of her career, her hopes, her dreams.

"I wish I were joking," I say, feeling stupid all over again. "Another red flag I missed. And sure, he never offered ideas for my business, but I just thought yoga wasn't his thing. And I told myself I was fine with it even as I tried to help him."

Trina lifts a glass of wine, knocks some back then sets it down with panache. "So, you're going to enter, right?"

I scoff. Shake my head. "One, I know nothing about what makes a great boyfriend. Two, I don't want to be associated with him."

Ivy grabs my phone and peers at the email, studying it intensely. Then grinning wickedly. She spins the phone around and points to some text on the screen. "Does this change your mind?"

I read the fine print. Holy shit. That absolutely does.

20

I AM A SPONGE

Hollis

It's official. I'm a dog with a bone, and I can't let it go. I can't stop googling *how to help a woman orgasm, what to do for a woman who doesn't climax easily,* and *techniques for the non-comer.*

Those are names of articles I've read—or really, had the text-to-speech app read back to me—on my run. I found a quiet back road to get my miles in and managed to slip out of the cottage while Rhys and Gavin were checking out the first day of the festival.

I am a goddamn sponge, soaking up all the intel on how to improve a woman's pleasure. Everything from better communication, to mixing things up, to taking more breaks for kissing, to music, porn, and kink.

As I run up a hill, passing lush, rolling vineyards, my mind is swimming with bedroom ideas. My running playlist reverberates in my earbuds, and the pump-me-up tunes take on a new meaning. It's not to inspire *me* to run faster or harder.

But to inspire me to *please* Briar better.

I don't even feel like I'm keeping a secret from Rhys. Briar's request that I say nothing trumps everything. So I've been exonerated from telling him the truth.

I am not, however, exonerated from failure to launch.

Thanks to my research, I have an idea about how to help her, and it just might be borderline brilliant.

When I reach the top of the hill, my heart is slamming hard against my rib cage. I pace along the quiet road so I can ask Google for the nearest location of a certain store. Then I turn around and head back. It's fun to run downhill, but you have to pace yourself. That's a metaphor that will serve me well, or so I hope, in bed.

When I reach the rental, I'm sweat-soaked and energized. Since I don't have anywhere to be for a while, I unlock my car with the app, peel away from the cottage, and head off on my errand.

Forty-five minutes later, I've returned with a gift wrapped in pretty pink paper and a card to go with it. When I trot up the porch, my heart is pounding hard again, this time with hope that no one else is here. Quietly, I open the door. I check for signs of Briar in the living room, then the kitchen. She's not in either room, and Donut doesn't greet me.

Good.

But Gavin's standing in front of the cupboards in the kitchen, staring intently at a video on his phone—

looks like someone's cooking on it—as he taps in notes at the same time.

The shower's running, so Rhys must be in it.

Perfect. I just need to slip past Gavin. Maybe he won't notice me tiptoeing down the hall. His focus is legendary, after all, so hopefully it works in my favor. Without making a sound, I break right, beelining to Briar's room.

I'm a cat. I'm a spy. I'm a silent superhero.

"Aww. You got me a gift. It looks so pretty."

Damn. I straighten at her door, calling back to him. "Yup. It's the perfume you like, Worthy."

If I'm lucky, the convo will end there. I rap lightly on Briar's door. No one answers. I twist the handle and cross the room to the nightstand, then I leave the gift there with the card and the note inside.

There. Pulled it off. But when I spin around, Gavin stands in the doorway, arms crossed.

"Dude." It's a stern correction.

That one word says everything, so with a sigh, I answer his unasked question. "Yes, I'm gonna fucking tell Rhys I'm into her."

"Good. You'd better." He looks at his watch. "Maybe soon?"

I roll my eyes. "Yes, Dad."

I get an eye roll right back as he asks doubtfully, "Were you really going to?"

"Yes, I really was." I leave then shut the door, nodding toward the scene of the gift. "Maybe don't mention *that* though?"

"That?" he asks, seeming a little confused.

"Yes. That." I don't need to spell it out.

"So you don't want me to mention...*that?*" He sketches air quotes.

"Yeah. That."

"You can say it, Hollis."

"Say what?" I ask, feigning innocence.

He shakes his head, amused. "You really think I don't know you bought her a sex toy?"

I groan in frustration—with myself. "Just hoping you hadn't figured it out."

He snorts. "I'd already figured out you were into her from the way you looked at her like a hungry dog. Really, the sex-toy gift was just basic context clues. The pink paper, the nightstand, the sneaky walk down the hall like you thought you were pulling it off."

Jesus. How transparent am I?

At least he doesn't know what the note says. That's just for her.

Ten minutes later, Rhys is dressed and the three of us are ready to hit the grocery store. Once we're down the produce aisle and Gavin is pawing the butternut squash, it seems as good a time to talk to Rhys as any.

21

LET'S ALL DO FACE MASKS
TOGETHER

Gavin

I'm not in the habit of policing my friends. But I'm also not in the mood for the next week to be awkward as hell. Best to get Hollis's crush as out in the open as Rhys's.

As I'm picking the main attraction for this awesome butternut squash bowl recipe I know I will make so much better than the guy on the video, Hollis clears his throat. "So listen, Viscount, there's something I wanted to let you know."

Rhys gives him a faux thoughtful look. "You don't like to wear pants around the house?"

"Nope. It's shirts Hollis doesn't like to wear," I correct as we head toward the kale.

"Thanks for the reminder. I never would have known," Rhys deadpans.

"Anyway," Hollis says, like he's trying again as I grab some of the leafy vegetable.

"Wait, wait. Is this when you admit you've been hoping we'd all do face masks together tonight, Hollis?" Rhys asks.

I snap my gaze to Rhys. "What's wrong with face masks?"

"Nothing," Hollis says, answering first. "The ones with aloe vera vitamins are great for puffy eyes."

"Yeah, those are good. But caffeine eye masks are better for puffiness," I put in.

"Shit. Really?" Hollis asks with genuine curiosity.

I nod. "Definitely. You gotta try some."

Rhys peers at us like we're putting him on. "Both of you do face masks? *Both*?"

Hollis claps a hand on Rhys's shoulder. "I think the more apt question is—*you don't?*"

Rhys shakes his head. "No. I bloody don't."

"Just for that, I'm getting face masks for everyone tonight. Yes, I am *that* generous," I say, then I navigate the cart out of produce and toward the toiletry aisle, hoping Hollis gets his crush confession out now.

It's complicated enough that they're both into our temporary roommate. Worse that I am too. But I'm not going to do a damn thing about my own nascent feelings other than quash them. Nothing gets in the way of hockey for me.

Some guys say hockey is life. I say it and I mean it. Hockey isn't just my job. It's how I survived that house where I grew up. I won't ever call that two-bedroom ranch house a home. After a semi-truck jackknifed into my parents' car one snowy day in Madison, Wisconsin when I was five and my mom's never-wanted-kids sister and her mean-as-a-cobra husband reluctantly took me in, the only home I've ever had is the one I found on the ice.

The teams I play with.

The guys who depend on me on the rink.

No way am I going to pursue a woman who teaches our cross-town rivals, who my center is obsessed with, who my team's winger has a crush on. These guys are my closest friends on the team—hell, they're like the brothers I never had. Chasing a woman we're all connected to in a tangled way is just asking for trouble.

What Hollis does is his business, but he'd better deal with the topic soon. I shoot him a *get on with it* look.

He gives a quick nod of acknowledgement, then shifts his focus to Rhys. "Anyway, Rhys, I could wait till we have charcoal and grapefruit on our faces, but listen," he says, squaring his shoulders, but not like he's posturing—more like he knows it's time to man up. "I'm into Briar too."

I brace myself for the fallout. I want everyone to get along. That's why I insisted Hollis do this when we were all running the errand. So I could run interference if need be.

I pause the cart, watching Rhys. His expression is blank for several long seconds. This is bad.

"That so?" Rhys asks Hollis with zero emotions.

"And I know you are too," Hollis says, unperturbed by Rhys's cool reaction. "So I wanted you to know."

"That's very interesting." It's said like Rhys is gearing up for...something.

Before things get heated, I cut in. "Guys, she's a friend of ours and a guest. You can't just compete for her."

Hollis snort-laughs as he turns my way. "Who said anything about competing?"

I jerk my gaze back and forth to Rhys's dark eyes, then Hollis's light ones. "Well, aren't you?"

Am I reading the room all wrong?

Rhys chuckles too. "Just because we both like her doesn't mean we have to compete."

"Okaaaay." I'm lost.

Rhys claps Hollis on the shoulder with an approving smile. "We always did have great taste, didn't we?"

"Still do," Hollis says with a laugh.

I'm so lost. "What the fuck is happening here?"

Hollis gives me a shrug and a smile. "We sometimes share."

I...freeze. I was not expecting that answer, and I'm unsteady as I respond with a strangled, "You...do? Like girlfriends? You share a girlfriend? Like Stefan and Hayes with their wife?"

Presumably, Ivy was their girlfriend first. I'm not sure how Ivy, Stefan, and Hayes all came together, just that they were a throuple when I landed on the team. Maybe that's what Rhys and Hollis mean?

Rhys shakes his head. "Nothing that serious. More like a night out, a party—that sort of thing. Well, once we realized we had the same excellent taste."

I can't let this go. "When was that?"

"Back in college," Hollis answers easily.

"You didn't go to the same school." I point at his chest, like I've caught them on a technicality, but really, I'm just intrigued.

"But we played each other a lot," Rhys says. "So..."

Translation: we hung out together after and met women.

Which, yeah. I've done that after games too. But never in tandem with another guy.

There's a funny tightness in my chest. Not because they shared. But because they never mentioned it to me. "You never said—"

"Dude. We don't kiss and tell. Or fuck and tell," Hollis says to me, like he's explaining how basic arithmetic works.

Then it hits me—I'm not annoyed they didn't mention their kinks. I feel a little foolish. Like they have access to some secret room I never knew existed. A hidden library behind the stairs that they were sneaking into while I slept. "Are you two actually planning to share Briar?"

Rhys laughs, not meanly. Still, I can't help but feel he's laughing at me. "That, mate, is entirely up to her. It's always up to the woman," he says, like the cool expert who knows how sharing is done.

And, really, I suppose he does.

"It's Briar's call," Hollis adds. "Whatever she wants.

Whether it's him. Or me. Or neither. It's all up to her. Nothing...or everything. Right, Viscount?"

"Right," Rhys confirms.

I'm suddenly getting an unexpected education. But I'm finding rules aren't all I want to know. There's a question that keeps repeating in my brain like a snippet of a song you hear over and over.

I should hold back. Really, I should. But curiosity has gotten the better of me. "Why? Why do you like to share?"

The question makes me feel vulnerable, but I've got to sate this curiosity.

Rhys smiles fondly, like he's remembering a good night. "Because there's nothing hotter than a woman overwhelmed by pleasure."

Hollis clears his throat importantly. "Well, the only thing hotter is when you're the ones to overwhelm her."

Rhys lifts a finger his way, like he's saying Hollis has made an excellent point. "Yes. You're right. *That.* That is hotter."

I wheel around and grab a bunch of face masks so they can't see me as I picture our guest. Good thing we'll have these masks tonight. Maybe underneath this pink grapefruit goo, it won't be obvious that I'm imagining how Briar would look...overwhelmed.

* * *

When we return home, Briar is stretched out on the couch, tapping away on her laptop, a pleased look on her face. Is that how she looks when she's devastated by pleasure?

Her gaze lands on me. "Ready, Gavin?"

I gulp.

I have no idea what I'm ready for. All I know is this next week in the cottage just got a whole lot more interesting.

22

GOING FISHING

Rhys

Do mustard flowers even work in a vase?

I'm standing in the lush front yard, asking Siri if I should cut these, but the answers range from *no, you daft idiot* to *caramelize them with onions*.

The Internet is seriously maddening, but Amira would be amused with these robot results. I've got half a mind to text her and tell her Siri's reply, but I don't want to look like I'm inventing excuses to touch base.

Like I need to send cute little reminders that I'm knocking about, still champing at the bit for a contract. Or just a morsel of intel about my future.

With scissors in hand, I try one more time to find out if I should put these flowers in a vase. Though, I suppose, what I really want to know is if Briar likes flowers. She and Gavin are busy cooking and Hollis is setting the table. Or at least, I thought she was cooking, but the rustle of feet in the grass tells me otherwise.

I catch a glimpse of her walking toward me. "Yes, you can cut them," she says. "Yes, they look pretty on the table. Yes, you can even cook with them."

Well, someone is a mind reader. "Are you living rent-free in my head?" Though the answer is—yes.

"No," she says, laughing. "I saw you talking into the phone and standing there with scissors so figured I'd pop out and help."

I shrug casually, like I wasn't trying to impress her. "I thought they might look nice on the table. What do you think?"

Translation: *do you like flowers?*

"My dad used to get flowers for my mom every week."

Used. Past tense. "Did she pass away?" I ask, since I've learned from personal experience that it's best to be direct about loss.

"No. She just took off when I was ten." She waves a dismissive hand. "I don't know why I brought that up. I guess flowers sometimes make me think of her, since Dad tried to romance her every week with them. They're nice though."

And I am *not* cutting flowers for her now.

I look to the swaths of yellow flowers, swaying gently, spreading a vanilla scent across the breeze. "I'll leave them here then," I say, grateful that Siri's haphazard answers saved my ass.

Briar lifts her nose to the air, inhaling. "I love fresh flowers though. I've always loved to do yoga outside, but especially here, because it smells so good. This place felt a little bit like an escape when I arrived."

It can't possibly be an escape now. Maybe the last thing she wants is one man coming on to her, let alone two. "It's probably the opposite now with us crashing into the cottage?"

There. I'm fishing for intel without being obvious.

"I don't mind."

"Hmm. You sure? It can't have been on your bingo card to share a tiny cottage with three obnoxious hockey players who argue constantly, trash talk incessantly, and eat all the time."

"You're not obnoxious. Trust me," she says.

"We could try to be obnoxious," I tease.

"Is that a threat? Will you attempt to be rude to scare me away?" she challenges, but she seems unperturbed. No, that ferocity in her eyes, the raise of her chin—she seems fearless. Tough.

"I can try. If you really want me to," I say. "But it'll be hard because I'm naturally charming."

She smiles, relaxed, easy. "You sure are, Rhys Corbyn." She holds my gaze for a beat longer than I'd expected. "And you're right. It definitely wasn't on my bingo card. But I don't think I'm going to mind it at all."

Okay, that's intel too. She likes our company possibly. As I consider that, she gives me another important look. One that says there's something on her mind. Like her brain is turning over possibilities.

No idea what though, so I return to the earlier topic. Seems rude not to acknowledge what she's shared.

"Sorry about your mom leaving. That couldn't have been easy."

"It wasn't, but it was a long time ago. And hey, I'm a daddy's girl. He owns a garage, so I know how to change a tire and fix an engine."

I whistle. "That's right fucking hot."

"Wait till you see what I can do with a screwdriver." Then she tips her forehead toward the cottage. "I should go. I left Gavin in the kitchen."

I want to tell her he's Mister Independent. He'd make the whole meal himself, then serve us all, making sure everyone had gotten enough. But it's nice that he's letting someone help him cook.

"See you at the table," I say.

"See you inside," she says, and her blue eyes twinkle as they roam up and down my body, like she's assessing me.

What the hell is on that beautiful mind of hers?

Flowers might not be the way to her heart, but dammit, I'm going to figure out what is.

A minute later, I head back inside with the scissors, putting them away in the kitchen drawer as Briar helps Gavin slice veggies.

When he sets the knife down as she heads to the sink to wash kale, he lets his gaze linger on her too.

For a good, long time.

23

TIME TO WINE DOWN

Briar

I have two things on my mind tonight. First, the absolutely tempting offer that Hollis has made me along with the gift that I'm, admittedly, dying to use. The note put me in a giddy mood and has been playing on a loop since I found it when I returned home this afternoon.

If you want to teach me what you like, I'd like to learn. I am an excellent student. —H

I'm also totally fixated on the ten-thousand-dollar cash prize from Steven's contest and what I could do with it. I already have plans.

But those tempting twin thoughts have oddly taken a backseat to Gavin's absolute prowess in the kitchen.

I don't know why it's such a surprise. He did say he could cook. But I wasn't expecting him to cook with so much skill and ease. Gavin moves fluidly through the kitchen, slicing carrots, seasoning squash, and boiling quinoa all while I operate as his sous chef.

I've been happily following his orders as he's peppered me with questions about my day.

Did I catch any of the bands?

How did my class go?

What's the hardest pose to do?

My answers? *I've added some bands to my playlists. Excellent. And Shavasana.*

Of course, the last one is telling—Shavasana is the relaxing pose and, well, I suck at relaxing. But that's a matter for later.

For now, Gavin gestures to the oven as the timer beeps. "Grab the squash, 'kay?" he asks as he hands me a red pot holder with an illustration of a wine bottle on it along with the words *Time to Wine Down.*

"Yes, sir," I say, giving him a saucy little smile as I take the pot holder. There's a pause in his kitchen routine. A furrow in his brow. Like he's replaying my words, weighing them.

When his eyes darken, I'm pretty sure he likes my *yes, sir.*

I like his reaction, judging from the way my pulse skitters.

Then, he closes his eyes for a flash of a second, as if he's pushing off whatever thoughts invaded his mind.

When he opens them, he wheels around, tending to the skillet with the kale in it. That's my cue to brush off the moment too, so I snag the baking tray with the squash on it.

Hollis already set the table, and now he's outside

shooting hoops with Rhys while Donut watches them through the window. As I set the tray down on the counter, Gavin hits me with another question. "How did you get into yoga?"

"I needed it for rehab. I actually played soccer in high school," I explain. "But I tore my ACL my junior year."

He winces as he snags the pot of quinoa and drains it in the sink. "Ouch. That's one of my nightmares."

"It usually is for athletes."

His smile is sympathetic but also sad. "That sucks, Briar. Were you hoping to become a pro soccer player?"

I appreciate that the question is straightforward. That he asks it with no doubt that I'd have been one if that was what I'd wanted. "I did hope to at the time," I say, moving to the stove to stir the creamy pesto sauce that goes with the "squash bowl" he's making. "I love running and competing. And I did everything I could to rehab so I could play soccer again. Including yoga."

"And was it a perfect fit?"

I shake my head. "I actually hated it at first. Because it wasn't soccer. But I kept doing yoga, hoping it'd help me play soccer again. When it became clear that I wasn't going to be able to do it at the level I wanted to, I realized over time I'd somehow fallen in love with yoga."

As he scoops the quinoa into a pre-seasoned mixing bowl, he seems to mull that over before he asks, "Why do you love it?"

"Nearly anyone can do yoga. If you've had an injury. If you haven't had an injury. If you're an athlete. Or if

you've never played sports in your life. If you're coordi-
nated. If you don't know your left foot from your right
foot. And any one of any size can do it too. It's one of
the most accessible physical activities that exist. All it
takes is practice. And I like that it's called a practice
because that really tells you everything you need to
know about yoga as a form of exercise. You practice and
the more you practice, the more it gives back to you."

Gavin looks up from the mixing bowl and gives me a
soft smile—one that I don't often see from him. He has
some hard edges. He's more like sandpaper than the
other guys. But it's sweet to see he has a soft side even if
he rarely shows it. "I like that," he says thoughtfully. "The
idea that you're in charge. You make it happen. Just you."

"Exactly!"

As he adds the kale to the quinoa mix, his gaze
swings briefly to me, like he's weighing something. He
looks back down at the bowl, then says, a little quietly,
"I've seen some of your videos."

"You have?" I'm kind of ridiculously touched.

"I do them," he says, like it's hard for him to admit.

"I love that." I don't bother to mask my excitement.
I'm always thrilled when I learn someone watches *and*
likes my videos.

"I sort of missed it when you went to the Sea Dogs."
It not *me*, but that's okay. I can tell opening up isn't easy
for him.

"I'm just happy you're doing them," I say.

Gavin's suddenly intensely focused on tending to
the saucepan, and it's clear he's hit his limit for this

topic, so I take the wheel. I wave a hand to the mouth-watering spread in front of me on the counter. "I need to know where you learned to cook like this. I feel like you should be on one of those thirty-minute-chef shows or something."

"I taught myself." There's real pride there. But I hear the subtext too. Like there was nobody else to do it for him. Like he had no other choice.

"Books? Recipes? Cooking shows?"

"I just watch cooking videos on YouTube and I try to do it better."

I laugh. That's such an athlete approach. "So you're competitive?"

His hazel eyes twinkle. "Just a little bit," he says dryly, like he's glad to be understood.

"Well, I can't wait to try this feast."

"I think you'll like it," he says.

"Cocky."

"Just a little bit there too."

The verdict? Everyone likes it. When it's time for dinner, Hollis is the first to unleash a food moan. "This is amazing," Hollis says, pointing his fork approvingly to the butternut squash bowl, bursting with quinoa, kale, and pesto goodness. Donut even perks up her head from the couch. "Why are we getting tacos at hole-in-the-wall joints when you can cook like this?" Hollis asks.

Gavin scowls. "Because then I'd have to cook for you clowns every night."

Before I can ask why, Rhys meets my gaze and explains: "Gavin believes in eating the same thing when you're on a streak. We were on a sushi streak the night of the cat rescue."

"How fortuitous for the fish-loving Frances Furbottom," I say, then make a mental note to show them the pictures of her that my dad sent me. My cat's been living the spoiled life with her granddad all right. I'm surprised he hasn't built her a canopy bed. I take another bite of the bowl, and join Hollis in the chorus of praise for the chef. "This is as good as I predicted, Gavin. No, it's better. And I love bowls."

"I know," Gavin says, like a cat with a mouth full of canaries.

"How'd you know that?" Rhys asks, tilting his head.

Gavin meets Rhys's inquisitive gaze straight on. "It says so in her bio." Gavin clears his throat. "Briar Delaney has been teaching a blend of yoga, Pilates, and flexibility since college where she studied exercise science. She loves playlists, bowls, and her rescue pets. And she believes in the power of a good pair of boots."

Wow...he memorized my bio.

Hollis whistles in appreciation. "Look at you. Showing us up."

Rhys slow claps. "Someone can read."

I lift a glass of champagne. "To Gavin's cooking. Rhys's planning, and Hollis's..." I take a beat, since I've got a secret with Hollis and I don't want to make it too obvious to the others as I pick his toast. "Hollis's ears.

He's a very good listener." That earns me a flirty and dirty grin from the guy across from me. "Let's toast to a good week," I add.

All at once, the four of us clink glasses and say, "To a good week."

I take a sip of the bubbly. It's fresh and tingly on my tongue and it's chased by a memory of the last class of mine that Rhys came to in the city. We talked after and I happened to mention that champagne was my favorite. I look at the glass, then steal a glance at the handsome Brit. His gaze lands on my flute, then rises...to my mouth.

My skin tingles everywhere. He bought this champagne...*for me*. Gavin made bowls...*for me*. Hollis left a gift...*for me*.

All throughout the rest of the meal, my thoughts return to the contest. To the prize money Steven is offering. To the three men I'm sharing a house with. My mind is a pinball game, the silver ball slamming into flippers, bumpers, ramps. Then, it lights up.

Maybe it's the champagne. Possibly it's the gifts. It could be the sweet lure of revenge. Or perhaps it's the way they treat me like a very special guest. Whatever it is, it's unlocked me. And I know exactly how I can win that prize money.

I lift my fork and tap it gently against the flute. Three pairs of eyes turn to me and I waste no time. "So my ex's site is offering a contest for a female columnist on what makes for a great boyfriend, and I want to enter. Anonymously. An independent firm picks the winners, so he won't know it's me, even though the idea for the contest was one I gave him. The prize is ten thousand dollars and it would be enough to help me launch my yoga and flexibility app." I pause, then dive off the cliff. "The only thing is—I really need someone to run my ideas past. Like to discuss them, vet them, make sure they seem like things a guy *might* actually do if he truly wanted to impress a girl."

Rhys's hand shoots up. "We'll help you," he says, just like he did with the cat rescue.

I wasn't expecting that kind of speed, but I love it. "You will? Can we do it this week? It just seems practical since we're all here."

"Let me check my schedule. Ah yes, seems I can make myself available this week," Rhys says with a grin —one that makes me smile right back. "I'm a great fucking boyfriend. In fact, I can walk you to your yoga workshop tomorrow. That's something a great boyfriend would do, don't you think?"

I can picture it clearly, the two of us, heading into town together in the morning. "Yes, I do," I say, my cheeks going warm.

"Good. We can grab a cuppa if you want afterward too. Talk about your day," he adds, and his confidence is like a zap of electricity down my body. He's a man who knows what he wants. Who's unafraid to say it. Who puts himself out there.

In front of me *and* in front of his friends.

I feel a little shivery all over, almost like we're the only ones here. Rhys certainly looks at me that way. I flash back to the text messages the four of us exchanged last week, when they teased him about how often he goes to my classes. Is this something he's been wanting for a while?

That thought is as heady as it is risky. We still work for rival teams. I don't want to cause problems or draw attention to myself by dating a rival. Nova has given me a great opportunity with the Sea Dogs. It's a plum post, one I'll benefit from as I launch my app.

But just like Hollis offered to help me in the bedroom, Rhys is only offering to help me with a contest. And really, who better to help than a man who *truly* wants to show me what a great boyfriend is? I smile at Rhys, and it feels like a private grin until worry settles into my gut. Will Hollis be jealous of Rhys's role? I look across the table to the laid-back guy who got me closer to climax than anyone ever has. His expression is easygoing, a smile tipping his lips as he says, "I think you'll find we're *both* pretty happy to help you any way that you want."

Both.

Just this morning, Hollis said *we're good at sharing.* I didn't think he meant sharing a woman. But only because I didn't want to let myself believe that that was what he meant.

The evidence is adding up that I was wrong. And as my breath hitches, the clues are saying I like being wrong too.

What about the third guy? Is Gavin good at sharing? Is he part of the *both?* But Gavin is quiet. I try not to read anything into his silence.

I want to say yes to *both* of them but Donut is

jumping at the door. Whining too. I scoot back in the chair. "I need to take her for a quick walk."

"I'll join you," Hollis says without missing a beat.

"Perfect."

Once we're outside, I'm alone with Hollis for the first time since the other guys showed up this morning.

But unlike this morning, orgasms are exactly what I want to talk about with him.

24

THE TOY COLLECTOR

Briar

After I shimmy Donut into the harness my dad gave her for Christmas—it's covered in illustrations of sprinkled donuts—I take her leash in my hand, and we step out into the night. The moon hangs low in the sky, casting a soft glow over the quiet neighborhood as we leave the stone path and head onto the sidewalk. There's a gentle breeze rustling through the trees, carrying with it the faint scent of freshly cut grass and grapes, the promise of a rich merlot, the possibility of a crisp chardonnay.

Hollis walks beside me as Donut pulls eagerly at the leash, her tail wagging. I glance at the man by my side, catching the hopeful twinkle in his eyes.

The moonlight illuminates his features, high-lighting the strong lines of his face, the fullness of his lush lips, the scruff coasting over his jaw. Even with Rhys's attention at the table, Hollis's note still repeats in my head—*If you want to teach me what you like, I'd like to learn*—and anticipation flutters in my chest all over again.

"So, about your note..." I begin, searching for the right next words.

Hollis chuckles softly, his warm breath mingling with the night air. "I was hoping you'd bring that up."

"It took me by surprise. The gift and the note."

"Why?"

Because no one has ever offered. Most of all because no one has ever noticed I fake it.

But the words stick in my throat. Saying them requires opening up in ways I just don't like. Ways that are terribly uncomfortable. After my dad's warnings came true with Steven—I opened up to that *man's man* about my hopes and dreams and then he tried to steal my cat—I'm gun-shy. Vulnerability's always been hard for me though, given the way I was raised, the guardrails my father erected with his words, the way I saw my parents' romance splinter then leave shards in all of us.

My father who's resigned himself to being alone, my brother who barely dates, and me who dates... badly.

This isn't romance Hollis is offering though. It's sex, it's communication, and it's experimentation. Isn't communication part of what this whole contest is about too? Rhys is offering to play my boyfriend and Hollis is offering to be...a sex student. Takes a lot for a man to say *teach me*. I dig down and admit the hard truth. "No one has ever noticed before."

"Have you always faked it?"

"Yes," I say, and it feels even sadder to say it out loud.

"Briar," he says, then wraps an arm around me. It's a friendly gesture—affectionate, from the guy I play pool with. "We have to get you a happy ending."

I laugh at his playful way of speaking, then swallow my laughter, digging down once more. I meet his blue eyes and whisper another confession: "I can't stop thinking about it though. Your offer."

His smile burns off too, his deep voice resonating through the quiet night as he rubs his hand across my shoulder sensually, igniting sparks across my skin. "Same here."

My chest flips, my body urging me to say yes. But something nags at me. Is he offering because he thinks he's failed? If this is an ego thing for him...I don't think his plan will work. "But why? Why do you want to get me there?" I ask.

He stops, tilts his head, studies my face. "Because, call me crazy, but I have a feeling you've been dating the wrong kind of guys."

"What gave it away?"

"I've dated the wrong people too."

I was not expecting that. He seems so carefree, the kind of guy who breezes through life and rarely makes choices that irk him. "Really?" I ask as we resume our pace.

"Yeah. Really." He takes a deep breath, looks away, then back at me. "I don't trust a lot of people. I trust my family. My friends. My team. But when I date, I wind up...forgetting that. Trusting the wrong people. People who want the idea of the athlete rather than the reality."

That's an interesting way to put it. "The fantasy of the hot hockey player?"

"Your words."

I let my eyes roam pointedly up and down his muscular body. "You're hot. Empirically."

An eyebrow arches in challenge. "Just empirically?"

"Fine. Empirically and actually," I say, faux begrudgingly.

"There. That wasn't so hard." He squeezes my shoulder, and I do like this affectionate side of him— the way touching comes naturally to him in a way it doesn't to me. He continues, "Anyway, I wind up dating women who don't want the reality. The guy who's traveling, who's dealing with tired muscles, needing lots of sleep, time to practice. Someone who's obsessed with the job. But I have to be. I take care of my family. I'm the one who's going to put my little sisters through college. I'm the one who helps my mom out because she deserves it." There's passion in his voice, but frustration too.

"You do that for them?" I ask, touched by his caretaking.

"Of course," he says, but not like there was no choice—more like it's one he was grateful to make. "My mom's the best. She's my biggest fan. All of our biggest fans. She came to every single game of mine, and she went to every play Maggie performed in, and helped on every science project Maya worked on, and she made sure we helped around the house, and she was just... *there*."

My heart squeezes from the lovely, affectionate way he talks about the women in his life. He's the opposite of my ex. Hollis is the kind of guy who seems to deeply understand what makes a woman tick.

"That's what matters most of the time, I think," I say slowly, thoughtfully. "That someone is *there*."

He nods, meeting my gaze with fondness in his eyes. "Definitely."

"But you find people don't really understand what makes you tick?"

He sighs, resigned. "Yeah. I do. Most women, for whatever reason, don't want the real guy behind the jersey. They don't want to hear about how I feel when we lose. When everything in my body aches after a game. When the media rips us apart." He offers a *what can you do* shrug. "So I became the guy who's happy all the time."

A new realization clangs loudly, like a gong. Hollis *is* the easygoing athlete, but he's also carrying a heavy weight of responsibility. I'm the calm and confident yoga teacher, but I'm wary of people. We both wear masks. "You know something about faking it too," I say gently, bumping his shoulder in solidarity, I suppose.

"I do. Sometimes it's easier to be that happy guy than show what stresses me out. So I get it. I've wound up with the wrong people as well." We turn down the block, Donut sniffing trim hedges in front of a bungalow with a red mailbox. "I guess...I see a little of myself in you."

It's a little scary, this connection between us. But what's even scarier is the possibility of showing him how I want to be touched.

And yet, I desperately want to be touched. I draw a deep breath, and even as dread fills me, I say the hard thing anyway. "I want to feel good in bed. I want to say what I like. To open up. I just don't know if I can." I swallow past my nerves and my fears. "But I'd like to try."

His smile is like the morning sun—bright and unstoppable. He leans into me and sweeps a few strands of hair over my ear, his fingers gliding across my skin. "I'm very, very patient," he whispers, in a husky voice that thrums through my bones.

Then settles between my thighs like a pulse.

"Me too," I say, and it feels like a promise we've both made—to be real.

"And, you know, I'm pretty sure a good boyfriend would listen in bed," he adds, making it crystal clear he's RSVPing to the contest too.

It's not just sex he's offering.

It's sex and patience.

Sex and vulnerability.

Sex and listening.

"I think he would too," I say, but before my hormones take my brain hostage—and they're marching up there to lay siege to my head pretty damn fast—I add, "So, just for the week, right? Then we go back to...friends?"

That just makes sense given what he's shared about trust and his job. Neither one of us is in the market for romance. But we're both interested in the business of orgasms.

His full lips curve up in a grin. "We can stay friends, too, even as you teach me what you like."

Teach me what you like.

His words vibrate through my body, making my heart rate speed up. "Let's start tonight."

We turn around, walking faster toward the cottage, my girl leading the way. As we reach the yard, I say, "So that toy you got...I'm intrigued. I don't have that one."

"Do you have a lot of toys?"

"I'm something of a collector," I say as we step onto the porch.

Hollis's eyes light up, even against the inky blue starlit sky. "I'm going to need to hear all about this collection of sex toys. Every single detail."

Blood rushes hot and fast in my body. Talking about toys feels a little like foreplay. "I have so many toys I might as well buy stock in batteries," I say as we reach the back deck where Rhys is lounging in an Adirondack chair, a tumbler of amber liquid in his hand, and a curious expression on his magazine model face.

"I'd love to hear about these toys too," he says, making my breath catch.

25
___

WANT COMPANY?

Rhys

I meant it when I said the choice is Briar's. That didn't mean, though, that I was going to retreat into a corner.

Resistance might have worked fine back in San Francisco. It's clearly no longer an option this week now that we're talking about great boyfriends and battery-operated ones too.

And if my friend and the woman I want are talking about sex toys, then I'm damn well going to toss my hat in the ring.

Under the soft light of the deck, I knock back some scotch, then set the glass down on the arm of the wooden chair, my eyes on the blonde beauty in front of me. "Do you want to tell me about these toys?" I add. An invitation, I hope.

Her pupils dilate. Her lips part. But she's quiet, her breath just gusting across her lips.

Then, after a few potent seconds where the only sounds are branches rustling and the skitter of paws as Donut settles onto the deck, Briar tosses a question back at me. "Do you want to hear about them?"

It's asked as if she wants to be certain where I stand. Fair enough. She deserves clarity.

"I absolutely do," I say.

She shifts her gaze to Hollis, checking in with him. "Do you want me to tell him? About the gift?"

Now I'm even more intrigued.

But not surprised that Hollis nods immediately. Hollis is a gamer. "Yeah. Tell him," he says. Then the confident fucker runs a hand down her hair.

She shudders and dear god, it's beautiful. *She's* beautiful.

Briar takes a beat, possibly to emerge from a fog of lust. "Hollis got me a toy," she says to me, her breath a little raspy, like she's turned on from the talking and from his touch.

I barely have time to think about the boldness of Hollis buying her a sex toy. I'm keener on her reaction —she's aroused from his hand in her hair. He knows it too. He sweeps those blonde strands off her shoulder. "It's going to be so fun to play with," he murmurs to her.

"It is," she says, her breath feathery.

"Sounds like a perfect night," I say, then let my gaze linger on her a little longer. Briefly, my mind whirls to contracts, to the meetings my agent has coming up after the break, to her suggestions I see a therapist. To romance and all its awfulness. To the future. But I've had enough of all that. This is one week away from reality. I stop holding back. "Want company?"

Her eyes say yes before her mouth can form the word. Her gaze shifts to Hollis. "Is that cool with you?"

Hollis slides a hand down her back. "Absolutely."

She gasps, part excitement, part lust. "You guys... want to share?"

There it is. The most wonderful question ever. An opportunity. A curiosity. A match lit and a forbidden desire kindled.

"I do," I say, plainly, so there's nothing unclear.

Hollis curls his hand over her ass. "We do. Would you be into us sharing you, Briar?"

She shudders out a sexy breath, her eyes locking with mine as he touches her. "I would. But...I don't know how this works."

I take this one, answering with, "We know how to do this."

"We're pretty fucking good at it," Hollis adds, his fingers traveling down her lush locks again. "Want to know why?"

"Yes." She sounds desperate, like how I feel.

Hollis nods to me, a hand off.

I rise, close the distance to Briar, and for the first time ever, touch the woman I've been craving in the way I want to, tucking a finger under her chin. "Because we're both obsessed with making you feel good."

She sways closer to me, and it takes all the restraint in the world for me *not* to kiss her right now.

But there will be time.

She straightens her shoulders, glances down at her

dog. "Let me get Donut settled in." With her dog popping up and following, Briar heads to the door leading inside, stopping before she opens it, turning back to us. "What about Gavin? Is it weird that he's here?"

Hollis chuckles. "He's probably doing a face mask."

That makes her smile. "I'm almost tempted to join him." Then her eyes flicker, darkening with the thrill of what's to come. "Almost, but not quite."

"We'll be more fun than face masks," I say.

She grabs the doorknob. "Meet me in my room in five minutes."

I'm counting down.

26

THE DISTRACTION ARMADILLO

Briar

As soon as I shut the door to my room, I lean back against it, trying desperately to catch my breath and calm down. I'm too excited. Too nervous. Too hopeful.

Too turned on.

Is that a thing?

I shake my head to shake off the barrage of questions. Questions are the last thing I need before *two freaking men* come into my room to service me while another guy does...who even knows what Gavin's doing upstairs?

Donut is wandering around the room, a little restless, sniffing the carpet, peering under the bed. I have to deal with her too.

I rush over to my suitcase—hers too—and grab a dog toy, then toss her a stuffed armadillo that she pounces on. Then I urge her into her dog bed, a little cuddler cup that Trina gave me since her dog's obsessed with them too.

Donut hops in with her toy, thoroughly distracted by the stuffies squeaker now. Maybe I need an armadillo too. Instead, I head to the bathroom, freshen up, then go to the nightstand and take out *my* toy, setting it on a white pillow on the king-size bed. The toy mimics a tongue, so color me intrigued. But as I prep, picking a playlist I title Hot Summer Nights, even though it's February, I feel too practical.

What do I even do when they show up in a minute?

Everything's happening too quickly in my head. Closing my eyes, I just breathe.

In, out, in, out.

And, dammit, I add an affirmation. Admittedly, it's one I've never used in class. Or, well, ever.

But why the hell not start?

Tonight, I will come. Tonight, I will come. Tonight, I will come.

When I open my eyes, I hear two sets of footsteps outside my door, then a rap. My stomach flips right as Donut barks.

"We have...visitors," I say to my pup, smiling devilishly at the plural.

I have visitors and guess what, world? This girl is going to come tonight.

Yes, that's how an affirmation works.

I pop up, cross the room, and open the door. My stomach jumps, but screw nerves. In the hall are two big, strapping hockey studs who want to make me feel good.

I drink them in—Rhys with his dark hair and his deep brown eyes. Hollis with his messy golden-brown locks and his flirty gaze. Rhys is wearing a Henley and jeans. Hollis is more casual, dressed in shorts and a T-shirt. Both are barefoot.

Briefly, I wonder what they did in the last five minutes. If they talked about me. Shot the breeze about their upcoming away games. Played hoops. Who knows? But I don't want to get caught up in my head.

I focus on action rather than questions.

"Come in," I say and before I lose my nerve, I grab the collar of Rhys's Henley, tug him close, and drop a kiss to his lips.

He's only taken by surprise for a slice of a second. There's an *oh,* then a pleased murmur as I coast my lips across his. His hands come up to my face and he cups my cheeks, kissing me back with hungry lips. I taste scotch on his tongue and it mingles with the cedar of his cologne or maybe his soap.

He drags the pad of his thumb across my cheek. A zing shoots down my spine.

I break the kiss, and turn to Hollis to gauge his reaction. Does he truly like sharing me? And wow. The verdict is self-evident—the man looks downright satisfied. His blue eyes spark.

Hollis nods to the door. "Maybe I'll just shut this now."

"You do that," Rhys says as Hollis closes it behind him, shutting out the rest of the house. Gavin's the lone man out. A pang of missing digs into my chest. What is he doing right now? Is he reading? Working out?

Listening to music? Watching a show? Does he know what we're up to here in the corner bedroom? But the questions break apart as Rhys's gaze drops to my mouth. "Need more of you. I've been wanting this for a long, long time."

I go still even as my blood rushes hot. "You have?"

"Yes." One word. An admission. A declaration.

Since he's being patently honest, I ought to do the same, so I turn to Hollis. "Did you tell him *why* you got me the toy?"

"No."

I asked Hollis not to say a word this morning. He honored my wish, and that means the world to me. But some secrets are meant to be shared.

"I want to tell him," I say.

"It's your call," Hollis adds. "Always."

It's an easy call. I turn to Rhys who lifts a brow, wary, but intrigued. Sure, these two men may like to share women, but what if one guy gets to her first? Does that change the score?

Time to find out. "Hollis and I...we had some fun last night," I begin, and Rhys's curiosity burns off.

He steps back before he bites out, "You two were together?"

A FILTHY CHALLENGE

Rhys

I turn away from Briar, huffing out a sharp breath as small flames of envy crackle inside me.

Last night, they hooked up. Last night, she was with him. Last night, he touched her.

Dragging a hand through my hair, I try to get a better handle on this jealousy. I have no right to feel it, and yet I can't help it as I think about Hollis and Briar.

What did they do? Did she wish I were there too? How did it happen? I've been wanting her for months, and he touched her first simply because he was here?

Then I replay my own thoughts.

Get a fucking grip, man.

This is foolish. I'd have scaled walls to get a chance to touch her too. A small laugh gusts past my lips.

Well, Hollis *did* scale a wall. He climbed up on the balcony to save her cat that very first night.

Perhaps he deserves the first touch. Better yet, maybe it isn't about what *we* deserve, but what *she* wants. Right now, that's both of us, and that's what matters. She's game to share. Hoarding her pleasure like a dragon with his gold won't make Briar feel incredible. I take one deep breath then another, letting go of these selfish wishes to plant a flag and instead focus on her.

I imagine last night. Her arching, moaning, panting.

Then, tonight.

Her begging, pleading...for both of us.

The fire burns higher in me, but this time it's stoked by lust.

"Rhys. Are you okay?" Her worried voice breaks my incendiary thoughts.

Fucking hell. She thinks I'm pissed.

Of course she does, you wanker.

I spin around, stalk over to her, and cup her face but with tender hands. "I only walked away so I could get a handle on *this*." Like that one word encompasses all manner of emotions—envy, lust, this little obsession. "It's hard to catch my breath around you."

Her shoulders relax. "I thought you were angry."

"Yeah, dude, me fucking too," Hollis says, border-line annoyed.

"Sorry, love," I say to her, then to him. "Sorry, mate. Just...jealous at first."

"I'd have been too," Hollis says, not quite back to his usual easygoing self.

Briar tilts her head, intrigued. "Why were you jealous?"

Of course she'd ask. She doesn't know exactly how front and center she's been in my mind. I drag my hand down the side of her neck, a tease of a touch. "Every time I see you, every time we talk, you've been in my head. And I'm dying to know what you like. What you crave. So *we* can give it to you."

A soft smile tips her lips and we're back in business. "That you're asking that question—that's what I like." She steals a glance at my friend, who's running a hand down her arm seductively, sensually. "I liked the way Hollis listened. I liked how he teased me. I liked how he paid attention." She stops, pauses, then like it costs her something, she says, "And it was fun. But I've never... well, I've never completely gotten there with a man. Only alone, with toys. But not while letting someone else take care of my pleasure completely. I would love you both to help me get over the cliff." Her voice is straightforward as she adds, "And I don't think it'll be easy."

Ah. I get it now. She needs both of us. "You came to the right teammates," I say, ready for the filthy challenge.

"Did I now?"

"You sure did," Hollis says, leaning closer to her, maybe to catch the scent of her hair since that's where he pauses, next to those blonde locks. "We're here for you. Just you, baby."

I meet her eager gaze, and serve up a sliver of my obsession. "You're so fucking gorgeous it's hard to be near you without...devouring you."

Hollis moves behind her, dragging his hands down

both her arms now. Goose bumps rise across her skin. She melts into his touch. He brushes a kiss to her hair, but then says to me, "Devour her. I bet she'd like it."

Briar shudders.

That's the answer to a question between Hollis and me from before we came into her room—*will she like it if we talk about her?*

Just to be sure though...

"You think so?" I ask him so I can test her reaction.

Hollis sweeps her hair off the back of her neck then kisses her there, eliciting a tremble. "Pretty sure, but you won't know till you try it, man." He kisses up her neck to her ear, nips on the lobe. "Want him to kiss you hard, baby? Make you forget the day?"

She swallows and breathes out a needy, "Yes."

Hollis's tone shifts. Firm. A command. "Then say *please* to my friend."

Briar looks up at me with lips parted, cheeks flushed, and hands bound. Hollis has clasped her wrists behind her back, like he's offering her to me.

Such a good fucking mate.

But she doesn't say please. Her eyes are glossy with desire, but there's a hint of skepticism etched in her irises. "You sure you're not mad we were together last night? I don't want this to be weird."

There's a toughness to her tone. Self-protection, I think. Makes sense, given the ways she's been screwed over recently. I know the feeling too, having been there myself. I run the back of my knuckles down her cheek, feeling terrible for my frustration moments ago. "I'm not at all mad," I assure her. "Not only have we shared before, we fucking love it. Let me show you how much I love it."

Her eyes float closed, and she tips up her chin, whispering, "Please."

I slide a thumb over her bottom lip. She gasps. I coast along her jaw. She moves with me, turning into my touch like she's in a trance.

I travel my hand over her throat. Touching her is such a privilege. "Can you feel how much I want you?"

She nods, soft breath escaping her lips.

I dust my lips along her cheek, inhaling her fresh, summer breeze scent. "Can you tell I *only* want to make you feel good?"

"Yes."

I can't wait any longer to taste her again. I crush my lips to hers.

I kiss her hard, thoroughly, covering her mouth with mine. Our tongues skate together. Her breath is soft, her lips lush. And her need—her hunger—is a beautiful thing.

I travel a hand down her loose T-shirt, along the wide neckline. I kiss her collarbone, roam across her soft flesh, tease at her with my teeth.

She moans and gasps, arching into me. Hollis reads her cues, asking, "You want to touch him now, baby?"

"I do," she murmurs to him, then he lets go of her wrists. The second they're free her hands fly up my stomach over my torso, grabbing at the neck of my shirt to tug me against her.

My chest molds to hers. She feels spectacular in my arms.

Hollis moves somewhere else. Makes himself scarce perhaps so we can have a moment to kiss like this.

Frenzied. Needy. Tangled up together. It's a wild kind of kiss. I pull on her lower lip. She bites mine. My fingers curl around her head, roping into her hair. I make a ponytail of it in my fist, then pull.

Her breath hitches against my lips, then she kisses back hard. She grabs at the waistband of my jeans, jerks me closer to her, no doubt so she can feel the outline of my cock.

Then she's grinding, seeking.

And I'm wanting...

She wrenches apart, lips shiny, eyes glittering. Wheeling away from me, she crosses the room to Hollis, who's lounging on the bed, feet crossed at the ankles.

The second she reaches him, he's sitting up and she's grabbing his face. Then kissing him.

But slower than she kissed me. More sensually. She takes her time, savoring the kiss in a different way.

She even sounds different, teasing me with softer sighs and murmurs until she breaks that kiss. Then, she says to both of us: "Can I please show you guys what I like?"

28

THE FIRST LESSON

Briar

They kiss so differently.

Hollis kisses like a slow dance, a sultry song that thrums through your cells, makes you feel like your outline is dissolving. He's the sun that warms me in the afternoon.

Rhys is the guy in the sleek bar who wants you, the one who kisses you in a dimly lit corner as the guitar amps up on the sound system. He's twilight, a dirty promise heading into the darkening night.

I crave both kisses. They each turn me on, and I'm a hot mess.

I'm ludicrously wet.

They've made me feel really good with no judgment. No issues. That gives me an idea. I back away from the bed a foot or so.

I like my body. It's strong. It's healthy. I can do handstands and backbends, and I can lift myself up on my hands and hover.

I want them to admire me. To stare at me. "Watch me."

Even though I'm in yoga pants and a T-shirt, I give them a show. I take my time stripping off the top, then I slide down the blue pants inch by inch, revealing my hips, then my pink panties.

Hollis growls from the bed. Rhys rumbles from next to me. I step out of my leggings. I'm in a tight sports bra and panties, then I take off my bra.

Rhys swallows roughly, his pupils darkening. "She's so fucking gorgeous."

"Isn't she ridiculously hot?" Hollis asks his friend, and the praise makes me wetter.

The fact that they aren't talking to me makes me ache. I'm the center of their attention, but there's space for my thoughts too. Maybe that's what I've needed? I go to the bed, then beckon Rhys so he can join us.

I move next to Hollis while Rhys sits at the foot of the bed.

"Take off your shirts," I tell them.

"Thank fuck," Hollis says, relieved. The man hates shirts.

Rhys rolls his eyes. "Surprised you didn't have it off already."

"Me too," he says.

I laugh, loving the way they tease each other even in the heat of this moment. I watch them both, drinking in the reveal of Rhys's chest. It's strong, carved, marked with scars. There's a tattoo across his right pec—a series of dates in black ink.

My heart catches, then hurts briefly. That has to be for a person he loved deeply and lost. I sit up, press a reverent kiss to it, then lie back on the pillows.

This is it.

All those nerves I shed as I stripped come roaring back.

I've never shown someone what I like in bed. I've never gotten myself off for a guy. I feel shaky, tense even as I reach for the toy. "I've never done this."

Hollis leans forward and kisses me. "Me neither," he admits.

"Same here," Rhys says.

They're both so surprisingly honest that some of the tightness in me vanishes.

You can do this. You're a teacher. It's time to teach.

I quirk up my lips in a saucy grin. "Is someone going to take off my panties or do I have to do everything myself?"

Hollis tips his chin to his friend. "Her pussy's fucking beautiful. You strip her, man."

Oh. My. Fucking. God.

I'm shivering from those filthy, gorgeous words. They're fueling me even as nerves rattle through me. Nerves and excitement.

Rhys moves between my thighs, kneeling, his strong hands coasting up my thighs, his fingers hooking into the waistband of my panties. He glides them down one hip, then the other. "Fuuuuuck."

Rhys's breath hisses, his eyes darkening, like he's walked into his hottest fantasy.

He looks savage as he peels them off then brings them to his nose. His eyes squeeze shut as he inhales the panel. "Mmm," he rumbles. "You were right."

When he opens his eyes, he tosses the panties...to Hollis. The man next to me catches the scrap of fabric, then inhales them too, murmuring, "Yessssss."

I think I just went from outrageously wet to a water-fall. Hollis drops my undies to the floor, then runs a hand down my arm. "Part those pretty legs more."

I comply.

Rhys's eyes practically turn black. "She's fucking perfect," he says, approvingly.

"I know, right?" Hollis says, like he's proud he discovered me, then he presses a firm kiss to my bare shoulder. "Show us, baby. Show us how you play with that pretty pussy."

That helps. His direction.

He moves down the bed so they're both at my feet, watching.

I turn on the toy. It's small and pretty—peach-colored. Shaped a little like a flower. It's The Flutter from Just for Her, designed to simulate a tongue. If Hollis had picked a huge dong, I'd be worried. A small bullet and I might have been bored.

This vibe says the gifter put some serious thought into it. It's easy to use, easier to teach.

When I teach poses in class, I show and I tell. With this toy, I start with a demonstration. I slide it down my chest first as two pairs of enrapt eyes stare at me like I'm the center of their world. It's heady, their gazes on me. Their hands on me too. Hollis runs a hand up my calf, fingers grazing behind my right knee. Rhys runs his warm palm along my left thigh.

The twin attention is all new. And so good because it's so much. I feel...surrounded.

I roam a thumb over my nipple, pinching it as my other hand travels down my stomach.

"Jesus," Hollis rasps out.

I grab my breast harder, getting into it.

"Fucking hell," Rhys grunts.

They like the show. I give them one, spreading my knees wider.

"Briar," Hollis groans, squeezing my calf, then dipping his face to my leg, planting a kiss there like he just can't resist touching me. "You're soaked."

"She's dripping," Rhys adds, and they sound mesmerized.

I feel like I'm glowing inside. Sparking. "I like...it like this," I say, letting the toy travel between my legs and pressing it to my clit. My hips shoot up. "Oh god," I groan.

"Yes," Hollis murmurs.

Rhys drops his face to kiss my hip.

I slide the toy up and down in tiny motions, gliding over my eager clit. Showing them what I like—laser attention on that one spot.

I'm not sure how to say this to them, but most men eat a woman out like they're sucking the juice out of a whole piece of fruit and that's just...not my thing. I need a man who's not afraid to love on my clit.

I close my eyes, apply a little pressure, then find the guts to say what I want. "I like all the focus on my clit," I say.

"Do you like it fast? Hard? Firm?" Rhys's voice is thick with lust.

"Start off slow, but don't suck it." All the things I've never said come out of my mouth in raspy little breaths as I show them. "It's like a symphony of the clit. It should grow louder, bolder, more beautiful. But I want all the attention centered here, right here."

"Do you like fingers, love?" Rhys asks, his hands, dancing closer to my wet center.

That's a good question. "I don't know," I admit, then shrug as I knead my breast with my left hand, rub my clit with the toy in my right hand, electricity shooting higher in my cells as I turn up the speed. "I don't fuck myself with my fingers."

But I think I do know what I want. "Will you go down on me?" I ask Rhys, then I say to Hollis, "While you—"

I barely have to say *play with my tits*.

Hollis moves like The Flash. He's wedging his body behind me in no time, pulling my back against his chest, his arms roping around me. "I get to play with these beauties," he gloats as he fondles my tits while Rhys settles between my thighs, his hands roaming down my legs as I turn off the toy, setting it on the mattress.

He meets my gaze, offering me a hopeful, dirty grin. "And now I attempt to turn my tongue into a sex toy."

I laugh, the sound reverberating joyfully through my body, then fading away when he kisses my clit.

Oh god.

It's soft and passionate at the same time.

It's focused.

It's precise and fluttery.

It's exactly what I wanted. It feels so right, I could cry.

He kisses me, then flicks his tongue against that swollen bundle of nerves. And wow. Just wow. I'm lifting my hips, and reaching for his head.

I'm grabbing onto his thick hair. He's licking my clit exactly like I told him.

Up, down, determined.

And Hollis, behind me, is kissing my neck and squeezing my tits. His strong hands cup my breasts like he's weighing them, then he rolls my nipples between his fingers.

It's sharp and hot.

Wild, thrilling sensations run through me.

Wicked bliss. Then a wave of pleasure. Hands, tongue, lips.

And Hollis's rumbly voice in my ear. "You like it, baby? You want anything different?"

"A little faster," I say breathily.

Rhys ups the speed, his tongue flicking along my clit, making my thighs shake. I feel like I'm liquid. Like I'm melting under his kiss.

Under Hollis's firm hands.

I'm trembling, and a wave of pleasure crashes into me.

Tonight, I will come.

I'm close. So close. I can feel the curl in my belly, the pull in my cells, the hot, thrilling pulse in my pussy —the tantalizing closeness to the edge.

This is how I feel when I'm alone. When I touch myself. When I *know* I'll get there. When I have no doubt the *O* is happening and can just let go and give in to the feelings.

I'm so freaking close. I can get there. I can reach for it.

But...*what if?*

In the blink of an eye, I shove my hand back between my thighs. I refuse to lose this orgasm. Even with Rhys's face right there, I lend a hand, fingers flying and taking me to the brink. My toes curl, my body tenses deliciously, then I'm shouting, crying, falling apart. An orgasm slams into me as Rhys shares me with my fingers and his friend's hands.

"Yes, yes, yes!"

I'm loud, so loud. Louder than I've ever been. And it is a symphony. Them and me. Me and them. Their groans, their grunts, their muttered *fuck yeses.*

It's all of us, playing together.

When I open my eyes, sighing woozily, the two men look seriously satisfied.

Like how I feel. "That was so good," I say, sounding a little drunk to my own ears. "I love coming."

Laughing, Hollis moves out from behind me, laying me gently on the pillows as he moves next to me. Rhys climbs up, settling on my other side. "Told you you deserved a happy ending," Hollis says.

I sigh happily, wiggling a little in the afterglow, feeling all kinds of intoxicated. "You were right."

"Just wait till you see what we'll do tomorrow night," Rhys adds.

They're already making plans for a next time. That's presumptuous in ways I like.

But it's also risky. Plans can lead to expectations. Expectations can lead to hurt. After the way Steven tossed me out like I was trash—literally—I don't want to put my heart on the line again. "I want tomorrow night," I begin, looking to Rhys, then Hollis. "But this is just for this week, right?"

There are a few seconds—no, several, where the whole earth seems to go still. I can almost hear a commentator whisper *awkward*. But then, Hollis chuckles. "Of course."

"Right. Yeah. I mean, we have a stretch of away games starting at the end of next week. The break is a bit shorter this year, so we start up again sooner. And we're actually leaving town a little early for a charity thing in Chicago. Where our next game is," Rhys says, then quickly adds, "And there's so much going on. Contracts and trade rumors and whatnot."

I flash back to Hollis's remarks from our dog walk—his family responsibilities, his focus on his mom and sisters. Rhys has his laser vision too.

"Totally," Hollis adds.

Do they mean it? But then these guys have meant everything they've said so far. They meant it when they helped me with the cat. They meant it when they offered to share this cottage. I take this *offer* at face value too.

It's safer this way. Nothing lasts anyway. And besides, next week I have to return to the city, find a place to live, and keep putting one foot in front of the other with my yoga plans.

"It'll be a good week then, and next week we'll be... friends again," I add.

"Friends again," Hollis repeats, and Rhys echoes the promise saying *friends again* too.

I smile, grateful for this plan. I'm eager, though, to return to the fun and games of this bed. I look to one guy, then the other, my tone light and flirty as I say, "I guess you guys really don't mind sharing."

Rhys slides his hand down my bare arm. "Not with a friend. Not with a toy, and never with you and your fantastic fingers."

That's a relief. I wasn't sure if Rhys would be annoyed that I called for last-minute backup—from me.

I meet his heated gaze, then Hollis's before my eyes drift down their bodies. "Let me take care of you two."

They don't protest. They shed their underwear, but before I can enjoy their cocks, I hear a noise outside. My mind snaps back to reality.

The sound of a car door slamming shut carries across the yard to the window. Tires crunch along gravel. I move quickly, turning to the window, pulling back the curtain a sliver.

Gavin's gone.

29

INSTAGRAM BOYFRIEND

Gavin

Are you kidding me?

It's seven-thirty. She got banged six ways to Sunday last night. And she's outside doing yoga this early?

What does a guy have to do to be alone?

I clench my jaw, hissing out a breath as I dip my spoon into the carton of yogurt, then take a bite at the kitchen counter.

I'd thought everyone was asleep when I returned from my morning run a few minutes ago. The house was still so I padded in quietly, sneakers off, and headed straight for the fridge to grab my yogurt.

Now that I've got a view of the deck, I can see Briar outside, set up at the far end of it on her yoga mat with her faithful dog at the top. Briar's back is to me as she lifts her arms to the sun, her long, lush golden waves cascading down her spine. She folds her body forward, then glides like water into a plank, then an upward dog.

Fuck me.

She looks too good like that. Too sexy. With her black yoga pants and some strappy little sports bra, and her pup watching her.

Donut has the right idea.

But this is the last thing I need—to see her looking this sexy after hearing her come last night. I can*not* give in. I cannot get involved. My teammates are already playing with fire. I can't add kerosene to the flames.

Should have picked the tiny house to stay in instead of the damn loft. When I slept in the tiny home last night, the damage had already been done. I *finally* returned to the property well after midnight. Took a long walk around town with a podcast in my ears, trying to wash away the sound of her climax.

Maybe I'll take my breakfast and eat it on the front porch. I spoon some more yogurt and granola into my mouth. Yup. I'll do that in one more second.

After I watch this next pose.

But she stops midway through her downward dog, sinks to her knees, then knee-walks over to…a tripod.

Oh. She's shooting a video.

Damn, she's a worker bee. But she always has fresh content on her channel, so it makes sense she'd be shooting all the time. Her tripod is set up on a low stool on the deck, but it's tilted at an odd angle.

I scoop another spoonful of yogurt.

When she reaches for the tripod, it topples to the deck before she even touches it or her phone.

I stop the spoon midway to my mouth to peer out the window. It looks like the leg is loose on the tripod? Briar's trying to put it back in position, setting it down gingerly again on the stool when the leg goes kersplat.

As she grabs it, her gaze catches me staring at her through the window. And I'm busted. Her brow knits, then her lips quirk up in an unasked question. *Have you been watching me?*

Can't stay here like a helpless jackass now. Besides, it's not like my secret's written across my forehead—*I jacked off hard to you last night.*

No. Ferociously is more like it.

When I returned late last night, crashing in the tiny house alone with my lust and the soundtrack of Briar's orgasm, I took matters into my own hand.

Twice.

She won't be able to tell though. My poker face is stellar.

With my yogurt in hand, I head outside. Donut pops up, tilting her snout, then barking like she doesn't know me. But when she charges over to me, she licks my leg in a hello instead.

"Hey, girl," I say to the dog.

"I guess she likes you," Briar says.

"Dogs do more than people."

"I don't know if I believe that."

"Believe it," I say.

"Well, I think it's a good sign she likes you. She didn't like Steven. That should have been a sign to me."

"Steven's a dick." I should know. I looked him up last week. Even his bio screams asshole. He bragged about liking Macallan. Who the fuck does that? "Bet he's a name-dropper. Bet he's the type of guy who makes plans with his girlfriend but not the kind of plans you want. Bet he doesn't take care of you when you're sick since he's afraid he'll catch it. Bet he says he believes in you but doesn't really know what you do for a living. Also I bet he grunts while doing arm curls at the gym."

She blinks, her lips parted in surprise. "How did you know about the grunting?"

"Took a guess."

"Impressive," she says, shifting to sit on her knees. "But actually, I don't know about that. I didn't go to the gym with him."

"Trust me—he's the type of guy who grunts while doing arm curls." Then I stage-whisper, "There's no need to unless you're lifting cars." But enough about him. I nod toward her camera setup. "Is your tripod broken?"

"The leg is loose," she says. "But I can fix it. If there's a Phillips-head screwdriver here in the house or garage."

"I can look for a toolbox for you," I say, since I get the impression she's not the kind of woman who wants a guy to mansplain how to fix it or to man-fix it.

"The leg is too wobbly though," she says, after examining it. "I'm pretty sure the screw is stripped." She sighs heavily and I set down the yogurt on the table and walk over to her. "Steven jammed it in a garbage bag when he so helpfully packed up my stuff."

I groan, dragging a hand down my face. When I

meet her gaze, I don't think of the sounds she made last night. I think of how tough she is, how resilient, how determined. "You deserve so much better than that guy," I say.

"I know," she says with some resignation.

I give her a curious look since I figured she'd say *you think so* or *he was a jerk*. Glad she knows though. Still, I add, "A good boyfriend should show you he deserves you every goddamn day."

"Ooh, intel for my column. I'll write that down."

"You do that. And don't forget it," I say, and before I'm tempted to sit with her and ask a million questions about who she is—a million tempting questions—I tip my chin toward the wounded tripod. "Want me to hold it for you while you shoot?"

"I can just grab a couple yoga blocks and stack it on that. I don't want to bother you." She says the last line like she feels guilty.

But why? Because she doesn't want help from me? Or because I didn't volunteer for her boyfriend project? It's not that I didn't want to. It's that I wanted to *too much*.

"I'd like to help you with this," I say, since it's the least I can do.

She shoots me a doubtful look. It's a little challenging—the look of someone who doesn't suffer fools. "Are you sure? You seem...irritated."

How do I seem irritated? But I don't want to ask that question. Because I don't want to get into *why* I had to take off late last night. Because I'm so fucking attracted to her, and every little thing I learn makes me like her more.

Like the fact that she wanted to cook with me. Like the fact that she's so goddamn determined to make it on her own. Like the way she takes care of her little dog like the dog's her bestie.

"I had a dog growing up," I say impulsively, the words rolling out before I can even get control of them. "A shepherd mix. Rascal was a good boy. My best friend."

"Is this going to be a sad story? Did someone take him away from you?"

"No," I reassure her. "He was like...Donut. Not a Dachshund, but my shadow."

She smiles warmly, instantly. "Donut's a shadow dog for sure."

I scratch my jaw. I don't love sharing my stories. But I say the next thing anyway. "He was my uncle's dog, but my uncle ignored the dog too. I trained him, Rascal. Taught him to shake, sit, stay, come. The dog felt like the only one I could rely on sometimes, you know?"

She meets my gaze with understanding in her eyes. "I do. I feel that way sometimes too about Donut. She's been mine for a few years now, and she makes her loyalties clear. Which I love." She takes a moment, then adds, "So I get it."

"Yeah?" I ask, a little hopeful.

"Yes. I do." There's a pause, then a tilt of her head. "You taught yourself to cook because no one else would do it, right?"

"You're exactly right."

"I had a feeling. I had to...figure out a lot on my own too. My mom left when I was young. I'm only saying that so you know I can kind of understand."

Ah, shit. That sucks. "I'm sorry." And I don't want to hog the parental trauma cards, but there's something about Briar—the way she talks, how she shares —that almost makes me want to open up. She may be a teacher, but her style of teaching is actually to share, to listen, to connect. My chest tightens uncomfortably, but still I say, "I was raised by my aunt and uncle." It's uncomfortable to say, but it feels necessary. It's also as far as I want to go right now. "Anyway, so that's that."

"That helps," she says, meeting my gaze with a smile, the sentence unfinished but I'm pretty sure she means *that helps me understand you*.

It's a good feeling—to be understood. But a dangerous one too. The kind that leads to closeness and that leads nowhere good. I gesture to the broken tripod again. "I don't mind holding your phone. It's what a good boyfriend would do."

Her smile says I'm recused. "I appreciate it, but I get that it's not your thing. The contest."

I pinch the bridge of my nose. How do I even explain why I want to do it?

Since I do.

Truly, I do.

I hate when people treat women badly, like my uncle did to my aunt. Then my aunt treated me badly because shit rolls downhill. "Your ex tossed all your things out in garbage bags because he cheated on you.

He tried to keep your cat. He stole your ideas. I'm offering to be your tripod. Just let me, Briar."

She taps her chin playfully, as if considering it, then says, "Well, I suppose it is what an Instagram boyfriend would do."

I laugh and that feels good too. She hands me the phone and tells me what to shoot as she finishes a vinyasa.

Ten minutes later, we're done, and she pops up after a long, deep exhale that had me feeling connected to the earth and at peace in my body.

"How does it look?" She gestures to the phone.

I pretend to give it some serious thought, like an auteur would. "It could be better with a long establishing shot. Or maybe a crane shot if you'd like," I deadpan.

She bumps her shoulder to mine.

That should not send tingles across my skin.

It should *not*.

But it does.

"Are you Christopher Nolan or something? Greta Gerwig?" she teases.

"For my next career I'll be a director," I say, then pause to shift gears. "I mean it, Briar. Let me know what else I can help with." Running from her won't do me any good. Hiding is for weaker men. "I would like to."

"Thank you," she says with a smile, but then her expression turns serious as she says my name. "Gavin. I'm sorry about last night."

My brow furrows. "What about it?"

"I don't want to have this hanging between us. I

don't want things to be awkward. So I'm just going to say it," she says with a resolute nod. "I'm sorry if we kept you up."

My face flames. She knows I ran off. She knows I heard her coming. She knows that's why I left.

C'mon, poker face, do your thing. "It's fine," I grunt, trying to be tough and unaffected.

"Good. Because I'm grateful you're letting me stay here, and I don't want to be a rude roommate."

"You're not." *You're sexy, and funny, and direct, and you don't suffer fools.*

"Thanks," she says, then heads to the door with her dog, tossing me a look before she goes in—a long, lingering one that's like a match to the kindling in me. The flames lick my skin, then burn hotter as she says, "You can direct me anytime."

Then she goes inside, leaving me with those parting words.

Does she mean in the bedroom? It's all I can think about as I shower off the run. It's all I can think about as I engage in round three of my hand's tribute to Briar.

This is going to be a fucking problem.

Especially since thirty minutes later as I finish getting dressed, there's a text from her blinking up at me on my phone.

With a very naughty emoticon.

30

BREAKFAST IS SERVED

Hollis

When I open the fridge, my eyes pop.

Is that my favorite breakfast? Pretty sure it is. I take out the bowl of chia seed pudding and find a Post-it note on it.

You guys are seriously the best. From the cat rescue to the boyfriend lessons, I can't thank you enough.

But consider breakfast a start. After I did some morning yoga, I made something for all of you. It's chia seed pudding —chia seeds, coconut milk, and mangoes. I left a bag of ground beans from the local coffee shop on the counter, too, and some Earl Grey for Rhys.

Good luck at the obstacle course today. Donut is staying at the house, so if you can let her out to do her business before you go I would be so grateful.

And thanks for being such great temporary boyfriends. There's a picture in the group text for you.

On a yawn, I grab my phone and open it, clicking on the icon of a cat and a shocked cat face emoticon.

> Briar: I call this her boudoir series.

Laughing, I click open the pic of Frances Furbottom. "Holy shit," I mutter.

> Hollis: You didn't tell us Mrs. Furry Butt had a second career.

> Briar: She didn't tell me.

> Rhys: You really need to work on her confidence.

Briar's silver tabby is lounging on a fluffy white pillow, stretched on her side, looking like a painting.

> Hollis: She looks like Odalisque.

> Gavin: Do you do that on purpose?

> Hollis: Do what?

> Gavin: Use those fancy words.

Hollis: Yes. I do it to communicate. Is that hard for you?

Gavin: Odalisque, dude? Really, who says that?

Hollis: It's the name of a fucking painting. La Grande Odalisque to be precise.

Gavin: My point exactly.

Hollis: By Ingres.

Gavin: Dude. Doily was bad enough. Now a painter?

Hollis: I took art history in college!

Gavin: Oh well, look at you.

Hollis: Yes, mock me for being educated.

Rhys: Briar, it's like watching a tennis match, isn't it?

Briar: It sure is. Impressive, too, that you can walk, text, and drink tea.

Rhys: I'm good at multitasking.

Ah, that explains where Rhys is right now. He must be walking her to her yoga workshop. My phone pings again.

> Gavin: Yes, thank you, Briar. I can't wait.

> Hollis: And I'm about to dig into the breakfast. Thank you!

A few minutes later, I sit down with my coffee and some chia seed pudding when Gavin strolls into the kitchen, hair wet, fresh out of the shower by the looks of it.

"Hey," he grunts, setting down his phone at the table. "She did look Rubenesque."

I shake my head in amusement. "I knew you knew it."

But he sighs, seeming thrown off.

"You okay?"

"Fine," he says, but I'm not sure he means it.

Me though? I'm on top of the world thanks to last night. "Did you have a good night?" I ask.

He flips me the middle finger.

"You're so sweet."

He flips me his other middle finger.

I smile and eat breakfast. When I'm done, I say, "Well, I'm going to work on how to be a great boyfriend today. I have some excellent ideas."

He meets my gaze. "Me too."

He's in on this now?

31

A FULL-SERVICE BOYFRIEND

Briar

"Just so I'm clear—a full-service boyfriend should be able to provide a screaming orgasm and then walk you to work the next morning?" I ask as Rhys and I pass a cute shop peddling throw pillows with sayings on them like *You Had Me at Merlot* and *Listen to Riesling.*

Rhys takes a drink of the tea I made, like he's giving that some serious thought, then says, "Sounds about right."

"I'm taking notes for my column," I say, tapping my temple like I'm recording these tips.

"But honestly, what kind of boyfriend *wouldn't* do that?"

"A bad one?" I ask, like I'm offering the answer in class.

"You already know the right answers."

"Probably because I've known the *wrong* guys," I say as we near the town square. The faint sounds of folk music in the distance tickle the air. "But why does this —walking—make for a great boyfriend? Or, put another way, how do I convince the men that might read this column that these tips will benefit them? His site is a little...*how to get laid.*"

"Lovely."

"Technically it's dating tips for real men. But same thing."

After a pause, Rhys says, "So you need to be a little bit subversive with the column. Like when your mum puts butter on peas to get you to eat them."

"Spoiler alert: nothing would get me to eat peas."

"Bet you've never tried sugar snap peas." He makes a good point.

"Fine. I will reserve judgment on sugar snap peas. And yes, I'll need to butter up the peas. Steven's readership will want to know what's in it for them." My brow knits as I noodle on how to present the *why* of all this in the column. "Do I make it seem like they could get more sex if they follow these tips?" I say, but as soon as I ask the question, my stomach twists in an answer. I shake my head. "I don't want to do that. I don't want to present *what makes a great boyfriend* in terms of *only* what's in it for them. What if some guy takes the advice and really messes with his partner's head?"

"Nothing worse than that."

That's said clearly from experience. "Did you have an ex who did something similar?"

He downs some tea from the travel mug, then answers, "In a way, yes. Turned out Samantha still kept all her dating profiles and was quite active with them while we were together," he says dryly, like he's reporting the news, but it's clear he's masking real hurt. Or shame.

I growl, instantly protective of this clever, caring man. "Why are people like that?"

"I wish I knew. I just know they are," he says, but he moves on swiftly as we turn the corner. "But to answer why a good boyfriend would walk you to work..." His gaze swings to me, his eyes curious. "I would turn it back to you. Do you actually want someone walking you to work?"

He doesn't ask it weakly as if he's doubting himself for walking me to yoga today. But more because he seems legitimately interested in my answer.

As we turn onto a bustling block where the festival's spread out on this Friday morning, taking over more of the town, I mull on an answer—one that makes me feel a little vulnerable. "Yes, because it gives us a chance to talk," I say.

He stops in front of a cheese shop, the scent of Gouda and cheddar drifting past the open door. Rhys lifts a hand, casually brushes some hair off my shoulder, his fingers trailing sensually over my hoodie. The fabric does nothing to stop the sensations from flowing through me.

"Screaming orgasms are great but I'm pretty sure they're better when you actually talk to the person you're sharing them with," he says, and my stomach swoops.

Impulsively, I set a hand on his chest over his right pec. I desperately want to know him more. To understand what makes him tick. "Your tattoo. I noticed the dates on it last night," I say, a start and an end. "For someone who must have mattered to you a lot?"

I leave it open-ended so he can answer or not.

"Yes. *A lot*," he says. Sadness flickers in his deep brown eyes, as he swings his gaze away from me to the town square across the street. Green wooden benches line the square on all sides, and the grass is dotted with a few early morning picnickers.

It's not hard to read the room. Or to give him what he's given me so far—a welcome ear. "Hey," I say gently. "I've got a few minutes before I need to set up my tent. Do you want to sit and chat?"

He's careful as he asks the question. "Are you sure? It's not a pretty story."

"I didn't think it was, Rhys." I squeeze his arm, trying to reassure him that I'm here if he needs to talk.

He gives a long exhale, then he says, "My brother died when I was sixteen. Daniel. He was my only sibling."

My heart lurches. "I'm so sorry for your loss," I say, emotion tightening my throat. "I have a brother I adore. I can't imagine."

"I hope you never have to," he says with so much kindness, my heart aches even more. "We don't have to sit and chat if you don't want to."

Rhys is trying to give me an out, but I don't need to take it. "It's not about me. If you want to talk, I want to listen."

His shoulders relax. Relief seems to pass over those soulful eyes. "I do."

32

THE LUCKY ONE

Rhys

If she's offering, I'm answering.

Samantha wasn't like this. She talked at me instead of with me. I take the opportunity Briar's giving, setting a hand on the small of her back as we head to the bench.

But a small part of me hates to be a downer after our fantastic night in bed. We didn't stop at her orgasm, though I'd have been content to. She insisted on returning the favor, and really, who was I to refuse? Then I learned she's a world-class cuddler, snuggling up with me while her dog curled under Hollis's neck.

There's something about actually sleeping with someone—slumbering—that brings you closer. She kissed my tattoo again before she fell asleep too. Maybe that's why I'm willing to sit on the bench with her and share.

"I don't usually share the worst thing that's ever happened to me on a third date," I say, trying to make light of...everything.

She gives me a curious look then asks, "The cat rescue was the first date? Dinner last night the second? And this is the third?"

"Sure," I say with a forced smile.

She sets a hand on my arm, takes a moment. "You don't have to do that."

"Do what?"

"Be charming all the time," she says, seeing through me.

Fucking hell.

I should have known she'd be able to. Her radar's maddeningly good. "My older brother, Daniel, had cystic fibrosis," I say, and even though it's been a decade, even though I've been to grief counseling, I still miss him. "He died when he was twenty. He was sick *a lot*. We never expected him to even get that much time. But still, we wanted it. I wanted it all."

"Of course you did." She pauses but doesn't look away or try to hide from whatever grief might be on my face. "What was Daniel like?"

Hearing her say his name does something funny to my chest. "He was funny and delightfully mean. But in a hilarious way. He loved to make me laugh with his nicknames for doctors. Doctor Prick. Doctor Knob," I say, furrowing my brow. "I guess he mostly named doctors after penises. There was one named Doctor Ball Sack though." Briar snort-laughs and I point at her. "You're a snort-laugher?"

She swats my arm. "It was funny. That's your fault."

"Well, imagine if you had to see Doctor Ball Sack."

"I'll try not to imagine that," she says.

I let out a relieved breath then go on, a touch more serious now. "He was in and out of hospitals when we were growing up. Some months, some years were better than others. Some were hard. *For him*," I add quickly.

"Sure, for him. But for everyone," she says, kindly.

I close my eyes as a kernel of guilt swirls in me. I open them and with a wince, I admit, "It's selfish, though, to think that it was hard for me. What was hard, really? Being able to run? To play sports? To do anything I wanted?"

She squeezes my arm, her eyes brimming with sympathy. "I have to imagine it was hard to be able to do that when he couldn't? To be able to do anything, physically, you wanted?"

Yes. Fucking yes. She gets it without me having to overexplain it. But still, she deserves an answer. I wasn't the only one who put the pressure on me. My mum and dad did. They never let me forget that I was the lucky one. "My parents always reminded me that it was a gift to be able to walk. To run. To skate. I never want to squander it. I don't ever want to lose it," I say with an intensity, but a fear I've never been able to shake either underlining my words. Especially with that ankle sprain last season. That only intensified my...tension.

"That drives you on. That's why hockey is precious to you?"

"Every day. Every practice. Every game," I say, and her

reaction is an absolute relief. When I told Samantha about my brother, her response was, "Good thing it wasn't you." I was a daft idiot to stay with her. The biggest fucking knob.

"I get it," Briar says, pulling me from my thoughts. "Your health feels like the gift your brother never had. You don't want to squander the things that matter most."

"Yes. Exactly," I say, and maybe Gavin was right in his assessment yesterday morning. I needed a distraction but not simply to get laid. I needed to be able to unburden myself.

Briar opened up easily last night about her mother. She's not someone I need to be afraid of sharing with so I don't stop. "And now my agent is talking to the Foxes about my contract, and it's winding me up. It's just a lot to think about."

"That is a lot," Briar says. "Let me know if I can help. We're friends, right?"

It's an offering. A promise that what we agreed to last night—to stay friends on the other side—was real. Something we can stick to.

"We are," I say.

"Good. And friends don't let friends worry alone."

I laugh. I'm not even sure why, but I do. Maybe because no one has ever said that to me before. Maybe because I only really let Amira and the guys know about my worries. Or maybe because she made it so damn easy to share.

I set a palm on her thigh, give it a squeeze. "Let's get you to your tent. This is your chance too, right? You're here to show people how brilliant Briar Delaney's brand of flowing and flexing is."

"So damn brilliant," she reiterates, then I walk her the rest of the way.

We reach her tent on the festival grounds. "Thanks for walking me," she says as she turns to face me. "I get it now. Why this is something a good boyfriend would do."

"So's this," I say, then I brush the faintest kiss to her cheek. It's chaste enough. A safe kiss.

But what's happening inside my body and heart doesn't feel safe.

I spend the next several hours at the obstacle course, demonstrating the rope climb, the tire run, and the water balloon dodge as I emcee the event with my closest mates.

When we have a break in the afternoon, the three of us grab our waters from a nearby table. After Hollis takes a drink, he sets down his bottle, then tips his chin toward the other end of the grounds where Briar's tent is. "I think I'll go tell Briar about what I found under the bed this morning that we can do tonight."

I flash back on the idea we devised, hoping she'll like it. "You do that, mate."

Hollis heads off to see the woman I'm already feeling way more than friendly for.

INDIANA JONES OF DATING

Hollis

Last night, I offered her sex.

But I need to make it crystal clear that I meant it, too, when I said I'd help her in all the ways, including the boyfriend way. Just like I looked up sex toys yesterday, this morning I researched "things a good boyfriend does."

I take my responsibilities very seriously. That's why I don't want to assume she'll want to hang out this evening. When I reach her tent, I ask, "Want to know what we found under the bed this morning that we can do tonight?"

"Was it a piggy bank? A creepy doll? A rope?"

"You want to play with creepy dolls, Briar?"

"So that's the one you think I want to play with?" Her smile is teasing.

"I was trying to be a gentleman," I say.

"Stop."

"Stop being a gentleman?"

Her eyes twinkle with mischief. She is feisty and flirty this afternoon, and I am here for it. "Yes. Just stop."

"Noted. You prefer ungentlemanly," I say.

I expect her to toss out a rapid-fire reply, but she seems to give my comment some real thought instead, her forehead crinkling. "Actually, I don't know. But I'm curious if I do."

I tug at the neckline of my T-shirt. "And I suddenly wish I had the afternoon off to help you figure that out."

As the sun peeks out from behind a cloud, she lifts a hand over her eyes, shielding them as she holds my gaze. "Me too," she says, her voice stripped bare.

There's a pause as the air crackles between us, a heated charge. "You're tempting," I say in a low whisper.

"So are you," she says, then leans a little closer and adds, "And your friend is too."

It's like she's testing how those words sound on her lips. Like she's figuring out what she wants. The thing is, I'm figuring her out too. I'm putting together the puzzle of Briar.

"Have you always been a hard worker?" I ask.

"What do you mean?"

"I think you work hard, you play by the rules, you try to do the right thing, you're tough, and you're strong." I hold up a finger, giving that last one a little more thought. "No, you're badass. Like your fitness brand."

"That's probably all true. But what are you getting at?" She doesn't ask defensively—more like she's truly intrigued.

I'm working through that right now, and I'm almost there. "You're all about doing things yourself. Taking everything on—your business, your life, your dog, your family..." I glance around, checking to make sure the festivalgoers aren't eavesdropping. "And your own pleasure."

She seems to turn that over in her head, then nods. "That's probably true."

"But I bet you'd really like it if you don't have to think at all. If you didn't have to worry. If you didn't have to work for it. Maybe you mentioned the ropes for a reason." *So you can surrender.*

Vulnerability flashes in her irises. "I'm trying to figure that out too—the reason."

"Do you want us to help you? Rhys and me?"

"Well, if you really found rope, you two could...tie me up with it tonight."

The images flip through my mind like a movie reel. Her, naked, bound to the bed. I *finally* manage to form a semi-coherent thought *and* get it past my lips. "We're going to Home Depot, stat, to get ropes."

She nibbles on the corner of her lips, then offers a hopeful, "Unless it was neckties you found under the bed?"

Well, that's clear. But before I can run off like the sex superhero I am to track down a fancy men's shop, she asks me again, "But what did you *really* find under the bed?"

Right. The reason I'm here. I shake off the lust and bondage. "A treasure trove. You could just call me the Indiana Jones of how to be a great boyfriend since I unearthed some vintage board games this morning with Rhys. Chutes and Ladders. Candy Land. That sort of thing. I wanted to ask if you had plans for tonight?"

Her smile is pure joy. It's so fucking adorable I want to kiss it off. Right here, right now. I have to remind myself we're just friends. Friends with a one-week lesson plan. At the end of this, we'll return to playing pool rather than *playing* boyfriend games.

"I believe I'm free," she says.

"Excellent." But then I hold up a stop-sign hand. It's not enough to make plans. "My bad. I didn't ask if there's something you'd rather do. Would you rather watch a movie? Play cards? Hang out in the hot tub? I want to make sure I'm planning something you actually like."

She's quiet for a beat, then she says softly, "Did you and Gavin talk about this?"

Why would she think that? Now I'm thrown off, and I don't like being unprepared. "What do you mean?"

"Gavin and I talked this morning, and he made a comment about how there are guys who think they're good boyfriends, but then they make plans a woman doesn't actually want. Sort of like what you just said."

That's very specific. But Gavin and I didn't talk in detail about Briar's boyfriend project. "He's a team player," I say, hedging my answer. My mind whirs with questions about Gavin even though I keep my focus on her. "Does that work for you? Vintage games?"

"Yes, but what can I do? Do you want snacks? I can pick some up," she offers.

I tsk her. "I want you *not* to work for it. Let me take care of tonight. Okay?"

She pauses, like letting go is hard for her, then sighs in faux resignation. "Bossy."

"And you like it."

She gives a playful bob of her shoulder. "I do."

"Now, tell me. What do you like in the snacks department? Chocolate? Ice cream? Candy?"

She winces like she has a terrible confession to make. "More like pretzels, popcorn, and chips."

"We've got board games, neckties, and savory snacks on the agenda tonight."

She pauses, as if she's weighing the next thing, then asks hopefully, "So is this a date with my three pretend boyfriends?"

That is a very good question, and one I don't have the answer to. I glance around, making sure the coast is still clear. It's just us here at her tent, and it's time to be as direct as we were with the ties. "Do you want Gavin there?"

"For the board games?" Her tone doesn't give anything away. She just sounds excited to hang out. "Definitely. It'll be fun."

That's a start. But *only* a start. Stripping all the flirtation out of my voice, I press on and ask, "And what about in the bedroom?"

Her blue eyes widen, but before she can give me an

answer, a curly-haired redhead in tie-dye yoga pants breezes past me and walks straight up to Briar. "Hi," she says, a little nervous, like she's meeting a star.

"Hey there. How are you?" Briar says, shifting into outgoing teacher mode.

"I love your videos," the woman says, and damn, that's cute to see someone fangirling over Briar.

"I'm so glad to hear that," Briar says warmly.

"But I can't for the life of me figure out how to do those flows from downward dog to plank and then back, and it feels like I'm doing the tango with two left feet."

"It can seem daunting at first. But I've got you. Let's do it together."

That's my cue to go. I give a subtle wave then take off, not knowing if it's a yes or a no to Gavin joining us later.

But I know this—I started this whole thing with Briar. Her happiness feels like my responsibility. I weave through the festival grounds with one goal in mind—to track down Gavin. Trouble is when I find my teammate near a booth peddling handmade kites, Gavin's not alone. He's shaking his head adamantly at Wesley, who plays for the rival hockey team.

The Sea Dog digs his heels into whatever the argument is, declaring, "No, it was the episode where he drove the car into the lake. One hundred percent."

Gavin scoffs at the dark-haired dude with inked arms, saying, "It was the one where he drove it to the edge of the cliff—"

I don't have time for this debate. "It was a forest.

They left the car at the edge of the forest when the nightwalkers arrived. Which was a dumbass move if you ask me. I saw that episode of *Twisted Nights* the other week," I say, ready to move this convo from bingeable TV thrillers on Webflix to another kind of twisted night.

Wesley's eyes register shock, then resignation as he looks my way. "Ah, shit. You're right, Bouchard."

Gavin gives me an approving nod. "From art history to pop culture. What would we do without you?"

Wesley arches a brow my way. "Art history?"

I'm not in the mood for this again. "I took the class in college. I don't know why this is such a thing."

"You just don't look like the class type," Wesley says with an easy shrug, like that explains that.

"I went to class. All of them," I say, because I wanted to make my mom proud and I fucking did—scored mostly A's. But that is not for them to know. I turn to Gavin, since we need to get down to business. "When you're done debating TV plotlines and whether you're tall enough to ride any of these rides, we need to get back to the obstacle course demo."

Gavin fist-bumps Wesley. "Catch you later."

"Don't do anything I wouldn't do," Wesley says to Gavin, returning the knock.

"That doesn't leave much," Gavin retorts.

"Don't I know it," Wesley says with his usual bravado, then takes off.

With the Sea Dog gone, Gavin swings his gaze my way, a crease in his brow. "What's that all about? You really coming to collect me for the course?"

I'm not surprised he saw through that but I don't have the time to mince words. I pull him behind the kite-making tent. "We need to talk about Briar."

His face turns stony. "We talked about her this morning."

I roll my eyes. "You said jack shit. You were like *yeah, I'm gonna help where I can with her column, now let's go*. That was it."

"Yes, because that *is* it," he says.

I might not be able to read his expression, but his tone is not merely emphatic. It's *too* emphatic.

"You're not just helping her out from time to time. The nuances of how to make plans with a girl you like is very, *very* specific. So...?" I hold out my arms in question. Can I make this any clearer?

Gavin stares at me blankly. "So what?"

He's going to make me spell it out. Fine. "Are you into her too?"

Gavin's not a defenseman for nothing. He doesn't give. Doesn't bend. "Why are you asking?"

"Why are you not answering?"

His shoulders tense. His eyes are hard. But his jaw ticks as he fires back, "Why do you need to know?"

"I'm asking you a simple question," I say, standing my ground. I'm strung tight, but it's not with jealousy. This gnawing in my chest is something different. It's a need that has surprised me. An insistent need to give Briar everything she wants.

She entrusted me with her bedroom secrets. She made herself vulnerable. If she's wanting more than

Rhys and me, I've got to make sure Gavin is going to treat her right. In and out of bed.

He crosses his arms, then sighs heavily. "Why do you want to know?"

"We're having a game night tonight. We're all playing vintage games. She wants you there, man," I say, putting *those* cards on the table. I might not know all Briar's answers, but I know that one. She wants him to hang with us, and I'd like to make that happen for her.

His stone facade cracks the slightest bit as his lips twitch in a smile. But he erases it in a second. "She... does?"

He says it like that's all he wants in the world—to be asked by her.

Good. That's a start.

But Gavin needs to know that I'll protect her. If he hurts her, he'll have to answer to me. "She just got out of a bad relationship. She's a friend. I don't want you messing with her head or her heart. Is that clear?"

"One hundred percent. And you don't have to worry about that. Just because I'm into her doesn't mean I'm going to let anything happen between us."

The thing is, I don't believe him.

34

SURPRISE ME

Gavin

Who invented cat-cow? That yoga pose on all fours is seriously distracting. You'd think I could handle it better since I've seen Briar do this pose countless times in her videos.

But nope. Watching her, on all fours, bowing her back like a cow, then arching it like a cat, is frying my brain as I walk to her tent.

I shouldn't even be heading to see her. This is the last place I should be. But as she demonstrates this pose for an older lady who's trying it out, too, on an extra mat in the tent, I keep walking.

Like this morning when I couldn't stay away from the deck, I can't stay away from *her*.

At least I have a reason though. That's what I tell myself as I close the distance between us, coming up behind her. When I reach her, Briar's saying to the woman, "You just take a deep breath, lift your head, then tilt your pelvis up. Like this."

Damn, Briar looks good like that. Like she's offering herself up. Which she isn't and which I should not be thinking.

"Perfect," the woman says, still on all fours. "I'm just never sure how deep to go."

"Listen to your body. Don't push it," Briar says. "So often we try to do more than our body wants, but it's better if we can just listen to it. The body knows what it needs."

The woman gives a thoughtful nod, like that's exactly the advice she needed. "Thank you," she says as she kneels, then rises.

Briar stretches up, standing gracefully as she says goodbye. She moves like water, and it's too alluring.

She checks the time on her phone on the table, then must notice me out of the corner of her eye. Whirling around, she says, "Oh. Hi."

She sounds breathy. Can't be from the pose though. She does that one all the time.

I swallow roughly, hunting for words. Why didn't I plan better what to say? "Hey," I reply.

Get it together, man.

I clear my throat, try again. "Uh, I wanted to see what...games you like."

"You did?" She sounds intrigued.

I scratch my jaw, trying to seem nonchalant. "Hollis mentioned game night. So I figured I'd ask. Settlers of Catan? Go Fish? Charades? Cards Against Humanity?"

She taps her chin, going all thoughtful, teasing me a

LAUREN BLAKELY

little. Then she tilts her head, holds my gaze, and says, "Surprise me."

My chest is a furnace. My skin is too tight. I can't breathe.

All I want is to surprise her.

But it's a bad idea to get involved. Not just with her. She's in some sort of situation with my teammates who are also my two best friends. The three of us rely on each other every goddamn day, nearly every play. It's already risky enough that they're adding fuel to the fire.

I won't take the chance of fanning it. I can't mess things up. The team comes first.

I find the will to break her captivating gaze and give a tight nod. "I'll get Twister then," I say, all deadpan, since I guess I can't resist the implication of that game.

Maybe she can't either.

Her eyes glitter with excitement, and I guess I've surprised her. Maybe I've surprised myself too.

35

MIND-BLOWING PLANKS

Briar

It's hard to focus on the update my brother is showing me when I know the three guys are coming back to the cottage in an hour.

I really should give Griffin all my attention. He popped by today since he was driving through on his way into the city. But even as he shows me the new content he's added to my app, my mind drifts. What do I wear tonight? Is it even a date? And the big question is —what's going on with Gavin?

Griffin points to the drop-down menu for classes on the prototype. "This is where I grouped together the new videos you uploaded. For the fourteen-day core-work class," Griffin says, then shudders.

That snaps my attention fully back to my brother. Donut's sitting with us, and she tilts her head his way too, ears perked.

"What's that for?" I point at him, indicating his reaction.

"Core work. AKA the devil's work."

"Core work feels so good," I insist.

"Keep telling yourself that."

"But it does," I say.

"You know what feels good? Resting at the end of a long day," he says, then kicks his feet up on the coffee table, like he's making his point.

I slump deeper onto the couch and turn to Donut. "There's no hope if I can't get my brother to do yoga."

"Well, what's in it for me if I don't want better core muscles?" Griffin challenges as he adjusts his black glasses.

I marinate on that for a second, flipping back to my conversation with Rhys this morning. We didn't want to use boyfriend tips as a way to lure men to get more sex. But yoga tips? That's a different kettle of fish. "Yoga can improve your sex life."

Griffin sits up like a jack-in-the-box. "What is this voodoo of which you speak?"

Ha! I've caught the fish. Time to reel him in. "A strong core means you can last longer in certain positions. Think about it. Missionary is like one long plank."

He stares at me with the biggest brown eyes I've ever seen. Mouth agape. "Mind. Blown."

"Now, go blow your next girlfriend's mind with that."

He makes a show of looking at his watch. "And I'm outta here to do some planks."

But he's one of the hardest workers I know so he stays thirty more minutes, till we've hammered out the details of the app menu. "This is going to be a beautiful, battle-tested app when you finally launch it," he says, understandably proud of his work.

"It is and you're awesome," I say, patting his shoulder affectionately.

"Now all you have to do is keep making a ton of videos. Oh, and you know, market it," he says, so dryly I have to laugh.

None of that's easy. Nothing worth having is. But if I win the contest on Steven's website, I'll have a head start on the marketing for Flow and Flex Fitness—a nice cash infusion. Right away, my mind swirls with all the things I need to do. The new video series I need to shoot. The coursework I want to develop for Nova and the Sea Dogs. The classes at Peak Performance in the city. The apartment I need to find. Then Rhys and Hollis and all they have going on. Good thing we set a time limit for this tryst, so I won't be their distraction.

I have enough distractions of my own. My brain's a depot, and too many trains are rolling through the station at once.

I try to let them all go as I walk Griffin to the door with my faithful girl trotting by my side. As he hoists his messenger bag onto his shoulder, he glances around the cottage one more time, checking it out. "So you're really staying here with three guys from the other team?"

A flush rises up my chest. I hope he doesn't notice. "Yes," I say in my calmest voice.

"Three guys," he says, shaking his head. "Must be a zoo. I bet it's loud."

I cough. I was the noisy one last night. "So loud," I say with a laugh.

"Good luck keeping them in line," he says, then waves goodbye to Donut.

Even after he leaves, my heart is still beating too fast. I shut the door, alone with my thoughts, only this time I'm thinking of the guys.

Last night was wild. Hot. I felt freer than I ever have before. But I'm a practical girl. I'm not a day dreamer. It'd be silly to think I'm suddenly "cured" of my...

Is it sex anxiety?

Yes, I think it must be sex anxiety. I've always felt a little tension, a little tightness in my belly before I'm intimate with a guy. I worry if I'll like it. If I'll let go. If I'll feel good. But also if I'll be any good at receiving pleasure. That's why I've tried so hard to focus on the guy I'm with. To learn how to make sex good for him. In the way I move, the way I use my body, how I use, well, my mouth and my hands. Just like I taught myself yoga, I researched how to make a man happy in bed.

It's been easier for me that way. But these hockey guys? They want to make me feel like the star of the show, and that's just uncharted terrain.

Setting a hand on my chest, I take the temperature of how I'm feeling. I still feel anxious tonight, but I feel something else too.

Something entirely new.

Hope.

Dirty, delicious hope.

"C'mon, girl. Let's get ready," I say to Donut, and she bounces down the hall with me.

I head to my room and as Donut watches, I change into something cute but casual. A distressed jean skirt and a pink crew-neck cropped sweatshirt. "What do you think?" I ask her.

I don't love shopping. It's never been my thing. I'd rather be outdoors. But Ivy picked these clothes for me at one of her favorite thrift shops and said pink was my color. Here's hoping she was right.

Donut yawns.

"What do you know? You're naked all the time," I tell her, then I touch up my makeup and hair and brush my teeth. I showered earlier.

We return to the living room and since the guys aren't home yet, I jump back onto my phone, texting Ivy. She mentioned she might have a lead on an apartment so I check in with her, and she tells me she thinks she'll have good news soon. *Keep your fingers crossed*, she adds.

And my toes, I reply.

Maybe I can let go of that worry for tonight. I try to since that chat with Griffin has me thinking.

Maybe I should move forward on the yoga for better sex idea. I'm not the first instructor to hit on the connection between the two. But I could incorporate yoga and sex into my videos and give it my particular... flare. I jot down some ideas for videos with cheeky titles, starting with Sex is a Plank.

A few minutes later, tires crunch on the gravel driveway. My chest flutters. I might as well jump at the door. Putting down my phone I try to get a grip on my excitement as Hollis and Rhys head up the porch, then step inside the cottage, greeted by my pogo pup.

They say hi to Donut first, which makes my heart feel a little fizzy, then they walk in, with Rhys carrying a bag from a men's shop.

Oh.

Oh.

"A good boyfriend listens," Hollis says, gesturing to the bag as he comes over to me on the couch. He drops a kiss to my cheek that's not chaste at all. That lingers. That makes my breath hitch. I turn my face and catch his lips. He murmurs as he gives me an intoxicating slow kiss, one that spreads like liquid down my body.

He breaks the kiss and I'm blinking up at Rhys.

"Yes, they do," Rhys seconds, then grabs my face and crushes my mouth in a hot, possessive kiss that makes me shiver.

When he lets go a few seconds later, I can barely breathe. "Are you guys competing with each other in the kissing Olympics?"

"I won the gold, right?" Hollis asks, then brushes a strand of hair from my face and devastates me with another kiss that makes me feel like I'm floating.

When Hollis lets go, Rhys comes in one more time. I'm swooning by the time he stops a few seconds later. "New gold medalist?" Rhys asks.

"You both win the tag team kissing event," I say, my voice feathery from their attention.

"Good. Because when it comes to you, we're definitely into teamwork," Rhys says as he removes a silky blue necktie from the bag, then dangles it in front of me. "Hollis told me you *might* want to try this tonight. Think this will work?"

What works is them talking about me. Them teaming up to make this night amazing. Them sharing me in more ways than one.

An image of them at the shop, picking out ties for me, Hollis telling him about our conversation earlier, sends a hot shiver to my core. I run my thumb across the soft fabric. "I do."

Gavin arrives a minute later. He looks freshly showered, his dark hair neatly combed. He wears a snug burgundy polo and jeans. Maybe he was here earlier before I returned home? He has a board game tucked under his arm. On the cover of it is a cartoonish man in a hospital bed. It's Operation. A better choice than Twister given my skirt. "Well, it *is* game night," he says, like he needs to make light of his contribution.

I hide my smile since Gavin clearly doesn't want his gift to seem like a big deal.

But Hollis isn't so subtle. He shoots Gavin the most *I told you so* smile I've ever seen. Gavin waves a dismissive hand, then sets the game on the table with a rough, "Here you go."

"Nice of you to join us for game night," Rhys remarks, then turns to me, strategy flickering in his brown eyes. He's entered playmaker mode, I suspect. Then, I'm certain of it when he asks, "Can we take Donut for a quick walk?"

Last night Hollis joined me for some alone time on a walk. Now it's Rhys's turn.

They're tag-teaming me here too. I never answered Hollis earlier when he asked whether I wanted another man in the bedroom or not.

I'm ready to answer Rhys now.

36

GAME NIGHT

Briar

We barely make it past the yard when I blurt out, "Yes."

"But you don't even know what I'm going to ask," Rhys teases.

As Donut sniffs the grass at the edge of the sidewalk, I say, "I'm pretty sure I do. The question Hollis asked me earlier. I never answered him."

"Is it about menswear?" he asks innocently.

I give him a look, then with my free hand I tug on the collar of his Henley, a needy pull. "Rhys. I know he told you. I know you guys talked about me."

Rhys drops the teasing, then covers my hand with both of his. "Because we want to take care of you this week."

The reminder of the expiration date—one we both need. We both have so much at stake beyond this tryst. Hollis, Rhys, and me. We're all on the same page.

But the page tonight is pleasure. "Yes," I say, nerves swooping through my entire body.

Rhys inches closer as Donut busies herself with ground exploration. "Of course we talked about you. Both of us want you to feel extraordinary," he says, and how could I not when he says things like that?

But I have something to say, too, about my desires. Ones I've barely come to terms with. Ones I'm still trying to understand. In just a couple days, Hollis, and then Hollis and Rhys together, have taken care of me in brand-new ways.

Hollis has made me feel safe every step of this thrilling new journey—safe in bed, and safe with my wants. He seems to understand me in ways I haven't even articulated yet.

Rhys came into the scene last night without any agenda except...me. He had one goal—to show me what it means to be adored. To be treated well. He's done that.

They're both an excellent team.

I should be a good teammate too.

Because Gavin understands me as well. Gavin has stepped up too. Gavin has shown me the type of man he is.

I want all three of them.

I dig down deep, ready to expose my raw wishes, my deepest fantasies. "I don't know what Gavin wants. Or if it bothers you or Hollis. This whole thing is so new to me," I say, in a bare admission.

Rhys's gaze softens as he comes close and cups my chin. "Hollis and I—we're good with whatever you want. We want to make you feel amazing. We want to overwhelm you with pleasure. We want you to feel adored in bed." He slides his thumb over my bottom lip, taking his time, seducing me with his firm touch. "Do you want him to join us too?"

What a question. What a freaking question I never thought a man would ask me. I might have dated the wrong men, but somehow I picked the right guys for this...*project*. "Only if he wants to. Don't ask him. Don't push him," I say, worry stitched in my voice.

"We won't, Briar," he says, reassuring me as he answers for the two of them. My fears fade away into the twilit air. "We'll just keep our eyes and ears open for an opportunity. How does that sound?"

My body answers first in a rush of heat that settles low in my belly. Then, in my words. "It sounds great."

"Good." He nods to the house. "You ready to play?"

Rhys is talking about Candy Land, but either way my answer is yes.

37

HOW TO ARRANGE A TABLE FOR FOUR

Rhys

I'm not sure *engineer an orgy* is on the list of how to be a great boyfriend.

But maybe it should be.

As we play Chutes and Ladders, my radar's on. Hollis and I flank her on the couch with Gavin parked on the floor, barely touching his wine. As he moves his piece around the board, eating up spaces, attacking the game, my mind whirs.

There's the direct approach. *Hey there, mate. Want to join the fun? Our girl's keen on you too.*

Too easy though for him to dismiss a spot-on question, though, with a growly *what the fuck.* The other issue is I don't want to pressure him. That's a shit thing to do to a friend. Don't want him to feel uncomfortable, like he has to jump in the water, even though the water's really, *really* nice.

I simply want to give him...an opportunity. Like I'd do on the ice in a game. Then, he can take it or leave it.

As we roll onto Operation, I noodle on how to do that. With humor? Sarcasm? A subtle hint?

When we shift to Candy Land, Gavin quickly pulls ahead while Briar's lagging. She flips the card, then groans when she lands on *another* licorice space in the board game. "Lord Licorice hates me," she says, since she's now stuck there for another turn.

That's as good a chance as any.

"Imagine if we were playing Adult Candy Land," I muse, keeping it nice and simple as I toss some bait in the water.

That catches his attention. His eyes swing to Briar and stay fixed on her. *Yes, there we go.*

"Is that a real game?" she asks, doubtful.

"Of course it is," Hollis offers, grabbing a handful of popcorn from the bowl on the coffee table.

Briar shakes her head. "You're pulling my leg again."

"Everything's an adult game if you just take off your clothes," Gavin suggests, his voice dry, giving nothing away. Except the fact that the words he's said give everything away.

Oh, Gavin, I can see right through you. And I can help.

"Is that your way of telling us something, mate?" I ask as I move my gingerbread pawn around Lollipop Woods, settling on an orange space.

He shrugs, but his gaze strays to Briar once more with something like longing in his eyes. "I was just saying I bet that's how it's played."

What a fantastic answer of a non-answer. And I know exactly what play to make now.

38

SHOW-OFF

Briar

Tonight, there's been a certain ease between Rhys and Hollis and me, but also a delicious tension as to *how* the night might unfold.

But when it comes to Gavin, I have no clue what's next or how Hollis and Rhys are going to figure out the third man.

Gavin has made the occasional remark, like the naked Candy Land one, but otherwise he's been quieter than usual. When he flips a card and moves three spots to an orange space dangerously near Candy Castle, he then clears his throat and looks my way. "When do you start writing the column?"

He sounds a little awkward, like he's not entirely sure what to say to me. But it's an easy enough question to answer, and I can do my part, too, in helping Gavin feel comfortable. "I started it earlier today before my brother came over."

"And what did you decide makes for a good boyfriend?" Rhys asks as he lifts his glass of wine and takes a drink.

"A good boyfriend listens," I say, remembering chatting with Rhys on the walk this morning. "But a good girlfriend should too," I tell him. Rhys's eyes spark, like he enjoys the memory too. I turn to Hollis by my side. "Making plans that she likes and sticking to them."

"Hell yes, Pretzel," Hollis says, then like the bold, outgoing man he is, he drops his hand to my thigh in front of everyone. My skin tingles from his touch.

Words gallop away from my brain for several seconds. Once I wrangle them, I nod toward Gavin, locking eyes with his hazel ones. "And a good boyfriend helps her with work."

He swallows roughly, looks down, then back at me. "Glad I was useful."

"Aww, did our guy help you?" Hollis asks.

"A leg on my tripod broke, so he played the role of the tripod."

Rhys hums knowingly. "Just like when we helped save the cat."

My smile brightens at his analogy. "Yes! Exactly."

"Seems you're good at that, Worthy," Rhys says to his friend on the floor. "Playing a critical part in a group project."

I sit up straighter, putting two and two together. This is how they keep their eyes and ears open? By dropping subtle hints? I purse my lips to contain my excitement. My thrill, too, at the way they're both playing their part as they lay the groundwork.

The Englishman unapologetically slides an arm around my shoulders. That's quite welcome, this kind of twin affection, even if they're showing off that they get to touch me.

Or maybe *because* they're showing me off. Because they're enjoying me. Because they're having fun for me. Since they know I want this.

They're not doing this for themselves. But once again, for me.

It's heady.

Like they promised earlier, they're doing the work. They're letting me surrender.

As we take the next set of turns in the game, Hollis touches my thigh, Rhys my shoulder, and Gavin the gingerbread pawn, landing first at Candy Castle. "I win," he declares.

But it sounds like a hollow victory. The other guys hardly seem to care. Hollis is busy languidly stroking my exposed leg, while Rhys threads his fingers into my hair. The board game is meaningless to them. They're playing the game of pleasing me.

I'm trembling as they touch me shamelessly in front of Gavin.

I'm not sure how to act as my body sparks and sizzles. But I try my best to play this thrilling new game.

"And how was the obstacle course?" I ask all of them, but my voice is wobbly since it's hard to concentrate while Rhys is running his fingers through my hair.

I didn't know my hair was such an erogenous zone till now.

"We had a ton of people show up," Rhys says. "People had a blast, wouldn't you say, Worthy?"

"Definitely," Gavin says, gritting out the answer.

"What did you think they liked best?" Rhys asks him. "You had a good view of the whole course from where you were, wouldn't you say?"

"The rope climb. Everyone likes the rope climb the best," he says, stoic, like he's not taking Rhys's bait.

Shame.

But I can't complain about a thing. Not with Rhys touching me, and Hollis roaming that talented hand higher up my leg. Still, I manage to say, "How fun," as Hollis draws dizzying circles with his thumb. I swing my gaze to Gavin, adding, "I had fun at my tent too."

There. I've said my part. Made an invitation of sorts. That's as far as I can go, especially since I'm under some kind of spell right now. My skin is buzzing, and my body is melting. If I was wet earlier, I'm pretty sure I'm a Slip 'N Slide right now. I squirm on the couch as Hollis lightly runs his strong fingers dangerously close to my center.

"Sounds like a good day. Like everyone had one," Hollis says, his voice lower, deeper than usual.

"It was...good." I'm barely aware of how I'm forming words.

Rhys cups the back of my head, stroking slowly and sensually. "Bet it's a good night too," he says, leaving that possibility crackling in the air as I melt into the couch.

"And Gav, you checked out some bands today?" Hollis asks innocently—too innocently. "Any good... *groups?*"

Even in my heightened state of arousal, I'm pretty sure Hollis is using his eyes, ears, and mouth now as he drops a not-so-subtle hint.

"Yeah. I did," Gavin says, and his voice sounds hoarse. Frayed even.

"Cool. If you like any, you should, you know, share them with Briar and us," Hollis adds.

An invitation.

I'm as turned on by Hollis and Rhys being willing to offer it up as I am by the possibility of Gavin RSVPing. I'm turned on by everything. By the rush of sensations hitting me all at once. Pretty sure my bones are dissolving. I'm even whimpering as the two men languidly tease me while Gavin tries not to stare at me.

Tries but fails.

His jaw tightens as he swallows roughly, checks the clock on the wall, then grits out, "I should...let you...do your thing."

He stands and turns toward the door, but not before I notice his jeans. And the hard ridge of his erection.

I'm even more aroused. So aroused that before the door clicks shut, I say, "Will you fuck me tonight?"

39

THE AUDIENCE

Briar

I'm not sure which guy I'm asking. I'm not sure it matters either. They both answer me at once—a gravelly *yessss* comes from Hollis as he sinks to the floor on his knees, running his hands down to my ankles, while Rhys gives a deep, smooth *anything for you*.

Then he shifts me around on the couch, pulling me onto him, my back to his chest, my body exposed for Hollis on the floor.

With me like that, Rhys wastes no time. Before I can blink, he's kissing my neck, my hair, my face while his hands slide down my arms, his fingers curling through mine.

Hollis's big hands travel up my legs, under my skirt, to my panties.

"Better take those off now, mate," Rhys instructs his friend.

"I'm on it," Hollis rasps out as he peels down my panties but stops midway. "Fuck, baby." His eyes darken as they meet mine. "Have you been like this all night?"

"Yes," I say, shuddering. I'm on the edge already. "Since you started touching me during the game."

"You loved that," Hollis observes.

"I did."

"Do you want us to tie you up tonight?" Hollis asks as Rhys flicks his tongue against the shell of my ear.

I ache too much. I crave too much. "I can't wait that long. I'm so turned on." I do want them to tie me up, but it feels like too much theater right now. I'm too raw, too needy. "Tomorrow. Please do it tomorrow."

As Hollis slides off my panties the rest of the way then pushes up my skirt to my waist, Rhys runs his nose along my neck. "Whatever you want. You'll get a long, slow tease tomorrow night," Rhys promises in a low rumble. "Now, do you want to ride my friend while I play with these perfect tits?"

God. Yes. That. But my throat is so dry I can barely get out the *yes*. Still, I manage, then add, "I want that so badly."

Rhys nods to Hollis curtly. "You heard our girl. Take care of her sweet pussy now."

I shudder from the command in Rhys's tone. From the way these two men seamlessly hand off to each other. Sometimes Hollis calls the shots. Sometimes Rhys. I never know which one will set the mood. Is that their style, this kind of switching? But before my mind tunnels down that rabbit hole, I dismiss the thought.

They're doing this for me to surprise me. So I don't

have to work for pleasure. So I don't *get* to think about it.

Another doubt slinks away and I arch my hips up, offering myself to Hollis. "I want you," I tell him, laying my wishes bare.

"Get a condom. Our girl needs to get on a dick right fucking now," Rhys adds as his hands travel under my sweatshirt, then beneath my bra.

"I do. God, I do," I say, breathless with lust.

Hollis presses a kiss to my inner thigh. "Then I'll eat this pretty pussy another time." He blows a soft, warm gust of air against my flesh, then pulls away.

Wait. Hold the hell on.

That's too tempting an offer.

I grab his head, not letting him stand. Hollis's eyes flicker with amusement, excitement. "What is it?"

"Eat me. Just for a minute," I demand desperately.

"Yes, ma'am," Hollis says like he's hit the jackpot as he sheds his shirt, strips off his shorts in seconds, then drops back to his knees, parting my thighs once more.

Rhys slides my sweatshirt up and over my head. "Need to suck on these gorgeous tits," he says.

"Yes. Please. Anything," I say, and I don't know if I'm saying it to the man behind me or the man on his knees. Or to everyone. All at once.

When Hollis presses a hot kiss to my center, I moan.

When Rhys kneads my breasts roughly, I cry out a long, "Yesssss."

I can hear Rhys smile smugly rather than see it. "Our girl likes it when we *all* play with her."

"No," Hollis corrects, taking his time to lap up my

wetness, making me tremble in every single cell. "She fucking loves it."

Hollis swirls his tongue there. Right there. Licking my needy clit, just like I taught them both last night.

My brain goes offline. I'm shaking. Shuddering. Everything feels so good. Rhys's big hands on my breasts.

Hollis's tender lips on my clit.

Rhys's stubble along my skin as he moves around me, shifting so he's kneeling next to me and drawing one tight, peaked nipple into his talented mouth, murmuring as he sucks.

Hollis groans, too, against my wetness.

I'm the loudest of them all. Gasps. Sighs. Whimpers.

After a minute or so, Rhys drops my nipple from his mouth, giving me a sly smile as he says, "You liked when we touched you earlier in front of him."

I arch my chest toward Rhys, thrust my hips toward Hollis. "I did," I admit.

"You liked the audience," Rhys adds as Hollis flicks his tongue faster, hungrier.

"So much," I say.

Hollis takes directions so well. He's doing it exactly like I asked last night. He's adoring my clit with his talented tongue. Then drawing a long, worshipful lick that makes my hips shoot up.

Pleasure zings through my whole body, sharp, hot, powerful.

It's good, so good, but I also ache desperately. I feel empty. I want to be filled now. Gently but firmly, I push his head away. His lips shine with my pleasure as I beg, "Please fuck me like this."

In seconds the rest of our clothes vanish, a condom appears, and everyone shifts like musical chairs. Hollis lies naked on the couch. Rhys stands behind the furniture, cock out, leaking at the tip. But he doesn't seem to care about his own arousal. The second I climb over Hollis, Rhys's hands are in my hair, then my shoulders, like he's guiding me.

I don't need any direction right now though. I know where I want to be. I sink down onto Hollis's dick in one move.

As he fills me deeply, I let out a long, blissful sigh. "It feels so good," I say.

"Then fuck her hard. Make her forget the day," Rhys tells his friend.

Hollis thrusts up into me, and I gasp so loudly it barely registers when the door creaks open.

And I'm looking right at Gavin. He locks eyes with me, then says, "Put her on all fours and fuck her from behind."

40

HANDS FREE

Gavin

Well, she did say I could direct her anytime. So I'm here to play that role. The role she cast me in. The role I've been resisting for the past two days. Feels like forever though. Feels like I'll suffocate if I spend another night in the tiny house, in a tiny bed, with my too big lust.

Now, with Briar in my crosshairs, I can finally breathe again. My lungs fill with air as she gazes at me with glittery eyes. I can't look away from the gorgeous woman, all heaving tits and bare skin, dewy from whatever they've been doing without me.

Which ends...now.

I took Briar's advice. I listened to my body. The body knows what it wants. I want her. I just do. So fuck it. Fuck everything else tonight.

Her lips part in a shuddery "yessss" as she bounces on Hollis's dick.

I tip my chin toward the naked trio, even though I only have eyes for her. "Get up, Bouchard. Flip her over," I tell Hollis. Then to Briar, I say, "Put your hands on the arm of the couch." Next, Rhys. "Smack that sweet ass before he fucks her again."

Briar's nipples tighten like hard diamonds on glorious teardrop tits. They bounce beautifully as she scrambles off Hollis, then stands next to the couch for a couple seconds, giving me a full view of her fantastic body. I stalk closer till I'm a few feet away. She's exactly as I pictured.

Strong.

Toned.

She takes care of herself in every goddamn way, and I'm so fucking turned on I can barely handle it.

But what I can handle is *this*—this sexy, confident, feisty, strong-willed woman obeying my command. As Hollis moves off the couch, Briar returns to the blue cushions, getting down on her hands and knees, her throat stretching as she looks up at me, curling her hands around the arm of the couch at the end. "This what you want?"

"Yes," I bite out.

She lifts her chin in an offering. "Are you going to touch me?"

It's a taunt. A challenge.

I come over to her, willing myself not to kiss her till I lose all control. "No. I'm going to take you up on your offer from this morning," I say, then turn my attention briefly to Rhys, who looks a little stunned standing there behind the couch. "Well, get to it. I believe the lady wants you to spank her. Don't you, Briar?"

"I do."

"I thought so," I say, then turn around, even though it pains me not to look at her. But if I'm too close I'll have my hands all the fuck over her. And that'll kill my resolve.

Watching is all I'll allow.

I park myself in the chair a few feet away as Rhys's palm comes down on her ass. A sharp sting rends the air, chased by her yelp. "Ohhh!"

"Now, soothe it," I tell him.

Seeming a little stunned, he rubs his palm against her flesh. "That better, love?" he asks her.

She nods. "Yes."

"Do it again," I grit out.

Rhys lifts his hand a second time, swats the other cheek. Another needy cry escapes her pretty lips.

My dick throbs at the sound. Just fucking throbs, demanding attention.

I fight off the lust twisting in my body as I turn to Hollis. "Now fuck her hard."

But he looks to her first. "You want that, baby?" Hollis asks the woman of the hour—no, the whole damn week—as he kneels behind her, tenderly rubbing her ass.

Something like trust flashes in her eyes, in her entire expression, when he asks her that. It floors me for a second to witness it. She turns away from me, looking back at him to answer in a matching tone, "I think I do."

"Good. We want you to have everything." He dips his face to the top of her spine, presses a soft kiss there that makes her shudder, then the fucker looks at me smugly with so much satisfaction. "You're missing out, Worthy. She tastes fucking incredible. *Everywhere.*"

I hiss in annoyance and jealousy, then look to Rhys. "Then kiss her while he fucks her."

Rhys doesn't miss a beat. He comes over to the end of the couch, grabs Briar's chin, and covers her mouth fiercely as Hollis lines up, then shoves in. Hollis finds a rhythm quickly. His hands curl around her hips, keeping her in place as he rocks into her. Rhys devours her lips and fondles her tits.

Her whole body shakes as they pleasure her.

I'm shaking under my skin. With red-hot desire.

My cock is made of stone as I watch the sexiest show I've ever seen.

Briar, losing her mind.

Briar, being fucked within an inch of her life.

Briar, moaning, panting, and crying.

Briar's tits swaying as Rhys kneads them. Her ass writhing as Hollis pounds into her.

Then Rhys breaks the kiss and whispers something in her ear. She smiles, filthy and beautiful, nodding.

Absently, I palm the ridge of my cock, aching in my jeans. Rhys moves alongside her, gathers her hair in his fist, then tugs hard. She's staring right at me. "You like watching?" she asks, that challenging tone again.

I grit my teeth. Swallow roughly. But nod my obvious assent as I rub my palm over my hard-on.

She nibbles on the corner of her lips. Rhys tugs her hair harder, squeezes her tit.

Her lips part in an O. Her shoulders shake. Then, with her eyes on me, she says, or maybe begs, "Take it out."

I burn.

I am a forest, and I go up in a wildfire. With the flames go my resistance. I unzip my jeans, push down my boxer briefs, and free my cock.

Her eyes glitter with excitement. They shine as I wrap a hand around my shaft. "You wanted me to watch you," I say as I shuttle my fist fast.

"Yes," she gasps.

"Fucking yes," Hollis grunts.

"Play with her clit," Rhys tells him.

"Already fucking there," Hollis answers, roping his arm around her waist, sliding his hand between her thighs and out of view.

But not out of my imagination.

I bet her pussy is beautiful. Pink, pretty, and ludicrously wet right now since I've never seen anyone look more aroused than Briar as she stares at me stroking my cock.

"But you really wanted to watch me," I grit out.

She doesn't even answer. Her shoulders shake, and her eyes squeeze shut as she unleashes the hottest moan I've ever heard in my life.

41

THE PARTY CRASHER

Briar

My belly tightens once, twice. A familiar pressure that tightens. Pulses. Turns into a thrilling ache in my core.

A tantalizing promise.

Yes, please, yes.

I want this so badly. It feels so good. Everything. All of this. Hollis fucking and stroking. Rhys tugging my hair and squeezing my breasts. It's all so much. My mind is short-circuiting. My body is buzzing. It's like liquid silver and gold flowing through my veins. Colors burst behind my eyes.

But I can't stop watching the man in the chair. Gavin's fist is a blur, his hand flying over his hard length as he watches one man fuck me, the other man play with me.

I am the center of their world, all three men, and I am utterly overwhelmed.

Pleasure hits me like a tidal wave, and then, I shatter. From the center of my body out to my fingers, to my toes, to the ends of my hair, I break in bliss.

And it's spectacular here on the other side. It's like sex and magic and starlight all crashing into me. I'm floating on endorphins as adrenaline and joy spin inside my body. I'm so high on this sensation that it takes a few beats for me to fully realize Hollis is still fucking me.

His fingers dig into my hips as he drives into me on a savage grunt, jerking, shuddering, then unleashing a strangled, "Coming."

Seconds later, I swing my gaze back to the new guy, who's gritting his teeth as his fist flies. His eyes squeeze shut, then he spills all over his hand.

It's the hottest thing I've felt. The hottest thing I've seen. I'm surrounded by my guys coming.

Except Rhys.

My lovely, cheeky, thoughtful Rhys who's gotten zero attention for his beautiful cock tonight. The second Hollis pulls out, I move to my knees, grab Rhys's hips, and jerk him toward my face. "Give it to me," I urge.

He's as helpless to the lust as the rest of us.

"Take it," he says, feeding me his cock.

I open wide and let him fuck my mouth, knowing it won't take long till he's coming down my throat.

His hands rope through my hair, and he pumps. I nearly gag, but I nod for him to keep going, and he gives another thrust, then groans.

I taste his release—salty, musky, and all for me.

And when he eases out and comes down, he dips his face and kisses my mouth. He's tender—reverent even.

When he breaks the kiss, I look up at him and say, "Thank you."

My throat tightens with unexpected emotion. It's silly. Really, it is—to feel this overjoyed about something as meaningless, in the scheme of things, as an orgasm.

And yet I feel this wonderful connection with my body. Like my body is doing what it's supposed to do—playing nicely with my mind.

Not fighting it.

I swallow past the knot of emotions in my throat, fighting off the threat of happy tears. I'm not going to cry because I came. Deep breath.

I take another, then turn around to a woozy, happy Hollis and say, "Thank you too." My heart beats faster as I look at both of these men who were so determined to turn me on and send me over the cliff.

They made it happen even though tonight, it took a village. It took all of them to break my brain. To overwhelm my too busy mind. To shut off the noise.

I dare to look at Gavin again, and he's still breathing hard in that chair. "Umm...thanks for letting me crash your party," he says as he shifts around, probably looking for a tissue.

Yeah, I guess we all need to clean up. I look away, giving him what little privacy there is in this home to find one.

"Glad you got the hint," Hollis says to him as I hear the rustle of a Kleenex box.

"Took him long enough," Rhys remarks, then gives all his attention to me. "Let's get you cleaned up, love. You worked hard tonight."

Hollis soothes a hand up my back. "You did so good, baby."

"I feel so good," I say, my voice breaking for a few seconds.

I take another breath and stave off the flood of feelings, standing, looking for my clothes, something to cover up, to clean up. "I should shower," I say, then my stomach rumbles. "I guess I'm hungry too."

"We'll take care of that," Rhys says, and as I grab my sweatshirt and skirt, Gavin strides over, jeans buttoned, tissue tossed.

"Can I take her to the shower?"

He's not asking me. He's asking them. And there's something so respectful in the question. He's the welcomed party crasher, and sure, he swaggered in and hit the ground running. Now, he seems to sense he shouldn't just barrel into this new scene like a bull in a china shop.

Rhys smirks.

Hollis laughs, then says, "You're asking the wrong person."

There's nothing stoic in Gavin's expression anymore as he turns to me. The softness of his mouth shows real vulnerability. So does his tone as he asks, "May I?"

42

THAT SHOWER THOUGH

Briar

There's no question. My answer comes without a second thought. "Yes."

Gavin scoops me up, grabbing my clothes too, and carries me to the bathroom we're all sharing. He sets me down on the tiled floor, then hands me a fluffy towel he's taken from the linen closet as we passed it. "Do you want me to get you something else to wear?"

"Sure. Jammies would be nice," I say as I hang the towel on the hook next to the shower. "There's a pair of sleep shorts with donuts on them on my bed. I left them there."

"I'll get them," he says, eager to help.

A laugh bubbles up inside me, but I stifle it quickly. I don't think he'd want me to laugh right now, even though I'm not laughing at him.

I'm still intoxicated from the most exhilarating night.

"Thanks," I say, then I reach into the shower and turn the water to high as he leaves. Before I get in, I grab a hair tie from the vanity, twist my strands onto the top of my head, then look in the mirror, kind of amazed. "You just had sex with three guys."

Fine, technically I *didn't*. But that's splitting hairs. For all intents and purposes, I did.

Somehow, three men are exactly what I needed to get over the hump.

Life is funny that way. I never expected Steven stealing my cat would lead to my first O with a man. It's a bright new world.

I step into the shower and let the hot water sluice over me, lifting my face to the stream, savoring every sensation of this side of O-Land.

The door creaks open. Gavin's back, setting the jammies on the vanity in a neat, folded pile. He's not alone. Donut's at his feet, waggling her little booty as she trots inside, headed straight for the shower. "Hey, girl," I say to my pooch.

She shimmies in excitement.

She must have been in the bedroom the whole time. Probably for the best. She's young and impressionable, after all.

After she finishes her greeting, she flops down on the bath mat.

Gavin gestures to the door with some reluctance. "I'll leave you alone," he says.

I almost want to ask him to stay, but he might need

his space. "Sounds good," I say, closing my eyes and lifting my face to the water as he exits.

Footsteps sound on the hardwood. But seconds later, the door swings open in a loud, definitive thunk. Startled, I blink open my eyes.

Gavin's outside the shower stall barefoot, still dressed in jeans and a polo, and with determination etched in his sinful hazel eyes. He grabs the handle on the shower door and jerks it open, muttering, "Fuck it."

"Fuck what and why?"

The corner of his lips twitches as he gives a *what can you do* shrug, then stretches an arm into the shower and curls his hand around the back of my head.

His arm's right in the stream, getting soaked. Then, the rest of him as he steps into the shower and covers my lips with his.

It's a hot, deep kiss that makes my knees weak. He steadies me, roping a strong hand around my hip, settling it there as he crushes my mouth. He's unforgiving in his kiss. Merciless as he sucks on my bottom lip, then my tongue.

I taste the wine he drank earlier, then catch the faint scent of whatever cologne or aftershave he slapped on after his shower before game night.

The taste and the scent mingle deliciously.

A low rumble emanates from his chest as he kisses me harder. My belly swoops. Then, I say screw it too, grabbing his shirt collar and tugging him closer to me.

He seals his body to mine and kisses me under the scalding stream. I'm naked and he's fully dressed. His polo shirt sticks to his strong chest, his jeans turn sopping wet, his hair is slick, and still, he doesn't break the kiss for long, dizzying seconds.

When he does, his breathing is staggered, his eyes fiery. I push wet strands of hair off my face, catching my breath as he steps back and out of the shower, dripping water onto the floor.

"Guess I need a towel," he deadpans.

This time I don't smother my laugh.

* * *

A little later, I'm dried off, lotioned up, and dressed in sleep shorts and a comfy T-shirt.

I'm hungry too.

But also a little unsure. What happens next? Well, besides food. Do we pick positions for tomorrow? Does Gavin join us again? Was this a one-night-only foursome? Was this even technically a quartet?

Four people got off, girl. It was a foursome.

With a strange new burst of nerves, I pad down the hall, turn into the kitchen.

"Dude, that is not how you make an omelet. Stop, just stop. You're hurting my eyes," Gavin says to Hollis.

They're both at the stove. Gavin has changed into gym shorts and a T-shirt. Hollis is shirtless and sporting basketball shorts.

"This is fine," Hollis insists, pushing the eggs in the pan with a red spatula.

"The pan is too hot. Your omelet is going to be over-cooked. It'll be browned and burned and overdone."

"I like well-cooked omelets," Hollis fires back.

From the other side of the kitchen, Rhys scoffs as he washes blueberries in the sink. "No one likes well-cooked omelets."

"You're siding with Worthy?" Hollis asks, faux aggrieved.

"Yes, Bouchard. Because you, sir, are just plain wrong."

"Facts," Gavin says, then pushes Hollis aside to take over the pan.

Amused at the scene, I lean against the wall then play my ace. "I like well-cooked omelets," I announce.

Gavin hisses. Rhys shudders.

Hollis just grins, smug and cocky as he gestures proudly to me. "See? There you go. *Our guest* prefers my omelets."

Gavin lifts the spatula my way like he's going to make a point. "We're going to do a taste test then, Briar. My perfectly cooked fluffy omelet and his overcooked one. They'll be ready in five."

"Fair enough," I say, then head to the couch to wait for them to serve me.

Feels fitting.

I settle in, pick up my phone to open the novel for Trina's book club as they chat about tomorrow, mentioning they don't have to do the obstacle course in the afternoon, and I pipe in that I only have yoga in the morning. Then I yawn as I swipe on my e-reader and return to the chapter where I left off. It's a good story, but as the heroine debates the merits of banging her boss, my eyes flutter closed.

* * *

I rustle awake to the sun shining brightly through the window and Donut licking my face.

As I stretch, I glance down. There's a blanket covering me, and I'm not on the couch anymore. I'm on my bed.

I fling off the covers, scoop up my dog and walk around the cottage, but it's silent and I'm all alone.

43

A COUPLE OF ADDENDUMS

Hollis

I race up the steps, tapping the wooden railing on the porch, breathing out hard and victoriously.

"How's that for a streak?" Spinning around, I hold my arms out wide. "But really, I don't even need to gloat. It's too easy beating you guys every single time."

"And yet you gloated anyway," Rhys remarks as he flies across the yard, joining me seconds later.

Gavin's next, finishing the Saturday morning run, which turned into a race, naturally. A race I won, since I always do with them.

"It's okay," Gavin says dryly. "Men who need to gloat..."

I fold my arms across my chest. "Men who need to gloat...what? Have small feet?" I challenge. "You've seen my feet, and they're as spectacular as the rest of me."

"You think I was looking at *you* last night?" Gavin retorts as I tap in the code to unlock the door, excited to see Briar again.

"No, man. I just think my dick is impossible to miss," I say as I swing open the door. Briar was still sound asleep in her bed when we woke, so we texted her that we were going out for a run and that the first guy back would get to kiss her.

Donut's bouncing already behind it, jumping up to say hi. I give her a pat on the head, then a scratch on the chin while Briar leans against the counter, drinking a fruit smoothie, looking like all my sex dreams come to life.

My heart stutters. Then it does a race of its own, like it's trying to run to her. Or maybe I'm just amped up from the run. That must be it. But damn, she's pretty, so laid-back and carefree, dressed in sky-blue exercise clothes.

"Yes, Hollis's dick is fantastic," she says, setting down the tumbler.

I pump a fist.

"Briar, love. Wouldn't you say *I* have really big feet?" Rhys calls out as he enters the cottage right behind me.

"So big you need clown shoes," she says to Rhys as I close the distance to her and stop a foot in front of the beauty, my pulse speeding up all over again in double time. "I won. Do I get a morning kiss?"

She eyes me up and down, as if she's appraising my sweat-soaked shirt, the sheen on my face.

"C'mon. Sweat is sexy, baby," I goad.

Shaking her head, she grabs my shirt with her free hand. "No, what's sexy is you guys carrying me to my bed last night. Walking my dog this morning *and* putting her back in bed with me. Making me this smoothie. Letting me sleep in. So this kiss is for all that."

She drops her mouth to mine and kisses me hard, making my head spin with lust. Don't want to get her all sweaty, so I set a hand on the counter behind her, then give her a kiss that says I can't stop thinking about her.

I gather her hair in my other hand and pull it—not too hard, but just hard enough to jerk her head back more.

Something I'm learning she likes.

To surrender.

To give in. To be...consumed.

She murmurs into my mouth and I swallow the sound, then somehow find the will to wrench away.

When I stop, she blows out a breath. "Wow."

My chest swells with pride. That's the real streak I don't want to break—making her happy.

"How was your run?" she asks, like she's getting her bearings after that kiss.

Gavin strides past us and into the kitchen. "Good. Hollis beat us by five seconds, but I guess he usually comes first."

I turn around and stare him down. "Oh no you didn't."

Gavin flashes an evil smirk as he pours a glass of water. Rhys swings by to drop a quick kiss on Briar's cheek, like he's sneaking one in. She says hi to him and glances at Gavin. Hmm. He didn't kiss her. Not sure why. She stands straighter, looks around, like she's checking the mood. Maybe before she says something?

Shit.

Was last night a one-and-done? Did she want one night with all of us and that was it? The second that thought lands in my mind, I want to ball it up and toss it in the trash. That won't do. I need so much more than what we've already had.

No idea how the other guys feel since we deliberately didn't discuss her on the run this morning. When Rhys brought her up on the way back to the house, asking what would be next, I said I felt weird discussing that without her around. Making sex plans was entirely different.

But now we're here and I need to know where she stands, stat. "So, I was thinking—"

"Guys we should talk," she says at the same time, then gestures to me. "You go first."

I shake my head, hiding my worry that she's had enough. "No. You. Ladies first."

"What do you want to talk about?" Rhys asks, and he sounds strung tight too.

"About...us," Briar says, chin up, confident. "This project. After last night, I thought we should discuss it and what's next. Like, for tonight."

All my tension vanishes. I'm so damn proud of her instead. I wrap my arms around her waist and lift her up. "You fucking rock."

She laughs. "Why?"

"Two days ago you didn't want to talk about orgasms, and look at you now. Having one with us unlocked you, baby."

She rolls her eyes, but she's smiling as I put her down.

Gavin's not though. His brow is creased. "You. Never. Had. One?"

"Not with another person," she says. "Until the night before, and then last night."

"Oh. Well. That's good," he says, his lips twitching, like he's excited.

Well, yeah.

I rub my palms, ready to get down to business. "Last night. Tonight. What is on your mind?"

"The three of us set down the rules the other night. You, Rhys, and me," she says to me. "It seems we have an extra person so maybe we need an addendum. For the rest of this...boyfriend project."

It's like a noose tightens around my chest from the reminder. The first few days have flown by too fast. They can't be ending this soon. But yet, the calendar doesn't lie. It's Saturday. On Wednesday morning we take off. We have a charity thing in Chicago with the children's hospital there, then a stretch of road games that begins in the Windy City.

There's a heavy pause in the cottage, like we were all just slapped with the realization that this ends very, *very* soon. A darkness passes across Rhys's eyes. Gavin's mouth is a ruler. And Briar gives a little sigh.

But the clock only spins forward. "Time's a ticking," I say, trying to keep the mood light.

"It is," Briar says, then gestures to the table.

We sit and I grab a sheet of paper from a notebook that the property manager left here and a pen. "What's that for?" Gavin asks.

"It's paper," I say. "You use it to write things down. Like words and stuff."

"No shit. But what are you doing?"

"Making a new list of rules since you're the addendum."

Gavin's quiet for a beat, then nods, his expression somber. "Right. Of course."

Ah, shit. I realize what's going on. He's not giving me a hard time for fun. He's the guy who's never negotiated sharing a woman before. That's why he didn't kiss her a few minutes ago. This is new terrain for him. I ease up on the teasing, patting his shoulder. "Hey, this'll help. It'll be good to get everything out in the open. Okay?"

"Yeah. Sure. That's how it's done, right?" It's said earnestly, and I'm proud of him too—for being vulnerable and asking that kind of question.

"Communication is key," I say, then look to the blue-eyed beauty across from me, eager to learn what's on her mind. No, make that downright antsy. I want to know everything about her. Everything she wants. So we can give it to her. "What do you have in mind, baby?"

She's like a new woman. This is not the Briar who sorted wooden spoons when I called her on faking it. "Well, first," she begins, "it ends on Wednesday when the three of you leave. Like we talked about."

My chest twinges. A dull ache. Maybe that's from the run. "Right, done," I say, staying businesslike. Don't want to think about the end right now. Then I add a rule of my own. "We need to be safe and communicate. Like we've done so far."

"Like you and I did the first night," she adds.

Gavin's brow knits again.

Shit. I've been a bad friend. A bad leader. I give him an apologetic look. "Briar and I *hung out* the first night. Before you got here."

I brace myself for any fallout.

Gavin chuckles. "Yeah, I figured that already."

I blink. "You did?"

He flaps a hand at me. "Dude. You got her a sex toy. Yeah, I fucking figured."

Rhys cracks up, dropping his face into his palm. "You're so obvious, Bouchard."

"I guess that was a dead giveaway," Briar deadpans.

I hold out my hands in surrender. "I suppose it was," I say, then move things along. "Boundaries is another guideline. If someone doesn't want something, he or she will say it." Everyone nods, then Briar adds, "Here's one of mine. I'm on birth control, but I want to use condoms."

"Noted," I say, then I add, "And consent. Like last night when Gavin asked if Briar wanted to be spanked."

Briar's eyes sparkle. "I liked that."

"Good," Gavin says quietly.

Rhys clears his throat. "Here's a guideline. If someone wants to be alone with Briar, they don't need anyone else's permission. Just hers."

Doesn't surprise me that he says that. I just hope the man doesn't fall in love with her. That'd be a mess.

She doesn't want anything more, and as easy as it would be to fall for her—the easiest thing in the world since she's a feisty, strong, badass babe I can't get out of my head—falling is a bad idea.

"That works for me," she says, and I write those rules down too.

But there's something I want as well. I look her in the eyes. "I want you to win the 'what makes a great boyfriend' contest. I want you to get that prize money, show that jackass he can't steal your ideas, and then show all those dudes who read his site how to treat a woman well." I go for the kill. "Which means I want us to romance you too. Show you how a good boyfriend would do that. That work for you?"

Briar smiles, wide and bright, like it comes from the center of her soul. "Lucky me. I have three boyfriends this week to teach me."

Her response makes my heart beat fast again. Makes my skin go all warm. Makes me want to just tell her she's kind of amazing. Ah, hell. I can't just worry about my friends. I've got to look out for myself, too, since I'd better not fall in love with her either.

I really better not. Especially when she says to the other guys, "Does that work for you two? To romance me with Hollis?"

Rhys doesn't bother to hide a smile. The man is too far gone. "Yes."

Gavin gives a nod. "Same."

"Awesome," I say, writing that down, more excited

than I'd expected to be. But the more we all give her, the more she seems to glow.

I set down the pen. "Are we good?"

Briar reads the list, then looks up. "I'm good."

But Gavin raises a finger. "I just have one condition."

44

A VOW

Briar

I'm on the edge of my seat. "What's your condition?"

I cycle through possibilities at lightning speed. He doesn't want to have sex with me? He just wants to watch? He doesn't want to romance me after all?

I steel myself. I like the way I feel with all these guys —all three. There's something about us that just clicks as a foursome. A temporary foursome, but a damn good one.

Gavin licks his lips nervously. His eyes are wide, tone hopeful as he says, "I want us to stay friends. On the other side." He turns to the guys. "You're my closest friends. You're like family."

My heart thunders. My eyes shine with the threat of tears. I didn't expect *that*, but I love the sentiment. It makes me sad too.

Yesterday morning on the deck, he talked about his

aunt and uncle. I don't think they were good to him. But these guys are. They're like his home.

Rhys stretches out an arm, pats Gavin on the back. Hollis offers a fist for knocking. "We're fucking family. That's not going to change," Hollis assures him.

"Even if the team trades me," Rhys adds.

"They won't, man," Gavin says, reassuring him too.

I swallow past a knot in my throat. The fondness between the three of them has me reaching for a tissue and dabbing my eyes. I don't like showing too many emotions. But I have no choice right now. Discreetly, I tuck the tissue in my pocket.

Gavin shifts his focus to me, that same serious look in his hazel eyes. "My friends are everything to me. I never had a family I could count on. My parents died when I was five. I don't remember them."

I can't hold back the emotions now. Twin tears slip down my cheeks. "I'm so sorry."

"Thank you," he says quietly, then he rolls his lips and seems to shake off the hurt. "And I kind of think of you as a friend now too, Briar."

It's only been a few short days, but I think of myself that way too. "We'll stay friends," I say, reaching out to squeeze his hand.

This is a promise that feels vital for all of us to keep. It's one that's so important that we put our hands together in the middle of the table—the guys on the bottom, me on top.

"Friends," we say as we make our vow.

We might be rivals to the world, but here in this

cottage we're unconventional lovers, and we've all become friends.

When we let go, Rhys glances toward the clock on the wall. "Since we're all free this afternoon, maybe we could go to the festival just for fun." Then he adds, sealing the deal, "As friends."

Sounds like a perfect day.

* * *

That afternoon as we wander past a booth offering kits for making your own pickled radishes, my phone pings. I check it, and there's a text from Ivy.

> Ivy: My old apartment is available!!!! My friend Jackson just moved out. (I bought it a while ago and I've been subleasing it. You can have it for free though.)

I beam, writing back immediately to the great news.

> Briar: I won't take it for free. But I will take it.

> Ivy: You can pay me in yoga and playlists.

Briar: I will pay you in money! Yoga, playlists, and my awesome company are just a bonus.

Ivy: I love my bonuses. But there's only one issue. There's no furniture.

Briar: I don't even care. I'll sleep on the floor.

When I put the phone away, I tell the guys the good news, and they high-five me.

Like friends.

We spend the rest of the afternoon goofing off. We test out kites. Try hummus and chips. Nibble on crepes. Listen to music. Then we hit the rides. In the fun house, when the four of us stop in front of the warped mirror, I point to Rhys's shoes. "You do have clown feet."

"Told you so," he says.

It feels like we are a new friend group, one that can last beyond this week. I'm buoyed by the possibilities of these kinds of days when we're back in San Francisco, and I even say as much as we trot down the steps of the fun house as the sun dips lower in the late afternoon sky. "We have to do this in the city," I say to them, and I barely notice the woman walking toward me.

Until I smack right into Nova.

"Oh, I'm sorry," I say, taken aback, my breath knocked out of me.

"My bad," she says, then eyes my companions. One, two, three. "I didn't realize you were all—"

Before she can say anything more, I jump in with, "Friends. We're friends. We're all friends."

Do I sound like I'm covering something up or what? My stomach churns.

"Hey, Nova," Hollis says easily, stepping in perhaps to save me. "Good to see you."

I don't know how they know each other, but Hollis is the type of person who knows everyone.

"Good to see you, Hollis," she says, but her eyes are shrewd, curious still as she studies us, like we're a math problem she's determined to figure out.

"Can't wait to see you at the big cross-town rival game in a couple weeks," Hollis says. "We do plan to beat the Sea Dogs."

Nova scoffs. "We'll see about that." Then to me, she says, "And we have lots to work on when you get back."

Like I'm on a vacation when we're all here. "I'll be ready," I say, upbeat, and so damn eager to impress her.

"Have fun with your friends," she says, but her tone is a touch skeptical.

It's one thing to be friends with your rivals. It's entirely another to sleep with them. *Three of them.*

My neck prickles with worry. But that doesn't mean I want to pursue a...foursome relationship.

I have enough on my plate, and I need to do what my father always taught me. Focus on what's reliable— business and family. Not romance. Never romance.

When she's out of earshot, Rhys is the first to turn to me. "Are you okay?"

"That was a very close call," I say.

But for what? I don't even know. I just feel off. Weird. Like I've done something wrong.

I really need to get my mind off it. I glance around, spotting the Tilt-A-Whirl at the edge of the festival grounds. "I haven't ridden one of those in forever."

"Let's do it," Gavin says, and we head over, then climb the steps and onto the ride, where I try to put that odd encounter behind me.

But three minutes later, when I step off the ride, I'm so dizzy I can barely walk. I can barely see straight. My skin is both cold and sweaty, my stomach churning. I don't know which way is up.

I'm stumbling, and Rhys sets a hand on my shoulder. Gavin takes my other arm while Hollis leads us away from the crowds to a quiet bench on the outskirts of the festival where I sit and try to catch my breath.

It's not working though. The world is still upside down. My head aches and I feel like I'm going to throw up, but nothing happens—nothing except this cold, clammy feeling that won't leave me.

It looks like Gavin is tapping on his phone, but I can't focus as he rattles off some instructions.

In seconds, Rhys is scooping me up and carrying me away from the festival.

45

NURSE DOG

Briar

"I'm fine," I insist, even as the houses on both sides of the block sway toward me.

Rhys makes a soothing noise in his throat as he strides along the sidewalk, then says tenderly, "Of course you are."

"I swear I am. You don't have to carry me," I say as he turns onto the block with the cottage. At least, I think that's the cottage. Is the cottage sideways now?

"We're almost there," he says.

"I can make it the rest of the way." Sure, my hands are still clammy. But you don't walk with your hands, so I should be fine.

"I know you can. But I can also carry you."

This is so embarrassing. I'm a capable woman. I can do things. I don't need to be carried, but he hasn't let me go the whole way. "I don't mind," I point out, then breathe in quickly once, twice.

Another time.

He cuts a glance down at me, a swoop of his midnight hair falling across his forehead, his brown eyes assessing. "Motion sickness is no joke, Briar. The guys should be back soon with Dramamine," he says, since he sent Hollis and Gavin to the store in town.

I curl a hand tighter around his neck, tucking my face into his chest, my breath still short, the world still tilting, my skin still cold. "Did anyone see you carry me?" I whisper.

"Are you worried someone is going to figure out what's going on?"

"No. That's not it," I say as he reaches the cottage and cuts through the yard.

"What is it, love?"

Love. I know he just says that because he's English, but it's so...mesmerizing. The way the word curls on his tongue, gusts past his lips, floats to my ear.

"I hate being sick," I mutter.

He dips his face to my forehead, grazing me with a kiss. "Me too. I get it."

"I just didn't want anyone to see me like this. Like people I work with. Or might work with. That's all."

"I don't think anyone did. I didn't walk through the town square. I took some side streets through the neighborhoods. There weren't too many people."

"Thank you," I say into his chest.

Soon, we're at the front door, and he effortlessly unlocks it with one hand, then pushes it open.

Donut barks an excited hello. Then a concerned one. Then a *what the hell is going on with my person* yip as Rhys carries me to the couch. Gently, he lays me down, then kneels on the floor by my side and strokes my forehead while Donut jumps onto the couch and scurries right to my face, licking me. "It's okay, honey," I tell her.

"Is it? How are you feeling?" Rhys asks.

"So much better." I paste on a smile, even though I feel out of alignment with my body and my mind, like they're fighting each other. I'm sweaty and cold, and everything's still a little fuzzy.

"Why do I not believe you?" he asks.

I wrap my arms around Donut's little body, nuzzling into her soft fur. "You believe me, don't you?"

She licks my face in concern, then whimpers, and looks up at me with the biggest, sweetest eyes ever. I can't fake it with her. Or, really, with Rhys. "I don't like anyone seeing me like this," I whisper. "It makes me feel weak."

He runs a hand over my hair. "I get it."

"Like why would someone take my classes, or get my app, or trust me to teach them if I'm the teacher who's sick?"

"Teachers get sick too," he says.

"I know...but not me. I'm the designated driver, the chaperone." And, especially, I'm the girl who was abandoned by her mom and rose up stronger, better, tougher. "Did you know I had perfect attendance in high school?"

Rhys's smile is amused, but still so kind. "I'm not at all surprised."

"I never missed a day."

As I regale him with stories of my super-responsible self, the chill in my skin starts to subside, and the edges of the world are less blurry, and seconds later, the door groans open.

"We're back. We got you some things, baby." It's Hollis, ready to make me feel better.

I try to sit up and turn to him, but Donut licks my face, wiggling against me. "You're a nurse dog," I say to her.

That earns me another lick.

"Good girl," Rhys tells the Dachshund as Hollis and Gavin join Rhys on the floor by my side. I push up for real this time.

"Dramamine," Gavin says, showing me the box. "For motion sickness."

"I've never had motion sickness before," I point out, like that'll make it go away.

"Have you ridden the Tilt-A-Whirl before?" Gavin asks.

I wince. My mom was the amusement park fan. Dad never took us after she left. Maybe amusement parks were like bouquets of flowers for him. Too much of a reminder. "Not since I was young and my mom took me. I don't remember that though, going with her," I say. "But I don't get sick in cars, or boats, or even hot-air balloons."

Gavin's brow knits. "Hot-air balloons? That's random."

"I grew up around here. It's a thing."

"Well, so is motion sickness with some rides," Gavin adds. "I looked it up. And you should take some meds, okay?"

He's a little stern, but there's real caring in his tone too.

"And you need some tea," Hollis adds, waggling a tin of herbal tea and a plastic bear full of honey. "My mom always said tea and honey make everything better."

That's so him. "I'm sure she's right."

What's really starting to make me feel better is the three of them and how they take care of me. It can't be easy since I don't want anyone to take care of me at all.

But maybe I need them to.

* * *

A few hours of rest later, I stretch my arms, pop up from the couch, and spot the guys at the kitchen table, playing cards. "I'm all better. Does anyone want to..." I jut out my hip. Wiggle my brows. "...have another lesson?"

Three men look my way as if I'm nuts.

"No. You were sick. I have a better idea for tonight," Hollis offers, then sets down his cards and heads down the hall, waving us along. "Let me show you."

46

DIRTY DREAMS

Gavin

I sleep alone. It suits me.

So when Hollis explains his plan, I bristle. "You want us to drag the mattress from her room *and* your room into the living room?"

"Yes," he says. "Do you need a diagram?"

"Sure. Do you need me to carry all the mattresses since they're so heavy?" I fire back.

He stops outside Briar's room and tilts his head, like he's giving that question some serious thought. "Not a bad idea. You lift. I'll supervise."

I flip him the bird then turn to Briar. Maybe she won't want this. Maybe we can all go back to sleeping in our rooms like we did last night after Briar fell asleep.

Wouldn't that just be easier? We won't be all up in each other's business.

"You really want this?" I ask her. We did say consent

was key, so maybe she's dying for an out too. I haven't had a woman spend the night since my college girl-friend. She said I snored and bought me nose strips.

That was fun.

Briar pats my arm. "I'm fine with it. Rhys is a superior cuddler, so he's got that covered."

Rhys stretches, sighing in an oh-so-satisfied way. "But you don't have to," she says, giving me a reprieve, and fuck that.

I don't back down.

I'm the new guy in this sharing situation-ship. No way am I gonna chicken out of sharing a very big bed. Even if I snore. "I'm down with it."

A little later, we've lugged the mattresses to the living room, set up blankets and pillows, and made a giant mattress bed as the clock ticks to midnight. We're at the halfway point in our stay here, and it already feels like time is speeding up, like it does when you hit that midway point of a great vacation. I try not to think about Wednesday. There's no point. Besides, it'll be good to hit the ice again.

Hollis sets down his sleep mask then flops next to it, patting his special pillow a few times.

"You and your sleeping rituals," I say, since everyone on the team knows about his love affair with bedtime.

"I'm gonna marry sleep," he says with genuine affection.

"What's in that pillow?" Briar asks, settling in with her dog. "Angel dust? Virgin hair? Dandelions specially harvested by a devoted cult of sleep worshippers?"

"How did you know?" Hollis asks, all serious.

"I've heard good things about sleep worshippers," Briar says.

"And now you've met one." Hollis gives her an apologetic smile. "Sorry, baby. But I can't face anyone while I sleep. Even you."

She waves a hand his way. "Go, go. I don't need face-to-face sleep."

I don't either but I've got to know why he can't handle it. "What's that all about, Bouchard?"

He rustles around under the blankets, maybe buying some time, then he grumbles. "Just my thing."

"But why?" I press.

He moans, aggrieved, then drags a hand through his dark blond hair, a wild mess like always. "I just don't like...someone breathing on me."

A laugh bursts from me. A louder one from Rhys.

"Really?" Rhys asks.

"Yes, really," Hollis grumbles as he tugs on his sleep mask, adjusting it, then letting it sit on his forehead. "Everyone has their peculiarities. I'm sure you have yours."

Well, I don't like sleeping with anyone else. But no fucking way will I say that. It's more fun to give him hell. "But it's extra funny that Mister Easygoing has so many," I say.

"I like to sleep with my socks on then kick them off in the middle of the night," Briar offers, then paddles her fuzzy-socked feet under the covers in a demo. "Also, I spoon my dog."

I stare at the ceiling, trying not to smile over how

fucking cute that is. Especially as she brings Donut closer to her chest like I did with Rascal all those years ago.

"I like to sleep with a pillow over my face," Rhys offers, then adds, "Two, actually. I make a mountain of pillows on my head."

There's silence for several seconds. Everyone's waiting. It's my turn for a sleep confession. I hesitate as I pull the blanket up, casting a glance at Briar.

My new friend.

The woman I'm far too into.

I'm not sure I want everyone to know my sleep issue. But everyone served something up, so as foreign as this is to me, as bizarre as this entire situation is—four of us in a makeshift big bed—I push past the discomfort. "I have very dirty dreams."

Well, that's true.

But it's also a lie of omission. But they're going to find out one way or another. Fuck it. "And I snore loudly," I admit, then I say goodnight and turn the other way, plotting my escape to the futon as soon as I possibly can. This was a shitty idea.

"Don't worry. I sleep like the dead," Briar puts in.

"Me too," Hollis says.

"Same here," Rhys offers.

And I'm glad they can't see my expression in the dark—a stupid smile.

* * *

In the morning, I wake with my arms wrapped around Briar, my face in her hair, and the energy you get after having the best night of sleep ever.

It feels too good. Too right. That's a problem. I can't get used to her. I can't get hooked on her.

This is just sex.

That is all.

No matter how much I like sleeping with her.

It's time we refocus things on just sex. I leap out of bed, head to the kitchen, and make some coffee. We have three more days, then we're gone. A twinge of something like missing lodges in my chest, but I dismiss it quickly. No time for that. No space for missing. In seventy-two hours we'll be out of here and on our way to Chicago, then Detroit, then St. Louis.

But first, coffee.

A little later, when everyone's wandering into the kitchen, no doubt lured by the aroma, I go first, before anyone else can get a word in: "Anyone up for a round of morning Never Have I Ever?"

47

NEVER HAVE I EVER

Rhys

All things being equal, I'd rather be drinking scotch for this game.

But it is eight in the morning, so it's tea for me as Briar taps her chin, then goes first. "Never have I ever gone bungee jumping."

Hollis gives her a curious look. "Don't you know? This game is supposed to be dirty?"

"Bungee jumping is foreplay," Briar says with mischief in those blue eyes. "I mean, the adrenaline, guys. The adrenaline."

"Oh," Hollis says, nodding. "Good point."

But Briar is the only one who drinks, which surprises me. "You don't seem the type to go bungee jumping."

"Oh, I'm not. But my brother goaded me into it

once. He is the type, and I'm a sucker for him. So I did it," she says.

I add that nugget to the Briar intel file, her affection for her brother. It's getting bigger, the file. I like it too much for my own good, and yet I can't stop adding to it. "Never have I ever had a foursome," I say.

Hollis shoots me a doubtful look. "Was that a foursome though? Our guy Worthy fucked his own hand."

In no time, Gavin darts out said hand and thumps Hollis on the head.

"Ouch," Hollis says, rubbing the spot.

"Good. I hope it hurt," Gavin grumbles.

Hollis places his palm against his chest. "You hurt my feelings."

"You don't have any."

Briar grins like she's posing for a *pleased* meme as she lifts her mug. "I'll drink. It counts."

We all drink so fast.

When I set the mug down, I muse on my turn. Sure, it's fun to play dirty Never Have I Ever but yesterday morning at this table we vowed to romance her too, so fuck it. "Never have I ever gone on a date with...three guys."

Confused, she shoots me a look. "I haven't. I'm presuming you guys haven't either."

Feigning ignorance, I smack my forehead. "My mistake. I thought it also counted when it was for something you're about to do. Say, our last night here? Before we go?" I've already started forming the plan in my head.

Her grin is like melting chocolate, sweet and delicious. "I would love to," she says.

"It'll help with your column," I add, just so she doesn't think I've forgotten the rules we laid out. "We can romance you. Take you on the best date ever. Who's in?"

My mates all raise their mugs in our twist on the game.

Briar lifts her mug near her face, maybe to hide a smile. When it's her turn, she says, "Never have I ever gone on a hot-air balloon ride."

No one drinks except Briar. When she finishes, she says, "We'll change that. I'm going to take all of you on one. I know someone. I can get us a sunset ride no problem."

My heart stutters. This woman is a fucking romantic too. "I'm there," I say, the first man to RSVP.

Hollis is next, and Gavin says yes too.

My gaze strays to the clock. "We need to get to the obstacle course at ten-thirty. It's eight-thirty now."

"I have a class at eleven," Briar says.

Gavin clears his throat. "Never have I ever had morning sex."

We all scoff at the softball question and lift our cups, but before we can drink, Gavin raises his voice and adds, "Today."

48

A LINE CHANGE

Hollis

Fair's fair.

As much as it pains me, I gotta tap out. There's no *I* in team, and part of teamwork is helping a buddy.

I've been the lucky man who's been able to play with her the most. It's time for a line change.

"If our girl's game, you really should see if she'd want to ride your cock," I say to Rhys, since I'm helpful like that. Rhys's eyes flare. I turn to Gavin. "And if you're lucky, Worthy, maybe you can taste her sweet pussy. She's fucking delicious."

Gavin's chest rumbles. An obvious yes.

I shift my focus to Briar, who's stretched out on her bed again. We quickly reassembled her king-size bed. Fucking on a bed is way more fun than fucking on a mattress on the floor.

Angles and all.

She's wearing pink cotton panties and a pink sports bra. I never knew sports bras were sexy till I saw her in them. "Sure. As long as someone kisses me and plays with my tits," she says.

I have no choice. I climb onto the bed and cover her. "You're too fucking sexy. Look at you—asking for what you want," I say, then seal my lips to hers. Our mouths slip together easily, our tongues skating, our breath mingling.

She arches her hips, seeking me out, then spreads her legs for me.

I nearly say *fuck it* to the plan we just made. I'm so turned on I want to take her right now. But this week is about her. Being good to her. Learning from her. I wrench away, getting off the bed. "Show us what you like when Rhys fucks you, baby. So when it's Gavin's turn the next time he can fuck you the way you like. Okay?"

Briar shudders out a yes, and Gavin, who's standing on the other side of the bed, tries but fails to stifle a groan.

I retreat to a chair in the corner of the room, giving Rhys his chance and a break from choreographing. I can also help Gavin out. He'd never ask for it, but it can't hurt to give him a tip or two.

I should really win an award for being the friendliest fucker.

And also, the cleverest. Because I think I'm going to surprise them all right now.

"Briar, baby. Change of plans. How would you feel about fucking Rhys's face first? While Gavin plays with your tits? I know you love it when we play with those beauties."

A tremble moves down her body. "What a great idea."

A minute later, she's naked and sitting on Rhys's face, rocking against him, while Gavin stands behind her on the bed, fondling her tits, kissing her hair, and getting the hang of it like that.

"You're a fast learner, Worthy," I call out.

But he doesn't respond since Briar is moaning, gasping, and riding my friend like he's a wild mustang.

She looks close. She sounds close. I want her to come like this and I think I know the way. "Kiss her Worthy. Kiss her while she fucks his face. She fucking loves being kissed," I say.

"I do," Briar pants out as she grips the headboard and grinds against Rhys's stubble while Rhys curls his hands tighter around her hips, making sure she doesn't lose her footing.

Gavin grabs her chin, jerks her face to him, and kisses her while she rides my other teammate.

What a bunch of lucky guys.

But the best part is what she says when she breaks the kiss.

49

TAKE TWO

Briar

Never have I ever been kissed while being eaten.

Until now.

My belly tightens. My thighs shake. And the second I let go of Gavin's mouth, I can't help it. I'm shouting, "Coming."

A surprise orgasm crashes into me like an unexpected party guest, swinging the door wide open.

I cry out as this sharp and red-hot burst of ecstasy races through me, flooding every corner of my body. My fingers grab onto the headboard as I ride Rhys's hungry mouth to the ends of my pleasure.

It's a miracle I don't fall off him.

When I lean back into big, strong hands on my shoulders I realize why—Gavin's holding me, his palms spread across my shoulder blades, making sure I don't fall as I come.

I blink open my eyes. Is this really me? Yes, yes it is. I'm having sex like this. Sex I enjoy. Sex that isn't a chore. Sex that's fun and fiery.

And not at all over.

As an aftershock rips through me, I turn to Hollis and say, "I should ride him now and suck your other friend's dick, right?"

I flash the most fantastic partner-in-crime grin his way, and Hollis returns it right back. "You took the words right out of my mouth, baby," he says, a mastermind calling the shots.

Gavin, Rhys, and I play musical sex chairs, and after I slide a condom down Rhys's fantastic shaft, I whisper to him, "That was my first time unassisted."

His smile is downright swoony. "And you look so fucking gorgeous when you come, love."

"You deserve to come too," I say, then I spin around and sink down onto him reverse cowgirl.

I'm facing Gavin who's kneeling at the foot of the bed, watching me.

As Rhys fills me up, my thighs clench, and I moan from the delicious intrusion.

"Yesss," I murmur, never breaking eye contact with Gavin's deep hazel irises.

Rhys thrusts up, hard, powerful. "That what you wanted, love? My cock filling you all the fucking way?" He's making sure I feel every inch of him all while Gavin stares down at me, breathing ragged, a racehorse ready to tear down the tracks.

Gavin's cock is pointing at me, a bead of liquid arousal forming at the head. My mouth waters.

"I love it, Rhys," I say to the man under me while I lock eyes with the man in front of me. "I love when you fuck me hard. Do you think Gavin wants to fuck my mouth hard too?"

The sound Gavin makes is animalistic.

"Her mouth is heaven, mate," Rhys rasps out. "You're gonna lose your mind."

I curl a hand around Gavin's cock, then say to him, "Why don't you show me how you'd like to fuck my mouth?"

He shudders, and a drop of pre-come spills onto my hand.

"I will." Gavin stands, takes one step closer to me on the bed, gripping his cock in one hand, then gathering my hair into his fist. "Open, sweetheart," he demands.

"Show him how much you love giving head, baby," Hollis chimes in from his chair, and I steal a quick glance at him. He's a man in repose, with one leg crossed over the other knee. He might as well be smoking a cigar. He's a director in charge of a scene.

As Rhys fucks up into me, I part my lips for Gavin and take his cock in my mouth. The fat head slides down my throat while Rhys rocks up into my pussy. I'm being fucked from beneath me. I'm being fucked from in front of me.

Gavin coils a palm around my head, then closes his eyes. "Fuck, sweetheart. Your mouth. Your fucking mouth. My god."

I ache from those words. Pleasure pulses in me as I rock back and forth on Rhys's cock, as I relax my throat for Gavin's. He pushes a little deeper into my mouth. Spit dribbles down my chin.

Gavin grunts, a long, savage sound.

Rhys moans.

"Look at you. Owning them. Owning their pleasure," Hollis says, his tone deep and approving.

I lift my shoulders higher. I like being praised for what I've learned to do with my body in the last few days. *Listen to it.* And I like what that listening can do for me—bring me pleasure and bring pleasure to these men.

Their sounds grow louder. Their thrusts more erratic. Their dicks thrust deeper.

But almost too deep. As Gavin grips my hair tighter, his cock drives so far in that I gag.

"Shit, sweetheart. Are you okay?" he asks, jerking out his dick.

I cough one more time, my throat scraped, but I'm not ready to quit. "Come on my lips, okay?"

His eyes fall shut. "Yes, fucking yes," he bites out as I ride Rhys's cock till he's driving hard under me.

He's seconds away. Gavin is too.

My thoughts burn off. My brain hums. My nerves ripple with excitement as Gavin slides his cock between my lips halfway till he's growling then grunting, "Gonna come."

He pulls out, then comes on my mouth. I flick my tongue over my lips, tasting him while Rhys shoves up into me one more time, then stills.

As his sounds fill the air, I turn to Hollis, feeling

wicked, feeling wild as I squeeze my breasts together in an invitation.

He's up and out of the chair in no time. A minute later, I've eased off Rhys, and Gavin has backed away. I'm lying on the mattress, offering my tits for Hollis, who's now stripped naked.

Straddling my chest, he spits on his palm, then lubes up the valley of my breasts. A few quick pumps and he's saying on an upthrust, "Want to show you what I learned."

I have no idea what he means, but my head's full of too much static to care, my body bursting with too many endorphins to think. Hollis fucks my tits till a hot splash of his release paints my chest.

Mesmerized, I spread his release across my breasts as he slides next to me and coasts a hand down to my pussy.

Like he did the first night.

When I faked it.

This time, I part my legs, I arch my hips, and I give in to him.

This is what he meant. He's been learning what makes me tick all week, and now he's showing me. He touches me the way I've taught him, and I let go.

To this.

To the way I feel with these three men.

Free.

I move with his talented fingers, using them to seek the pleasure I deserve, chasing an orgasm fearlessly then surrendering when it jolts me and I come once again.

With them.

It feels like all three of them are doing everything to me.

And I don't want it any other way.

50

HOT RIDES

Hollis

The next evening as the day coasts toward sunset, we're standing in a field not far from a big, bright pink balloon that the ground crew for Hot Rides is inflating.

The balloon operator is an older woman named Clara with long fuchsia fingernails, lash extensions, and curly blonde hair. I don't know what I was expecting except, well, not a girlie girl my mom's age.

But I should know better. I was raised by a woman who played hockey, so it makes perfect sense that a hot-air balloon pilot is a woman with laugh lines etched in ivory skin and a penchant for pink.

"So, that's it. Just climb in when we tell you and up you go. But don't rock the basket," Clara says as she finishes her safety talk.

I appreciate the info and her thoroughness. Still, it's

my job to look out for my friends. "And you're saying we don't need safety harnesses or anything?"

She gives me a smile, genuine, but practiced. It's clearly not the first time she's gotten this question. But she turns to Briar. "You want to take this one, hun?"

Briar smiles at me, a twinkle in her eyes like she has a secret. "Nope. Hot-air balloons are one of the safest ways to travel."

Rhys takes off his shades, looks to me. "I'll be expecting you to land in the players' lot in your own balloon soon."

Gavin scoffs. "Don't tempt him, man. You know Hollis will be taking balloon lessons next weekend then getting his pilot's license."

Clara smiles like a cat. "If you want to get a license, you come find me. I'm an instructor. I've taught many people to fly one of these babies."

"My summers are free so consider it confirmed. And thank you for fitting us in at the last minute," I say, and even though Briar told us Clara is a friend of her dad's, I'm still amazed Briar pulled this off so quickly, booking us a sunset ride just a day after we first mentioned it.

"Anything for Briar," Clara says.

"I think you mean anything for my dad," Briar says to the older woman.

"Henry fixed the ignition in my van last week," she says, then frowns. "Too bad he can't fix the engines on these balloons."

I tense. "Wait. Is something wrong with the balloons?"

She laughs. "Just teasing. Everything is fine."

"Dude, they don't have engines," Gavin says.

"I know," I grumble.

Then Gavin pulls me aside and says in a low voice, "I looked up whether balloon rides are safe *and* allowed in our contracts. It's all good."

I breathe a sigh of relief. "Thanks, man."

I'm grateful he sensed my concern. I've focused so much on taking care of my mom and sisters that it's second nature to look out for Briar and the crew too. But I'm not the only one taking care of the four of us. We can share the responsibility. That's a strange new thought but not an unwelcome one. And it's digging roots inside me as Clara gestures to the big basket at the edge of the field. "Crew's about ready. Are you, gentlemen?"

We all nod.

She turns to Briar. "And are you ready for your, what is this, your fiftieth flight?"

"Something like that," Briar says, a smile turning her lips into a tease.

Like she has a secret.

Wait a second. I put two and two together. "Briar, are you a pilot?" I ask, incredulous.

She bobs a shoulder playfully. "I got my pilot's license in college. I used to work here on the weekends. Clara's the one who taught me to fly balloons."

The amount of Briar intel in those sentences is a year's worth. "I'm gonna need all the details later. But are you going to fly it?" I ask because that's kind of badass and totally Briar.

"No," Briar says with a laugh. "I have to do my biennial flight review before I'm comfortable doing that. I've been a bad girl and been a little lax. But I'll do it soon. For now, I'll go help the ground crew," she says, then heads off, her ponytail swishing as she goes. She adjusts some of the cables on the huge, majestic balloon, then with the help of the crew, she grabs the edges of the basket and tips it up.

I stare slack-jawed, my heart thudding hard. "Briar's a balloon pilot," I say, awed.

Rhys watches, shaking his head. "How is that so hot?"

Gavin lets out a low whistle, then murmurs, "Because she's capable and still wants us."

Yup. Nailed it.

A gravelly laugh rips through the air as Clara walks by. "Good luck fighting over her," she says, then passes us. The three of us smile like we have a secret too.

We don't have to fight over her whatsoever.

When the balloon is fully inflated and ready for liftoff, we jump inside the basket, joining our girl.

51

HOW TO FLOAT

Briar

It never gets old.

The view from a thousand feet. The vistas of Wine Country. The river, cutting a winding path through Lucky Falls. The sun is beginning to set, casting a warm, golden hue over the vineyards below us.

We're standing at the edge of the basket, Hollis on one side of me, Rhys the other, Gavin behind me. I point to the edge of the hills, a little town beyond. Maybe, just maybe, my childhood home. I can't really see it, but I can imagine it's there. "That's where I grew up."

"With your dad and brother?" Gavin asks, like he wants to picture it perfectly.

"Yeah. We were quite a trio. We were Sea Dogs fans though," I tell them. All three guys wince at once as if they've been mortally wounded. "But hey, at least they like hockey."

"Small consolation," Gavin mutters.

I laugh, then tell them more about my family. How my dad and brother came to all my soccer games growing up, then helped me with my rehab when I tore my ACL. How my brother encouraged me to learn yoga and Pilates, then how my dad suggested I study exercise science in college, catching them up to the present day and my dad's obsession with cats, and my brother's work helping me launch Flow and Flex Fitness. "And now Griffin helps me with my app. In exchange, I give him yoga for better sex tips."

"A fair trade," Hollis says with a laugh.

"What about your dad?" Rhys asks, then chuckles when he must realize how the question sounds.

"No yoga tips for him. He, however, does usually give me gruff life advice any chance he gets," I say, looking Rhys's way.

"What sort?"

"Focus on business. Business won't hurt you. Business won't leave you," I say, and while I don't want to dwell in that *romance is awful* space, it's also part of who I am. "And that romance can really let you down."

Maybe I ruined the vibe, since everyone goes quiet, thoughtful.

"It's good that we're friends then. That we made a vow," Hollis says.

"We won't let you down," Rhys seconds.

"We'll keep our promise," Gavin says, a solemn swear.

"I know we will. I believe that, guys," I say, a small hitch in my throat. For a while I thought working for rival teams would lead to a divide between them and me. But it hasn't at all. Instead, we've all become better friends, and I don't want to lose their friendship. "I feel like I can really depend on you guys. And I hope I'm not going out on a limb, but it almost seems like the three of you are even better friends after the last few days?"

It's a hopeful question. Maybe too hopeful.

But Gavin grunts out a *yes*, while Rhys says *absolutely* and Hollis echoes them with *we are*.

My heart swells with gratitude, especially when vulnerability shines in their eyes, both for me and perhaps for each other—for this unusual bond the four of us have formed in the cottage.

We all go quiet, soaring above Wine Country as the sunset paints the world below with warm oranges and deep purples.

"So, you can fly," Hollis observes a few minutes later, then runs a hand down my arm. He glances back at Clara, who's looking the other way.

"Maybe someday I'll take you all for a ride," I say.

Rhys takes his turn, sliding nimble fingers along my shoulder. "I'd say you are."

"I'm glad you're not flying right now, Briar," Gavin says in a low voice, then runs his nose along the back of my neck.

I tremble in his arms. "Why's that?"

Hollis lets his fingers drift over my hip. "Because we

like it when you can let go. When you're not worried about everything you have to do."

Isn't that what they've been teaching me this week? How to surrender? "With you guys I don't want to be in control," I say, an admission that's not easy to make. But I do it anyway, like I've been opening up all week. Sharing.

"Good. Just enjoy yourself with us," Rhys says, his voice thrumming over my skin as he slides a hand over my belly, then gently travels up one breast.

I glance back at Clara. Hot-air balloon rides are for families but also for lovers. We know the drill with lovers. Look away and give them a moment.

A moment is all I will take. Leaning back into Gavin. Enjoying Rhys. Savoring Hollis.

Up here, I'm floating. Up here, I can just feel. Hands on my hips, lips on my neck, a deep voice near my ear as Gavin asks, "Later, what do you want us to do to you?"

He ropes his arms around my waist, holding me tightly as the others touch and kiss me. Like that, surrounded and safe, I answer, "I want to...surrender."

I look down at the tiny houses and vineyards, their colors fading to shades of orange and pink as the day comes to an end.

And the night begins.

* * *

After we land in a field, Clara drives us back to Hot Rides in her hot pink van with a stencil of a balloon on the side.

Once she pulls into the lot outside the hangar and cuts the engine, I startle.

My father's on the other side of the asphalt, leaning against the hood of his restored Ford Mustang, waiting for me.

His eyes flicker with questions.

52

WHAT HAPPENS AT THE COTTAGE

Briar

"H-hi, Dad?" I ask it rather than say it.

Tension flares in every cell in my body. My dad hardly approves of romance at all. What would he think of me with three men?

You're not with them. They're just friends. No one needs to know what happens at the cottage.

As Clara putters in the van, my dad strides over to me, brow knitted across his weathered face, worn from the years and the work. "Hey, kiddo. What are you doing in these parts?" He goes with his standard greeting, but it means so much more as he glances at one, two, three guys with me, then adds, "Moonlighting?"

Yes, that's it! I grab onto the lifeline he likely doesn't even realize he's throwing. "I thought it'd be fun to show my friends how I fly a balloon," I say brightly.

But as soon as that excuse comes out of my mouth it

deflates, because of course that's not what actually happened. Clara flew the balloon while three hockey studs whispered sweet nothings in my ear and murmured promises of tying me up later.

Did she message him? Tell him what I was up to? Send him to check on me? My stomach churns with worry and I try again to explain what I'm up to. "I was…"

But the sentence dies on my tongue since I've got nothing. Can he tell I'm involved with these guys? He could always sense how I'm doing. Maybe because I don't hide my feelings from him. But I don't know what to say to him now.

Hollis takes over, striding across the asphalt, extending a hand to my dad. "I hear you're a big Sea Dogs fan, Mr. Delaney. And I'm wondering what we can do to get you to switch loyalties."

I'm so glad he's leading with sports. Sports is the universal lubricant.

Dad shakes his head, humming doubtfully. "Probably nothing. Once a Sea Dogs fan, always a Sea Dogs fan. I was pretty dang happy when my daughter switched to that team," he says, wary, like he doesn't trust them. "I never liked the Foxes even when they were the Avengers."

Okaaaay.

So much for that valiant attempt.

My dad tips his chin toward me. "Didn't realize you were taking a balloon ride."

A statement but really a question—what's going on?

Nerves prickle over my neck like I'm a kid caught stealing from his wallet, even though I never did that. I never took his car. Broke a curfew. Or drank a beer.

Is this my bad girl phase now? Hooking up with three guys?

"We thought it'd be fun," I say breezily, to cover up how unsettled I feel.

"We had a great time," Rhys seconds, but Gavin stays quiet. I get that. He's probably not great with parents. He'd rather let the other guys lead.

"It was really beautiful, Dad. The view was amazing. I think I even saw our home," I say, trying again to smooth over this uncomfortable moment. "I pointed it out to...my friends."

Maybe I'm selling the friendship too hard, but I don't want to have the *I'm having a fling with three hot hockey guys at once* convo.

"That's great," my dad says in his no-nonsense tone as Clara's work boots clunk across the driveway.

My dad's eyes swing to her immediately and then his mouth softens. "Hi, Clara," he says, his tone almost tender.

Hers turns playful. "You ready to go kick some butt at the pool hall, Henry?"

What the hell is going on?

My dad clears his throat, looking a little awkward before he meets my eyes again. "I'm just picking up Clara. We're on a team. We play pool together every other week. Tonight's our night."

My heart stutters then returns to its normal pace.

He's here for her. His friend. But the way his eyes sparked makes me wonder if there's more.

"I guess you weren't expecting to see me?" I ask to be sure.

He shakes his head. "No, but do you want to introduce me to all of your friends?"

I make quick introductions, then say, "Gavin is an amazing defenseman who protects his teammates to the ends of the earth. Rhys is a center, and he's going to play for the Foxes for a long time to come—I just know it. Hollis is a winger who busts his butt in every game to take care of his mom and sisters. Also, they saved my cat."

"My grandcat?" my dad asks, voice pitching up, eyes widening.

"This I need to hear," Clara demands.

"Dad, remember how much you hated Steven?" I ask.

My dad hooks his thumbs into the pockets of his jeans. "Sure do."

Rhys chuckles under his breath. "We all do."

"He was never good enough for Briar," Gavin says in a growl.

My dad locks eyes with Gavin. "Damn straight."

With pride bursting like the sun inside me, I tell my father the story of the night they rescued Frances Furbottom. When I'm done, my dad's impervious expression is a little less impervious as he nods to the three men. "I appreciate you looking out for my daughter. And my grandcat."

"We're happy to," Hollis says, speaking for the group.

Dad hooks his thumb toward his car. "We should go. But it was good seeing you, kiddo. And nice meeting you."

We hug goodbye and for a moment, I'm tempted to tell my dad that we're more than friends for now, that I care for them, that they're showing me what real affection is.

And for a moment, too, I think he'd be okay with it.

We say goodbye and he leaves, hopping into the front seat, but before Clara gets in, she trots back to me and squeezes me in a hug, then whispers, "I like them."

My heart catches in my throat. "Me too."

She lets go and leaves.

By the time I reach the cottage with the guys, I don't just want to surrender. I need to.

53

A WINDSOR KNOT

Briar

This time I want the theater.

The lights are low in the bedroom. Sexy music plays from my phone, a playlist I created just today.

I call it *When the Mood Strikes*.

Sultry vocals from whiskey-voiced women singing about longing weave around me as my men and I finish getting dressed, and I put on a gift they got me.

When we returned home, I found a pretty black box on the middle of the bed waiting for me, a silver bow tied around it. Inside it—a lavender demi-cup bra with a butterfly print and matching panties.

I check my reflection in the mirror. Is this really me? I've never been a lingerie girl. But maybe because I never felt like I was truly sexy. Now, with these men, I do. Because they listen.

I head to the door and open it. My dog's hanging

out in the living room with her new hedgehog. They bought her a toy too.

"I'm ready," I say.

I feel all glittery inside, lit up by fireworks and starlight as Rhys and Gavin come in, circling me.

Wearing jeans and nothing else, Rhys regards me with heat in his sinful eyes, then runs his fingers down my flushed chest before he moves past me, heading to the chair in the corner. Gavin, in gray sweats, runs his thumb along my bottom lip, then shoves it into my mouth. I suck, eyes closing, desire flaming. When he lets go, I flutter open my eyes as he moves next to me.

Hollis towers in the doorway, wearing something so incongruous and so hot. He's in his slacks and his dress shirt. That must be what he wore when he arrived the night we ran into each other in the hot tub. An emerald-green necktie is snug at his neck.

"You. Just fucking look at you," he says as he closes the distance between us, reaches for my hands, lifts them, and kisses one wrist.

I shudder.

Have I ever been kissed on my wrist before? I don't think so, and I don't ever want him to stop.

"Gavin, help him out. Kiss the back of her arm," Rhys instructs nonchalantly. Gavin plants a kiss on the underside of my elbow.

They kiss me more, treasure hunters discovering all the places on my body till I'm gasping, shivering.

Then, Hollis steps back and runs a hand down his tie, his blue eyes locked with mine. "Take it off me, Briar," he commands.

With eager fingers I undo the knot. Tug off the tie. Hand it to him.

"Gavin, worship our girl a little," Rhys says. "Maybe kiss her ankles. See if she likes that."

I look to Rhys, a heated charge zinging between the Englishman and me, all while Gavin drops to his knees, then wraps a big hand around my calf.

He kisses me, and I whimper.

But there's no time to linger in the new sensations of ankle kisses since Hollis crowds me, draping the tie around my neck. The silk slides against my skin. "You're going to look so fucking pretty wearing my tie," he says, his voice rough with lust as he adjusts the fabric, like he's going to make a knot.

But he stops abruptly. Turns to Rhys. "You know, I could use some help, man."

Rhys strides over to join the scene, coasting a hand ever so casually down my stomach to the lacy top of my panties. "What do you need exactly?" Rhys asks, like he doesn't know. Like they didn't script this.

Hollis eyes me up and down, humming thoughtfully. "Maybe unhook that bra. I think...yeah, I'd really like to see how the tie looks when it falls between her tits. What do you think, Gav?"

"Fuck yes," he rumbles from the floor.

Rhys moves behind me, sweeps my hair to the side, then presses a soft kiss between my shoulder blades. He unhooks the bra, tosses it gently to the bed, then walks in front of me but turns his attention to Hollis. "Better, mate?"

"Thanks, man," Hollis says, then loops one silky

piece of emerald fabric over the other, his big hands brushing against the hard points of my nipples.

He finishes the knot, then tightens it. "How does she look?" he asks Rhys, who's returned to the chair.

I shift subtly to him so he can drink me in. I'm wearing panties and a tie. That's it.

"Pretty good Windsor knot, but maybe move the tie just so." Rhys waves to the right.

Hollis centers the tie between my bare breasts. "Like that?"

"It's almost the perfect outfit." Rhys says.

"What would make it better?" I ask him, breathless.

Rhys sets his palms on his thighs, studying me. "If you were naked, love." He pauses. "Gavin, can you take care of that little issue?"

"I'm on it." Gavin peels down my panties, groaning as he goes. I step out of them, dressed in nothing but a necktie the color of a jewel.

"Do you like my outfit better now, Rhys?" I ask, playing along.

"It's the sexiest fucking thing I've ever seen you in," Rhys says, his voice thick with lust, then he shifts his focus to his friends. "You guys agree?"

Gavin rises and backs away from me, along with Hollis. They join Rhys by the wall. I've never felt more vulnerable than I do now with three pairs of eyes on me. Or more wanted.

"What do you guys think?" I ask Gavin and Hollis, having my fun too. Finally. *Finally*. I can have fun in bed, thanks to them.

"I fucking love," Hollis says.

"You're perfect," Gavin rasps out.

But Rhys likes to play. He taps his chin. "Run your hand down the tie," he instructs.

My chest goes hot as I comply.

"Lean your head back."

I obey, letting my hair fall down my spine.

"Fuuuuck," Rhys mutters. But he doesn't break. "Cup those tits. Want to see you play with yourself, love."

Heat pools in my core. I cover my tits with my hands, squeezing them, showing them how I touch myself when I'm wearing only my man's tie.

A rumble seems to climb up his chest as Rhys says, "I think I know what's missing."

"What is it?" I ask desperately.

"Gavin, put her on the bed."

In no time, Gavin tosses me over his shoulder and carries me the short distance to the mattress, then sets me down so my head's resting on a mountain of pillows.

"Ask her permission to tie her up."

Gavin climbs onto the bed, settling between my thighs as he pins me with a hot stare. "May I? Tie you to the bed?"

I'm molten. "Yes, please."

Rhys nods carelessly to Hollis. "Help our friend."

A few minutes later, Hollis checks the knot above my head. He's bound my wrists together with a sapphire blue tie—it must be the one they bought together the other day—and pinned them above the pillows and me, tying my wrists together to the headboard.

Rhys and Gavin are fastening my bare ankles to the footboard with more neckties. A pink one, and a cranberry-red one. They move off the bed and stare at me, naked, legs spread, bound.

"That's how you tie a tie," Rhys says, approvingly.

I sigh, smiling, eager, horny. "Except...you forgot one thing. What about my eyes?"

54

SOME OF OUR FRIENDS USE BATTERIES

Briar

Everything's dark. They've blindfolded me with Hollis's sleeping mask. Seductive music beats through my body. Hands slide up my legs. Lips trace my belly. A tongue flicks against the shell of my ear.

I *know* who's touching me. But I also don't. I can tell Rhys's scent—cedar and spice—as he nibbles on my earlobe, and I can feel Hollis's strong hands on my thighs, Gavin's rougher ones on my tits.

But then, everything in my mind scrambles as they move around. And I don't know who's doing what. I'm being touched everywhere and I can't move. All I can do is arch my hips. "Please," I whimper.

"Ask for it," Rhys demands, and I catalog that he's to my left.

"Touch me," I beg, and the second I say it I expect a mouth on my pussy.

But instead, there's the slide of a drawer opening. A clatter of plastic. Then Rhys's instructions. "For you. And you and you," Rhys says, like he's handing something to each man.

I shake, so eager, so ready.

Then moan when someone presses a toy to my center. I cant my hips, seeking out the vibrations. "That's right, baby," Hollis says, urging me on.

He must be between my thighs. Rhys is stroking my hair. A firm hand kneads my tits.

Lust pulses through my veins as I arch. "More, harder," I pant.

"Anything for you, baby," Hollis murmurs as hands roam over me and lips travel on my skin.

Feels like a brand-new toy that he's using. Maybe a bullet vibrator—I'm not sure. And I don't honestly care since my thighs clench and I cry out as an orgasm crashes into me.

Hot, fast, and bright.

And so loud. My sounds echo off the walls till I come down.

When Hollis turns off the toy, he brushes a tender kiss to my pussy before he moves away.

Several seconds later, the mattress dips. Men shift. I wait.

"Gonna fuck you with this toy," Gavin tells me, and I try to catch my breath. I barely can since he's turned it on and the buzzing sound is loud, a promise of a powerful orgasm. He rubs the head of a silicone cock against me.

I rock up into the new toy as Gavin works it over on

me. Hollis returns to my side, his fresh, soapy scent floating past me as Rhys kneads my breasts.

"Feels so good," I murmur as Gavin fucks me with the toy.

I'm shaking, shuddering, and they're all murmuring words like "yes" and "so sexy" and "look at you" and it's the perfect amount of praise—not too much, not too little. Just right.

They're not treating me like I've been perfectly cured of my O drought, but like they know sometimes a night just calls for extra friends that require batteries.

Gavin hits me so deep with the dildo that my brain just melts. "Yes!"

And I'm coming again, the kind of orgasm that's a hot rush, a molten cascade of sensations. It's so good, I'm sweating, and I'm sure they're going to untie me.

But a minute later, Rhys is kissing my thighs, rubbing his stubble against the soft skin, then turning on the very first toy they used on me.

The one that feels like a tongue.

He slides it up, down, up, down while Gavin sucks on my nipple and Hollis kisses me, and I am sure that this is part of what makes a great boyfriend.

The way they adore me.

The way they take care of me.

Like that, I shatter once more.

As I come down, they kiss me. I'm so drunk on coming that I can barely tell who's kissing me.

They all are.

And I know they orchestrated tonight solely for me. I know in the deepest part of my heart that they expect nothing in return. I could go to sleep and they'd tuck me in and turn off the lights, then bring me a coffee in the morning.

They are well and truly the most giving lovers.

But I've learned something else too.

These are the lovers I want to give myself to.

These are the men who deserve me.

So I ask them to untie me. When they're done, I tell Gavin to lie down on the bed and take off his clothes. He's naked in no time. I cover him with a condom and sink down on him.

He hisses in a breath then clamps his hands on my hips. A jolt of heat rushes down my body, and briefly I turn to Rhys, giving him a nod that I hope he knows means *he's next.*

Then, I turn my focus to Gavin, gazing at me the whole time as I ride him.

I fuck him for him. "Come for me," I urge when his breath turns shallow, frantic.

He grits his teeth, then groans.

Before I can even climb off him, Rhys is ready. "Put me on my hands and knees," I tell him.

"Anything for you," he says, then flips me over and fills me.

He takes me like that, hard, fast, determined. I claw at the covers, loving the way I feel when he fucks me. "Don't wait for me," I whisper.

Rhys listens to that too.

I'm so grateful. I don't want them to concentrate on me. I don't want them to try to make me come again. Right now, I want them to feel what I've felt. That incandescent rush of letting go when someone *only* gives to you.

When he's finished, I offer myself to Hollis, lying flat on my back, wrapping my legs around him, then watching the handsome face of the man who started this quest for me as he falls apart inside of me.

Tonight, I give them my body. But really, a piece of my heart.

* * *

A little later, we're in the hot tub with charcoal face masks on and champagne glasses in our hands, and I toast. "To cracking the case of the missing *O*."

Everyone clinks.

"Glad we could help you find it," Hollis says.

"Glad you wanted us to," Rhys adds.

"Glad you let me be a part of it," Gavin says.

My heart surges for my friends.

I repeat the word in my head—*friends*. I repeat it as a reminder of what's next. I repeat it because this week was so much more than friendship.

And I'm going to miss them when this ends in another day.

55

PARTY OF FOUR

Briar

Good thing I brought one cute outfit that does double duty as date attire. The next day, late in the afternoon, I strike a pose in the bedroom for Donut. "What do you think, girl?"

She whimpers a happy approval. I bend to give her a kiss. "Glad you like it," I say.

I'm wearing a pink skirt, a white top, and my favorite pair of boots. I picked them up one afternoon when Ivy dragged me out thrifting and I'm obsessed with them, but I haven't had a chance to wear them.

They're white, with chunky heels and pink hearts on the sides. She said they were perfect for me and even though I'm not a pink hearts gal I'm going to trust her.

I fluff out my hair, tell my girl I'll be back later, then leave the bedroom, trying not to stare wistfully at the bed. We dragged the mattresses out to the living room again last night, sleeping together, Gavin spooning me and, perhaps, snoring.

But like I tell him each morning, I sleep so deeply I don't notice. Besides, Donut snores too.

I'll miss seeing the makeshift Alaskan king-size bed —or close to it—on the living room floor.

I'll miss this cottage.

I'll miss our mornings and our nights.

When I reach the living room, I stop in my tracks. My heart sputters at the sight. Three suitcases. Neatly packed. Their flight is first thing in the morning. I glance at the clock, wishing the hands would unwind. But tonight is our last date.

All good things must come to an end.

Following the GPS directions the guys gave me, I drive down a long, winding road, past lush rolling hills, to a B&B at the end. I park, then get out, checking out the place. It's a gorgeous white inn with a red tile roof that glints in the setting sun. A sprawling vineyard stretches along the side of the inn and likely far into the hills. A slight breeze carries with it the scent of ripe grapes and fresh soil.

Up the steps is the main entrance to the inn, and next to it is a restaurant called Springtime. A wooden sign on the porch reads *Closed for private event.*

The next line reads—*Come to the back.*

I head along the porch to the back of the building

when my breath catches. On a patio, there's a string quartet playing. I train my ears, realizing it's not classical music.

It's pop. Girl pop. The kind of music the guys hear me listen to. The kind they know I love. Played on a cello, a viola, and two violins.

A door swings open and a hostess strides across the porch, down to the patio. "Briar Delaney? Your party is already here. Party of four," she says pleasantly, her nose ring sparkling against her bronze skin.

"That's me." I feel frothy and happy again. We are a party of four one more time.

She guides me along a cobbled path through the vineyard, toward a picnic table set up in the middle of the vines.

My heart surges. Three attentive, thoughtful, filthy, generous men chat animatedly in their seats, possibly arguing about their upcoming games as I pick up bits and pieces. When I reach them, they all stand. Like I'm the one they've been waiting their whole lives for.

That's silly to think. And yet I feel that way when Rhys comes up to me, ropes an arm around my waist, and kisses me passionately.

When Gavin grips my jaw and crushes my mouth.

When Hollis cups my cheeks and kisses me like he's putting a spell on me.

If Hollis's kisses are the sun and Rhys's are twilight, then Gavin kisses like it's after midnight.

Hard. Rough. Demanding.

They all kiss differently. I've grown to crave all their kisses. I've come to need all of them too.

When Hollis breaks the kiss at last, I blink. "Wow. Have I mentioned a good boyfriend is a great kisser?"

"You don't say," Hollis deadpans.

"And you all are," I add.

"It takes two," Gavin says, giving me credit where credit's due.

"Well, not to split hairs, but...*three*," Rhys corrects playfully.

"And that one goes to the Viscount," Hollis says, then gestures to the table, set with crystal glasses and ceramic plates along with plush cushions and soft blankets for us to relax on on the ground. A picnic basket is filled with an array of gourmet cheeses, fresh fruits, olives, nuts, and breads. My mouth waters.

"Sit. Have dinner with us," Hollis says.

This is so much more than just a meal. It's a wildly romantic private picnic with my three temporary boyfriends as my favorite tunes play.

This is the only place I want to be. I sit on the blanket, legs stretched out. Rhys grabs the basket, then pours a small glass of white wine and offers it to me. "Did the boyfriend project work out for you?"

It's a little wry, but there's a touch of vulnerability there too. Like he wants my yes. He deserves it. They all do.

I lift the glass, then say to all of them, "Yes. They showed me what it means to be good to a woman. They cherished me; they adored me; they romanced me."

"Good," Rhys says, while clearing his throat, like he needs to clear away emotions too. Gavin looks toward the never-ending stretch of vines. Hollis swallows roughly.

And I will miss all of you.

But I try to focus on the friendship, just the friendship. As we eat, we talk about the coming weeks. "You'll talk to Amira soon about her meeting, right?"

Rhys's eyes flicker with nerves but also some acceptance. He knows his fate is out of his hands. "I will."

"You better let me know," I say.

"Bossy," Hollis teases.

"And you know Rhys will when he shows up at your class again," Gavin adds. "He can't break that streak."

Hollis shoots a pointed look at Gavin. "I've no doubt you'll be making sure we wear face masks if we win this coming weekend."

"One hundred percent," Gavin says, but his tone says that's not the streak he wants.

Hollis sets a hand on my thigh. "You better send us cat pics *and* dog pics when you settle into your new place."

"Count on it," I say.

"And a copy of your column," he adds.

I'd nearly forgotten. Or maybe that's not quite right. I hadn't forgotten. The column just became the way of my life for the last several days. "I will," I say, and it's a promise—one that means we'll stay friends. We'll nurture this friendship.

Even though we're so much more. "Guys," I say, feeling all emotional and wistful at once.

"Yes?" Rhys asks.

"This was so much more than the missing O. You

have to know that." Their passionate gazes tell me they do. The way they look at me with fondness and genuine affection gives me the courage to say the next thing. "You made me feel...connected to my body in a way I never had—a way I wanted desperately to feel. You helped me relax. You helped me let go of...my anxiety. That means so much to me." But there's one thing we didn't do in bed. One thing I think about. *A lot.* "And I wanted to feel all of you at once. But I don't think I can, knowing it's ending. It's so intimate I'm afraid I won't be able to go back to friends."

No one says anything probably because no one disagrees. It is intimate, for all of us, and it would make the next part even harder.

When we clean up.

When we leave.

When we return to the cottage for our last night together.

When they say goodbye early in the morning before the sun rises, and they leave to catch their flight. When I do what I've been practicing all week—letting go.

I let them go.

56

DON'T EAT ALL THE TOILET PAPER

Briar

The walls are too close. The home is too silent. My mind is too loud. Everywhere I go, there are reminders of them.

The hot tub. The kitchen. The bedroom.

I try to settle onto the couch with Donut by my side and work on my column. But my mind is a tangled freeway. Everything is too tight, too close, too much. I try answering emails, letting the assisted living home know I'll stop by with Donut this week for stretching, then sending some stress-relief class ideas to Nova, but it's too hard to concentrate with all these memories pressing down on me.

I pop up. Pace the hall. Straighten towels in the bathroom even though they're hanging properly, fluff pillows in the bedroom even though they're fluffy enough, make sure the coffeepot is clean, even though we all cleaned up before the guys left this morning.

I have the place for one more night, but I don't think I can stay here without them.

After I set the squeaky-clean coffeepot on the counter, I rush down the hall to the bedroom and toss all my things in one of my suitcases. With the speed of a cheetah, I do a final double check of all the rooms. Donut follows me from room to room, tilting her head, asking questions in her anxious trot. I stop, kneel, and scratch her chin.

"We need to go," I tell her.

She licks my face.

A few minutes later, I'm yanking open the front door, my dog's leash wrapped around my wrist, wrestling with my suitcase when I spot Kailani walking along the cobblestone path.

She waves to me, bracelets jingling down her tanned skin. "Just wanted to check in and make sure everything went okay with the place? And to bring you a little thank you gift."

I blink. "A thank you gift?"

"Yes. I know it was kind of a pain to have to share. So I just wanted to say thanks for being so easy to deal with."

When she reaches me, she hands me a candle from her oversized tote.

I'm...stunned.

I don't deserve a gift for being a good sport. I let go of the suitcase handle and sniff the candle. It smells like the mustard flowers, vanilla, heady.

A lovely reminder, and I take it for what it is. A gift. A kindness. We need more of that in this world. More gratitude. More grace. Less taking. More giving.

"No, thank *you* for finding this place for me. Getting me into it early. It all worked out in the end. It was great."

She swipes her hand across her forehead. "I'm so glad. And maybe you can come back next year. The festival organizers said everyone loved your workshops. They were very popular."

I try to remind myself that's what I came here for. To build my business. To make a name for myself. "I'll be here whenever you need me."

I say goodbye and head to my father's house.

He's expecting me. But when he opens the door, he still lifts a brow curiously. "What are you doing in these parts?"

My heart climbs up my throat and I almost, *almost* tell him. Instead, I swallow down my emotions. Something I've done my whole life. Something I did when my mom left. When I learned how to grin and bear it. How to move on. How to hide what I'm truly feeling.

Trouble is, those tactics don't work so well anymore, I'm realizing.

I can't hide my feelings, and I'm not sure I want to. I shrug my shoulders, and instead of telling him I miss three men, I say something else that's equally true. "Sometimes I'm sad that Mom left."

He frowns, eyes shining. He nods, tight, hard, and true. He wraps his arms around me. "Me too, kiddo. Me too."

I stay like that for a while. Safe in his arms. Safe to give another admission. "I missed her for a long, long time," I say.

He strokes my hair. "I did too."

"But I'm glad you didn't leave."

I can feel him smile even as he chokes up. "I'd never leave you or your brother."

I let out a long, overdue breath, and some of the ache inside me starts to fade. Soon I let go of him because he'd never break a hug. We both clear our throats, like we're clearing away emotions that we aren't really used to showing. But maybe we need to.

"So how is my Frances Furbottom?" I ask, cheery and bright.

He sets a hand on my upper back and rubs it affectionately. "We had a good visit. I can cat-sit anytime."

With Donut at my feet, I follow Dad into the place I grew up, where he offers me an apple and an ear. As I eat the Cosmic Crisp, I tell him all the details about the festival, how it went, how I'm doing, and where I'm going to live. I tell him that Ivy got me into her old place, and she actually said I can move in right away.

"If you need any help let me know," he says.

There is something I need since I have zero furniture. "Actually, do you have an air mattress?"

"That I do." He's always been glad to be useful.

After he brings me the air mattress in a box, he retrieves his grandcat, carrying her in his arms, stroking her tabby head and cooing to her. It's the sweetest thing I've ever seen. "Now you be a good girl with my daughter, okay? Don't knock mugs off the counter like you did here. And don't eat all the toilet paper."

He's fighting a losing battle.

Gently, he tucks her into her cat carrier, adding a little pink blanket. He walks me to the door, pauses, then says, "Those boys seemed...nice enough."

"They really are."

It's not a blessing for a romance. But it doesn't have to be. It's enough that he likes my friends.

I head down the steps with my little pet family when something strikes me. I turn back to him. "Dad, you should really ask Clara out on a date."

His lips twitch. He tries to rearrange his expression. Maybe to hide his feelings. "We're just friends."

I shake my head, standing my ground. "No, you're not. And I'm pretty sure she'd say yes."

He's quiet for several seconds, then he gives a nod. "Maybe I will."

"You'd better."

I hop in my car with my fur babies, put on my shades, and blast my road-trip music.

I'm not that girl who's singing at the top of her lungs because she's exuberant. I'm singing at the top of my lungs so I don't cry as I drive.

* * *

That night I lie down in a too quiet apartment, in a too small bed in my new home, wishing I weren't so alone.

But at least there's a cat draped over my head and a dog curled up against me.

In the morning, I do something about all this alone-ness. I pick up my phone and send a text.

57

ALL HAIL THE QUEEN

Briar

I didn't expect *this* reaction.

I'm at Doctor Insomnia's on Fillmore Street, at a table in the back, finishing my story, when Trina makes the first move.

She pushes back in her chair. Stands, then bows down before me, *we are not worthy* style. Ivy abandons her vanilla latte to join her, like a supplicant. Aubrey goes next, setting down her mango smoothie with panache.

"All hail the queen," Aubrey says.

I laugh. "Stop! Just stop!"

But they keep going, bowing and hailing to me. I flap my hands, urging them to their feet. "Get up. You're in the middle of a coffee shop."

Finally, they rise as Trina purses her lips, then says,

like the words are candy in her mouth, "I guess it's a good thing that you're so...*flexible*."

I roll my eyes. "Why did I tell all of you?"

I just gave my friends the overview of the last week or so. I had to. I didn't want to feel all these feelings alone. And really, who would better understand than the women who know what it's like to fall for more than one guy at once?

"So what happens next?" Trina asks, lifting her coffee cup. "I mean, besides you getting a day-long massage after the pounding you took?"

"I guess we're just friends?"

Trina frowns. Ivy furrows her brow.

Aubrey hums then asks, "Is that what you want?"

"It's what we all agreed to," I say, a non-answer.

Aubrey fixes me with an intense stare in her brown eyes. "But is that what you want?"

It's a fair question. But I don't know if I can have what I want. But maybe I can have enough. "I want... them in my life. And I know they all have so much going on. Their careers, the team, the game," I say, and that barely covers the complication.

Ivy arches a brow doubtfully. "Don't lie to us. Don't fake your feelings."

I wince from her raw words. That's what I've done, in a way, for a long, long time. I stop doing it. "I want... more but that doesn't mean I'll get it."

Ivy squeezes my arm and gives me a soft, sad smile, understanding that you don't always get what you want.

We're quiet for a moment, nursing our drinks

before Aubrey asks, "So which yoga move was the most useful?"

I'm stone-faced as I answer. "All of them, Aubrey. All of them."

* * *

I go home, settle in at a cheap card table I bought at the thrift shop along with a hard metal chair, flip open my laptop, and spend the evening and the next day finishing my column for Steven's website, adding the byline *Just A Girl*. After I read it over ten times and show it to my friends for feedback, I hit submit on the piece titled *Cracking the Case of the Missing O—A Guide for the Great Boyfriend*.

That's done. And really, that was the point of the last week—to learn what makes a great boyfriend.

That's what I tell myself.

That's what I have to tell myself.

The next day I'm at the Sea Dogs arena, setting up mats in a workout room for the guys on the team, settling back into my regular routine.

One of the forwards strides in. Wesley was just recently traded to the team earlier this season, but he's settled in quickly and makes friends with everyone. He's dressed in shorts and a T-shirt with the arms lopped off. Ink crawls up his arms, black swirls and lines. "Briar, we've been having a debate," he says as the new team captain, a guy named Christian, comes in next. "Who is the best student in this class? It can't be anybody but me, right?"

Christian scoffs. "You need way too much praise."

"No. I just speak the truth."

"I never play. You're all excellent," I say.

"You heard her. I'm the best," Wesley says.

The rest of the guys wander in, including Trina's husbands—Chase, the former captain who stepped down so he'd have more free time for her and their dogs, and Ryker. The other guys filter in, too, and when everyone sets up, I say, "Now let's work on a little yoga for stress relief. You all work so hard as a team, and Nova and I thought it'd be good to help let go of some of that...also as a team."

They grumble but do the class anyway.

As they stretch, twist, and just breathe, I'm reminded of how important it is that all the guys rely on each other.

Like my guys. They're off in Chicago today, probably working out before their game this afternoon. Are they in sync even more than usual?

When I leave class, I send Rhys a note, asking if he met with his agent. It's what a friend would do, after all.

Briar: Hoping the Amira meeting went well!

I add a fingers-crossed emoticon. But he doesn't respond.

58

NO BIG DEAL

Rhys

I pace in my hotel room, my phone pressed to my skull, listening to every word from Amira and wishing she were saying something else. "No, I get it," I say, trying to mask my emotions. "It's fine."

But I close my eyes, pinch the bridge of my nose.

"This isn't the worst thing," she reassures me.

"Right. Right," I say with forced cheer. Don't want her to know that I'm a treacherous mess inside all over again. "Of course it's not."

"Rhys," she says, using her mum voice. "Are you hiding the way you're feeling?"

She's not in the same room as I am. She can't really tell. "I swear it's no big deal. I mean, I get it. They don't want to commit. I will remain trade bait. Hey, hopefully another team likes me."

"Just because there are trade rumors doesn't mean

you'll be traded. And just because the Foxes don't want to sign you *now* doesn't mean they won't at the end of the season," she says, calm and caring. "It's just business. Teams sometimes want to take their time. You really have to try to put it out of your head, hon. Did you give any more thought to what I suggested?"

I squeeze my eyes shut. I should have. But I was busy in Lucky Falls. "I don't really know," I say, avoiding the topic of seeing a sports psychologist. What athlete doesn't have anxiety? "I should probably go work out. Run. Something."

"The GM thinks you're a great center. They're glad to have you. A lot of teams don't do contract renewals in the middle of the season." She goes on to explain why and all of it makes perfect sense. But that doesn't change the fact that my chest feels too tight, and my muscles too tense, and my mind too damn busy.

I leave for the Chicago arena and hit the visitors' workout room early, pedaling fast and faster still on the exercise bike, trying to burn off all these feelings. When I hop off, I'm covered in sweat. And not at all relaxed. Gavin wanders in, giving me a once-over. "You doing okay, man?"

"Definitely. Absolutely," I lie.

"How did the call go?"

I don't feel like talking right now. "Fine."

"You sure about that?" he asks.

"Definitely. I'm thinking sushi if we win?"

"When we win," he says, and we head to the locker room, out of step.

59

THERE'S A GIRL

Hollis

The crowd jeers as we skate onto the ice for the Saturday afternoon game, but I tune it out. It's their barn. Their fans.

I head for the bench as the first line hits the ice for the face-off. My muscles are revved up, and I'm ready to jump in the second they need me.

My focus is the game. Only the game. That is all.

As soon as the puck drops, the Chicago team attacks it, skating fast and ferociously, weaving past our defenders and taking a shot on goal right away.

Dev saves it but barely. Chicago did not come to play.

Good. I didn't either. After a line shift a few minutes later, I'm chasing the puck, trying to wrangle it away from them, Gavin jostling in front of their guys, blocking for me. A surge of adrenaline courses through my veins, and I lunge for the puck with my stick, only to be called on a penalty on their D-man.

"That wasn't slashing," I mutter, but it's a moot point because...it fucking was.

In a huff, I make my way to the penalty box to serve my time. I rip off my helmet and fling it down, then stew, doing nothing, not a damn thing, as the other team scores the first goal, whipping the puck past Gavin, Rhys, and then Dev. "Fuck me," I grumble, flinging up my arms.

* * *

Near the end of the period I'm back out there again, ready to put something on the scoreboard.

The game's a chippy one, physical and mean, and I am going to be sore tomorrow, but I don't care when I snag the puck then fly on a breakaway, sending it screaming toward the goalie.

But he stops it with his leg.

I curse. I missed an easy shot.

When I hit the bench once more, I slam the stick against the floor.

"Bouchard, let it go. Let it fucking go," Stefan says, his tone firm and brooking no argument.

What's wrong with me? I'm not the guy who gets angry in a game. I'm the easygoing guy, even on the bench. I play hard, but I have fun. I work with my team-mates, not against them.

I grab my water bottle, chug some, then try to shake off my funk.

* * *

Deep into the second period, my blades cut through the ice as I try to sync up with my team, determined to atone for my earlier mistakes. The noise of the fans is deafening, the boos somehow even louder. Most nights, the din strangely quiets my thoughts. Tonight, the noise amplifies them. As I hunt for the puck, I'm wondering if Briar is watching back home. If she's cheering. If she's missing us too.

When Rhys slips the puck to me, I miss it.

Chicago doesn't though. Their players are relentless, their skates and sticks whipping around like the claws of a pack of wild animals taking us down.

At the end of the game, the horn blares and we've lost.

It's my fault.

I don't talk to anyone on the quick flight to Detroit on the team plane. Or in the hotel lobby. Or the elevator.

When I reach my room a little before eleven, I call my mom.

Her voice is sympathetic. "Hey there. Tough game."

"I know."

"Were you elsewhere?"

How does she know? "It was that obvious?" I ask, tugging at my tie, tossing it down on the couch.

"You don't usually play mad. Only when things aren't quite right in your life."

It *is* that obvious. "There's a girl," I admit.

"Yeah?" She brightens.

"It's complicated."

"It always is. Have you talked to her?"

No. But maybe I should. When I say goodbye, I hit Briar's number.

TELEPHONE TAG

Briar

After I leave the gym downstairs, I head to the elevator banks when my phone trills. Hollis's name appears across the screen along with the icon I assigned to him —a sunburst.

Giddy, I answer the call. "Hey there," I say, hoping he's doing okay but prepared for him to be in a funk post-game.

"Hey," he says, a little heavy.

Funk it is. "What's going on? You okay?" I ask gently as I hit the up button.

"Not really. The game was shitty. It was all my fault."

"It was a rough game. But there'll be another one tomorrow night," I say, trying to cheer him up.

"You watched it," he says, less a question, more a statement. A sort of dreamy one.

"I did. Are you surprised?"

"No. Just...weirdly happy?"

I smile as the elevator arrives and I step inside. "Why?"

"I don't know. I guess I just liked that you were there even though you weren't there. I'm not even sure that makes sense. A lot about today didn't make sense to me, Briar," he says, like the words are spilling out in a confession. "I felt off the whole time. Do you know what I mean? Didn't I seem off?"

From the sincerity in his tone, I can tell he wants an honest answer. "I sensed you felt a little out of sync," I say as the car chugs upward to the eighth floor.

"I did," he says, but he sounds relieved that I noticed, or really, that I told him the truth. "But I've got to do better, Briar. People depend on me," he says, and this is the side of him he doesn't usually show. This is the side of himself he fakes for others. He's being real with me though.

"And you will. It was a one-off game," I try to assure him.

"You think so?"

"I know so," I say as the car slows to a stop and I exit on my floor. "Everyone has a bad game. A bad class. A bad day. Even hockey studs like you."

He laughs, and it sounds like he's been carrying the world on his shoulders till now. "And I'm so freaking sore."

I remember him telling me that, too, in Lucky Falls. That he feels beaten up after a game. "You should get a massage. Do it tomorrow. And get some rest tonight, okay?"

"Okay," he says, and there's some light in his voice again. "I thought about you while I was on the ice."

"So it's *my* fault you guys didn't play well?" I tease as I open the door to my new apartment and say hi to my pogo dog.

"Sounds about right," he says.

"Well, the thinking about you is mutual," I say playfully.

Hollis lets out a big breath, then like it costs him something, he says, "My mom told me I should call you."

I startle. "Your mom knows about me?"

"Not really. But sort of. I just said I was thinking about a girl."

Warmth blooms in my chest at his words. This makes me unreasonably happy. We talk for another fifteen or twenty minutes about his mom, and the game, and Chicago, and this TV show he's watching and the music I'm listening to, and a funny video I saw, and the fact that the Sea Dogs won and my dad is probably thrilled. When the conversation winds down, he says, "I've missed this."

"Me too."

"This is us staying friends, right?" he asks, hopeful, but with real longing too.

"It sure is," I say, and before I can even hang up, my other line is ringing and it's Rhys. I say goodbye to Hollis and click over. "Hey, how are you?"

"I think I need to see a sports psychologist," he blurts out.

I'm taken aback but ready to listen. "Why do you think that is?"

The sound of his footsteps carries over the phone. He must be pacing in his room. "I'm wound up, and I get stressed, and I have anxiety. Like athlete anxiety or something. Is that a thing? I think it's a thing. Amira thinks it's a thing. I have it. I have to deal with it." He's talking at Mach speed, serving up pieces of his soul for me. "I haven't told anybody. I feel stupid about it. Really fucking stupid. Like a failure. And I stress, and I'm sure my stress is why we lost tonight."

"You're not a failure," I assure him. "You're the opposite. I'm really, really proud of you."

"Why would you be proud of me?"

"Because you called me. Because you told me. Because you realized you needed to talk to someone. Probably a lot more athletes need it. It's a stressful job. Hell, life can be stressful these days for anyone. And it's not your fault the team lost. But you do put a lot of pressure on yourself and your agent is right. It's a good idea, Rhys."

After a pause, he asks, in a less frantic tone, "You don't think it's like a weakness?"

"No, Rhys. I think it's a strength."

We look up names together of sports psychologists in San Francisco and I stay on the phone as he sends out a few inquiries. When he's done, it sounds like he can breathe again as he says, "I wish you were here tonight."

"I wish I were too."

When the call ends, I head to the bathroom to wash

my face and slather on night cream. After I switch into jammies, I slide under a T.J. Maxx blanket onto my twin-size air mattress.

My phone rings one more time, probably Rhys calling me back, but Gavin's name flashes across the screen. "Well, here you are," I say, and I can't hide the delight in my voice. I guess good things come in threes.

"Here I am," he says, and he sounds mostly happy too.

"How are you doing? I saw your game," I tell him.

"Not our finest showing."

"Not every game has to be."

"That's what I tried to tell the guys, but none of them felt like listening. But I don't want to talk about me. Or hockey. What are *you* up to tonight?"

I tell him about my day, my plans to stop by the assisted living home tomorrow with my dog, and that I moved into my new place.

"What's it like? Your new apartment?"

I almost offer to give him a tour, but it's too pathetic. This tiny air mattress, my creaky table, my hard chair.

"It's home enough for now," I say as the scent of vanilla drifts past my nose, reminding me of my week in the cottage. "I have a candle that smells like Lucky Falls."

"Mmm. Sounds really nice, Briar," he says, then stops, maybe because he's done or maybe because he's gearing up to say something else. "The funny thing is I thought getting involved with you would mess up the team dynamics. But we're not technically involved... and we still played like shit. Everyone was sort of lost today," he says. "I guess I was wrong. Sometimes you just have bad games."

I'm kind of amazed that Gavin sees so clearly what they don't. "Sometimes you do."

"But the thing is when the game ended all I wanted was to talk to you."

"I'm here anytime," I say, feeling a little glowy that they've all reached out to me. "I gave you an icon on my phone."

"What is it?"

"It's a starlit sky in the dark. Rhys has a twilight sky and Hollis, a sunburst."

He seems to give that some thought, then says, "I think you got that right."

When we're done talking I say goodnight but I don't set down the phone. I toggle over to the group chat. Maybe the team dynamic is off tonight, but I think I can fix it.

I send a message to all of them.

> Briar: It was good chatting with all of you separately. Now, let's talk together.

We chat for a good, long time. We chat the next day, too, as I walk with Donut to our stretching class at the assisted living home. We chat as I head over to Peak Performance. We chat as I work on my new Sea Dogs classes. We chat as I walk into my building in the afternoon and the doorman calls me over.

I put down the phone.

"Delivery for you," he says, then hands me an envelope.

I rip it open. Inside are tickets to the Golden State Foxes next home game.

61

LAST MAN STANDING

Gavin

The plan is simple—win.

But the execution will require a little finesse. Because my friends are knuckleheads.

Figures it's come down to me, but life is funny that way. Sometimes when you wait the longest for something, you're the first to know you want it.

But wanting something doesn't guarantee you'll get it.

I already got my game day nap in, so after I finish a light workout, I find the idiots I'm best friends with in the athletic trainer's room. Kelsey's working Hollis's shoulder, and Diego is stretching Rhys's quads.

"Didn't get enough flow and flex this week?" I drawl.

Rhys flips me the bird but he doesn't bite back.

Once they're done, I motion for them to follow me down a quieter hallway.

"What's up?" Hollis asks.

We all got her the tickets together. We sent them to her together. We invited her together. But that's as far as we've gotten. And it's not far enough. "Listen, we need to win tonight, guys."

"News flash: we need to win every night," Hollis retorts with a smirk.

I clap his shoulder. "But tonight we need to play like a team." We've been playing better the last few away games, but we've only won one out of three on the road, and by a hair at that. "We need to work together. I know it's not just the three of us out there, but when it comes to the three of us, we need to keep our heads in the game and our focus on."

Rhys gives me a dubious look. "Are you saying—?"

"That the woman we're obsessed with is distracting?" I finish for him since I know, I fucking know, that's where he was going.

"Yeah." He squares his shoulders, holding his ground.

I smother a smile as I shake my head. "No. I'm saying *we're* distracting. *We* distracted each other. *We're* up in our heads because we left Lucky Falls for this road trip acting like...well, like we're not totally into her."

There. Someone had to say it.

A smile tips Hollis's lips. "Look at you—last to fall, first to issue a call to arms."

I roll my eyes. "I wasn't the last—" I wave a hand

through the air, nixing that denial. "Whatever. It's not important. She knocked some sense into us over the last week in our chats, but we need to knock some sense into ourselves too. It wasn't Briar that distracted us from hockey. It was us not..."

Emotions lodge in my throat, shutting me up for a few seconds. Feels like I'm reaching my fist into my chest, squeezing my heart. But I've gotten better at letting myself feel, thanks to her. And at letting myself say what my heart wants. Before I can tell her though, I need to tell my friends. "It was us not having each other's backs on the ice. Before that week, we looked out for each other when we weren't playing. We did that while we were with her, but then when we left her, we stopped. It was like we all shut down as friends to get over her. To convince ourselves we could be just friends with her. But shutting each other out won't work either. Eating tacos or not eating tacos won't do the trick. It's up to us to play hard." I take a deep, fueling breath, then shrug in admission of this new truth. "And that's all we can do out there on the ice."

Denying my feelings won't make me play better.

Ignoring the ache in my heart won't make me a better teammate.

Eating the same meal every night won't make us win.

Putting my heart and soul into the game—that's what will make the difference. The only difference.

Rhys takes a moment, then nods somberly. "You're right."

"Of course I'm right," I say.

"We'll play like a team for us. And because she reminded us that we are," Hollis adds, a nod to our chats with Briar.

I'm glad we've cleared the air somewhat, but that's not all I wanted to say. We need to talk about her. Here. What's next, because I've missed her. I've missed her so damn much I feel hollow without her. *Here goes the hard part.* "She'll be here tonight. It's a big fucking deal."

"Yeah, because," Hollis says on a rough swallow, "I think...I'm a little in love with her."

Rhys snorts. "Try *a lot.*"

Hollis laughs. "Fucking showoff."

"I was saying you were *a lot* in love with her," Rhys corrects.

Clearing my throat I cut in, gesturing from Rhys to Hollis and back. "Pot. Kettle."

"Fine. *A lot,*" Hollis adds, like it was the easiest thing in the world to say.

Rhys blows out a breath, then shrugs in admission. "Yeah, me too. I'm in love with her too. *A lot.*"

I don't hide a smile this time. I can't hide it because I never expected this. I absolutely never thought *this* would happen. But if I've learned anything in my twenty-seven years on Earth, it's that life is what you make it, and you'd better make it everything you want. I offer a fist for knocking. "That makes three of us."

* * *

A little later we hit the ice, one by one. I race out first, my gaze swinging immediately to the seats on center ice.

There she is, wearing the cutest white knit cap I've ever seen, her long, blonde hair curling at the ends, and a plain black zip-up hoodie, along with a pink scarf. Too bad we couldn't send her a Golden State Foxes jersey, but her boss would flip if she wore one.

Briar's sitting next to her friends, Trina and Aubrey. We got tickets for them while Ivy works the game as the team's mascot, dressed up in her fox costume.

The three of us skate by Briar during warm-up drills, and she cheers for all of us together and each of us separately.

It's early in the first period and the crowd roars, their energy fueling me. Tension—and that hope for a win—crackles in the air, a palpable current that electrifies me.

Arizona's team is formidable. They're stacked up and down, but I've got something no one else in this rink of twenty thousand has—well except for two other guys.

I want it more.

I want it tonight.

I want it for her.

The puck zips across the ice, a blur of black amidst the swirling chaos of players. I zoom in on it, a rush of adrenaline charging through me as their forwards hoard it, passing it back and forth down the ice, chasing toward Dev in the net, but not on my watch. I'm there too, battling for the puck then...boom, I strip it from the Arizona player, spin away and sprint down the ice, flicking it quickly to Rhys.

In no time, he's flying toward their goal when a pack of D-men swarm him, so he slips the puck easily to Hollis, who sends it screaming into the net.

Just like that, the lamp lights and the crowd goes wild.

I turn to center ice. Briar's cheering us on, her voice echoing through the rink. It's not really echoing. Of course it's not. But I feel like I can hear only her.

When the game ends with a W, we all skate toward her without even planning it, like she's our North Star. She's what guides us. The three of us form a semi-circle in front of the glass where she is. She comes right up to us, glances around, checks to see who's watching, then satisfied it's safe, she unzips her hoodie, giving us—just us—a sneak peek.

Underneath, she was wearing a Foxes jersey after all.

There goes my last shred of resistance. I'm so far gone for this girl.

That's why we needed to win. We have her friendship, and now it's time to earn her heart.

62

THE SENTENCE FINISHERS

Hollis

Damn, I look good in a suit. "Check me out," I say to my reflection as I slide a hand down my teal-blue tie with fox illustrations on it. When in Rome, and all.

"How is there room for your ego and anyone else in this locker room?" Rhys deadpans as he walks past me.

"Wonders never cease," Gavin remarks from across the room.

"True. Being this handsome is a fucking miracle," I say, then spin around, ready to head out of the locker room when the captain calls out from in front of his stall.

"Bouchard. Do I need to fine you for being a cocky fucker?" It's Stefan, and he's knotting his tie too.

"Only if you fine yourself. I learned it from you," I toss back, then I give him a tip of the proverbial cap and head out with my friends, ready to put the game behind us and the night ahead of us.

Once we're alone in the hall, Gavin tugs us aside once more. "Here's the plan. We need to start a new streak."

I blink. That doesn't compute with what he said earlier.

Rhys tilts his head in question. "I thought you were over streaks. You gave a whole pre-game speech about tacos," Rhys says, like he's catching him on a technicality.

Gavin sighs. If a sigh could say *are you kidding me*, Gavin's does. "That was not a speech about tacos. You were missing the point."

"Right, right, tacos and love," Rhys says, making a rolling gesture for Gavin to speed it up.

"Which are sort of the same thing," I point out since I'm helpful like that.

"Fine. You got the point," Gavin grumbles, then quickly moves on. "What if the new streak is this—we can't just *tell her* we're in love with her. A few weeks ago, she got out of a terrible relationship with a jackass who tossed her stuff into garbage bags and tried to steal her pet and *did* steal her ideas. In Lucky Falls, we showed her what a great boyfriend does hypothetically. But now—"

"You beautiful bastard," I say, grabbing his shoulders. "You're right."

"I know," Gavin says dryly.

Rhys flicks his gaze from Gavin to me and back.

"What are you saying? That we show her what a great boyfriend does for real?"

I'm ready to do it now. Right now. "Let's show Briar what we can be for her," I say, unable to hold back a second longer.

For most of my career, I was sure romance would get in the way of my responsibilities to my family, to promises I made my mom to step up since my dad never did. Hell, Briar and I even bonded over this. She understood my fears in a way no one else ever has. But with these guys I've learned I don't have to shoulder all the work myself. I can lean on friends. Maybe, just maybe, I can lean on a partner too. And when you know what you want, it's fucking hard to wait. But we have to prove ourselves to Briar, so as much as I want to charge down the hall right now and scoop her up in my arms, I say, "Let's show her that we're not just trying to fuck her or touch her. That we can be her friends like we promised *and* that we can also love her."

"Like she deserves," Gavin adds, like a punctuation mark.

Rhys chuckles. "It's so bloody cute when you two finish each other's sentences." Then his expression grows solemn. "I'm in. And it starts with her dog."

63

SUPERFAN

Rhys

I've already logged one session with the sports psychologist. I'm not saying it cured my anxiety. I know I need many more, and I'm not sure I'll ever be *cured*.

I *want* many more.

But before I even walked in his door earlier this week and told him I play hockey like I'm afraid it'll be taken away, and that I want to play it like it's my favorite game, I realized that I was ready for a real romance with Briar.

I started to feel that certainty in Lucky Falls.

I was nearly sure of it when we peeled out of the driveway, leaving her behind.

And I knew it for good when I called her the other night and finally let her all the way in.

Now, we just need to show her.

It. Is. On.

Briar's hanging out down the corridor with Ivy, who's likely waiting for Hayes and Stefan to go home with them. When Briar spots us, she says something to her friend, then smiles and walks over. "Great game," she says, and for a second she leans in, like maybe she wants to kiss me, then Gavin, then Hollis.

She refrains.

I hold back, too, though it's hard. "I bet your dog needs a walk right now. How about we go with you?"

A smile spreads to her eyes, lighting them up. "She does. And I'd love that."

* * *

After she quickly runs up to her apartment to grab Donut we walk around her new neighborhood and she shows us all her haunts—the coffee shop she likes, the bookstore that hosts her book club, and the boutiques her friends frequent but she avoids like the plague since she's allergic to shopping, she says, as we pass one called Better with Pockets. "Thanks again for the ticket. That was really great. I'm not used to gifts...from *friends*." She says the last word with a lift in her brow and a tease in her tone.

Now is not yet the time to say *let's be so much more*, so instead I take the lead, saying, "Glad you could make it, and find something suitable to wear."

"Were you impressed with my secret superfan costume?" Briar asks as we turn onto her block.

"Yes, but it does raise the question of how far does the superfan costume go?" My hungry gaze drifts down her body. Fine, we're not trying to get her in bed...*yet*. But no one said I couldn't flirt with her. Loopholes and all.

Briar lifts a shoulder coyly as we head back to her building, Donut waggling her long, little body as she trots up the steps. "Hmm. Golden State Foxes panties. I have to be honest. I don't have a pair of those. But that'd be cute."

"That'd be hot," Gavin says.

"That'd be perfect," Hollis agrees.

"Well yeah," I rasp out.

This will be hard. But Gavin is right. We need to romance the hell out of her for real. Part of the way to her heart is through her pets. "Can we say hi to Frances Furbottom?" I ask.

"I thought you'd never ask," Briar says, then leads us into the building and to the elevator.

With the four of us in this small lift, it's tempting to take turns pinning her up against the wall and kissing the breath out of her. But I resist, and so do my friends. "Do you want to come to our next game? You're kind of a good luck charm," I say.

"You're really making it hard for me to keep up the narrative at work that I'm a Sea Dogs fan," she says.

"Imagine that," Gavin deadpans.

"So what'll it be, superfan?" Hollis asks.

"With you guys, it's a yes," Briar says.

I resist that undercurrent too.

We shift gears and chat briefly about the contest as we reach her floor. "Supposedly, the winner will be notified in a few more days."

"I bet it'll be you," I say.

"I hope so, but if not, I'll just keep moving forward with the app. It might take a little longer, but I don't mind," she says as she reaches her apartment and unlocks it.

Once the door's open, Briar unclips the dog, who races across the hardwood floor to retrieve a stuffed monkey toy in the corner of the room.

I step inside but stop in my tracks. Is this...really where she lives? It's an empty, echo-ey apartment with only an air mattress, a rickety card table, and a cold metal chair. This won't do for a friend, let alone the woman we're romancing.

This won't do at all.

But I hide my shock as we say hi to the cat, give her scratches on the chin, then tell Briar we'll see her at the next game.

When we leave, it takes all my willpower not to say a word till we get in the elevator. But once the doors snick shut, I point in the direction of her apartment and announce: "We have to do something about that right fucking away."

64

A LITTLE GIFT

Briar

The next morning as I'm taking an online Pilates class from Sandy Ho, one of my favorite instructors, my phone rings. I hit pause since it's the doorman. "There's someone here to see you. Her name is Charlotte Calloway."

I scrunch my brow. "I'm not expecting anyone by that name."

"She says that Rhys, Hollis, and Gavin sent her. As a gift for you."

That doesn't really clear things up either. "I'm intrigued but I still don't know who she is."

He chuckles. "She said to google her."

"Okay." I plug her name into the search engine.

Oh.

Oh.

Wow.

That's quite a gift. "Send her up."

A few minutes later, I open the door for the woman who looks just like her photo on her website—Charlotte Calloway Designs. A brunette in fashionable burgundy palazzo pants and a simple white sweater flashes me the warmest smile. A constellation of freckles crinkles across her nose. "I'm your new interior designer. I'm told you have no limits to the budget. Anything you want is yours. And to let you know that I can furnish this place as quickly as you want."

I'm a fish flapping its mouth open and closed. This is such a beautiful gift. I hate shopping so much, and I need furniture so badly, and I am so touched that they're giving me something I could never do for myself.

Something wonderful.

Something that makes me feel special.

But it's such a big gift. Sure, I truly appreciate them taking this whole we-stay-friends-on-the-other-side vow. I want to be certain, though, that I'm not just taking from them. "Hold on a second," I say, then turn around and grab my phone, quickly texting them.

> Briar: Guys! Seriously! This is huge. Are you sure? Like, truly sure? I know we promised to stay friends, but this is above and beyond.

> Rhys: What are friends for?

Briar: I've never had a friendship quite like this.

Hollis: Get used to it.

Briar: I don't want to just take things though. Even though this is amazing and so thoughtful.

Gavin: Take it, Briar.

I draw a deep inhale, and it feels like the biggest breath of fresh air. It feels like starting over. Like this is what it means to be seen. Listened to. Cared for. With my ex, I was his arm candy. He wasn't interested in the things I did or what made me who I am.

But with these three men, they see me. They truly see me for who I am, and they care not only about what I want, but what I need.

I turn back to Charlotte. "Where do we start?"

* * *

She's fast, well connected, and specializes in eco-design, which is important to me. She knows how to find pieces at consignment shops that are gently used or overstock from other stores. This means in three days, I have a couch, some throw pillows, a pretty white desk, and an actual bed.

Which my cat seriously enjoys.

I love this all so much that I pick up a small token of

my appreciation for them. A vintage edition of Candy Land. Before the next hockey game, I'm wrapping it for them when my phone brays. It's a local number—a familiar one, and it makes me freeze. A mix of terror and excitement courses through me all at once.

It's hard to contain my thrill at the hockey game that evening. Partly because they're winning. But partly because I kind of feel like I'm winning at life right now.

When the game ends with another victory for the Golden State Foxes, I'm that much closer to telling the guys the good news.

The call originated from Steven's office, but the caller was a woman named Zora, with a warm, husky voice. She said she ran the independent firm that handled the contest judging. *Of course* he did this too, hiring a woman-owned firm like I'd suggested. Not that I'm unhappy. I'm glad Zora got the gig since she said *Cracking the Case of the Missing O* was eye-opening and authentic, though I truly don't know if Steven has been informed that *Just A Girl* is his ex-girlfriend. Somehow I doubt it. If he knew it was me, he'd have nixed my prize.

I pace in the corridor after the game, waiting for the guys. When the three of them finally arrive, I practically vault into their arms, waggling my phone. "I won the contest!"

Hollis scoops me up first, wrapping me in a warm embrace that feels like home. I catch a whiff of his clean showery scent. It makes my head spin. Rhys is next, holding me like he doesn't want to let go. My skin tingles. Then Gavin embraces me, and his arms band around me, possessive, protective.

When they let go, I feel fizzy, frothy even. Like a bottle of champagne, bubbling over. I'm intoxicated by them. I don't know that I can last much longer just being friends. I don't know if they're ready for more than friendship though.

But I know this—I am. *Finally*. When I was with them in the cottage, I believed it was a mistake to get involved with three guys on the rival team.

That was what I needed to believe because I was afraid of being left again, not like Steven did, but like my mom did many years ago. I was afraid of not being enough for someone.

I'm not afraid anymore. I can handle whatever challenges the "rivalry" might bring because that's not the real issue. It was never the real issue. I was always strong. But I'm even stronger now that I know myself better.

There's another thing I know too—I *need* them by my side, however they'll have me. "There's a gala this weekend for the awards. I don't have a thing to wear. I have no clue if my ex will be there or not. I don't even know if they'll take away the prize when he figures out it's me. But I really want to go. I want everyone there to know what truly makes a great boyfriend. Do you want to come with me? As friends," I say quickly since I don't want them to be uncomfortable, but I want them with me. Desperately.

Rhys's lips twitch in a tease of a smile. "Yes."

Hollis nods solemnly. "Definitely."

Gavin says, "It's a plan."

I hand them the wrapped game of Candy Land. "Thank you," I tell them. "I couldn't have done it without you."

Without them, there'd be no boyfriend project. But without me, there'd be no piece. I told the story. I put it all together. I deserve the prize.

65

THAT'S IT

Rhys

Like hell are we settling for friendship.

66

PACKAGE PARADE

Briar

The next morning, the doorman buzzes me. "Package for you, Miss Delaney. It's from some fancy department store. Want me to send it up?"

"Yes," I say, and a minute later, Donut's trying to jump the door open when a building maintenance guy knocks on it.

I understand my dog so much right now. I'm bouncing with excitement as I yank open the door. "Thank you," I say, taking the box.

Once I shut the door, I undo the white satiny bow then carefully unfold the tissue to find a shimmery pink dress with a plunging neckline and a halter top tie. It's stunning, and I've never had anything like it before.

Gingerly, I pull it out, hold it up against me, and peer in the mirror. My heart gallops. "Wow."

I'm amazed at the dress but also the gift. The care in choosing it. The way I'm sure it'll fit. How they've once again solved a problem for me.

When I set down the dress in the box, I spot a card in the tissue paper. I open it. *Pink is your color.*

It's somehow sweet and filthy at the same time. Like three guys I know.

The next morning, the doorman rings. "Package for you."

Donut springs up and down at the door, and when I open it, the maintenance guy is handing me a silver box with a red bow. When I'm alone, I open it, shaking my head in amazement at the stunning pair of strappy silver shoes. There's a note too.

We won't be able to take our eyes off you.

My heart stutters. My mind races. And I see...my future. It's bright and unconventional, and entirely mine.

The next morning, I'm saying, "Send him up" as soon as I answer the call.

This time the package is a slim blue box, hardly bigger than my hand. When I open it, my breath catches. A silver necklace with what looks like a small diamond pendant at the throat sits elegantly in the soft tissue. They got me...a diamond?

This is too much. My fingers tremble as I open the note.

You deserve it.

I can barely breathe. I've never wanted a diamond before. But when I gently take it out, all the air rushes from my lungs. It's a diamond four-leaf clover. My throat tightens with beautiful emotions—ones I want to feel. Ones I never want to fake.

I clutch it to my chest, wanting not so much the diamond but what it stands for.

I'm not even sure how I'll make it through the rest of the day. All I want is tonight.

A few minutes later, the doorman buzzes one more time. One more time, Donut jumps at the door. One more time, I fling it open.

This time, the maintenance guy hands me only a card. I slide a finger under the flap, then read.

A limo will be here at seven to pick you up. See you at the gala...

Your three friends

* * *

I scratch Mrs. Frances Furbottom on the chin, kiss Donut on the snout, then fly out the door, down the hall, to the elevator, and out the lobby.

The gala is across the city at the Luxe Hotel. It should take twenty minutes in traffic to get there. Twenty minutes till I can see my guys, till I can tell them I want so much more than friendship, till I can ask if they'll take a chance on me.

I push through the doors and out into the San Francisco evening. The air is slightly chilly, but I have a black wrap around my shoulders to keep me warm enough as I drink in the lights and the glitter of the city. The shiny black limo glints from the curb even in the evening light.

I grin, shaking my head in amazement as I glance down at my pink shimmery dress, swishing against my legs.

I'm a leggings and ponytail gal, not a gown and glitter one. But tonight, Aubrey came over and styled my hair, twisting it up on the sides into a silvery barrette, curling it at the ends.

I'm used to fix-it cars, not stretch limos.

To air mattresses, not king-size beds.

To doing it all myself.

I near the limo, surprised the driver doesn't pop out and scurry around. I've seen enough movies to know that's kind of what they do. But when I reach for the handle, the door pushes open from the inside.

And out step my three men, dressed to the nines in tuxes.

67

KARMA IS THREE BOYFRIENDS

Briar

They don't look like my friends. They look like my men. "I don't want to go as friends," I blurt out.

Three pairs of eyes sparkle. Bright blue, deep brown, burnished hazel. Three mouths lift into smiles. Flirty, charming, daring. Three men step closer to me, their different scents catching in the night air, then wafting around me.

"Good," Hollis answers.

"We don't either," Rhys agrees.

"We want to take you as your boyfriends," Gavin says.

"Your real boyfriends," Hollis says.

"Not part of a project, not for a contest, not for a week," Rhys continues, and this romance Ping-Pong is making my heart spring wildly.

"For good," Gavin finishes.

There's a heady pause, full of crackling electricity as a breeze whips by, my skirt rustling around my ankles. I swallow past a gorgeous knot of emotions, then say, "I want to be your girlfriend."

Rhys lets out a long-held breath. "We want to be your boyfriends."

Hollis's bright blues glimmer with happiness. "We want you to be ours."

"Friends...and lovers," Gavin says, finishing as the hard lines of his mouth soften finally.

My heart is a roman candle, bursting with light and joy as I close the remaining distance between us and somehow throw my arms around all three of these big, strong hockey stars who have shown up for me over and over again. "You're mine," I whisper, my throat catching, my eyes shining, my emotions spilling over. "You're all mine."

For the longest time, I fervently believed romance was only for other people. I truly thought love would only hurt me. I thought my career was all I could depend on. But since the night they saved my cat, I've been learning slowly but surely that I can rely on people—the people who show up for me. These men who want only the best for me. Who let me be my best.

When I break the hug, I look from one to the other to the other. "I love you. All of you. All three of you."

Hollis reaches for my hand and threads his fingers through mine. "I love you so much, Briar."

Rhys cups one cheek. "I am madly in love with you."

Gavin slides a hand down my neck, over my shoulder. "I love you."

Their love professions are so very them, and with them I'm so very me.

We get in the car, and I spend the limo ride kissing my boyfriends. When we're a few blocks away, I shoo them off, then fix my lipstick and straighten my hair.

We arrive at the gala and head inside.

I am the one with the entourage—a queen with her court.

68

THE FAKE OUT

Rhys

Fifteen more minutes and the awards begin. Fifteen minutes till our woman takes the stage to receive the prize.

I'm going to cheer the loudest.

Right now, the four of us are standing at a high table in the corner of the ballroom, chatting, toasting, enjoying life, and just being together when my phone buzzes with a text. I thought I'd silenced it. Grabbing it from my pocket, I see it's the psychologist asking if Wednesday afternoon works for our next session.

Gavin shoots me an admonishing look. "Maybe turn that off."

He makes a good point. But this is also a good opportunity. I haven't told my friends yet. "I'm seeing a psychologist," I say. "He specializes in athletes. It's... helpful so far. I just need to confirm a time."

Chastened perhaps, Gavin's lips twitch in a curious grin. "Oh. My bad. And yeah, do it."

Hollis claps my shoulder. "Good for you, man."

I turn around, weave through the finely dressed crowds to the hall and tap out a reply when my attention snags on a man with perfectly gelled black hair, a straight nose, and a ticking jaw. I catch his profile, but his back is to me as he talks to a woman with box braids and leopard-print glasses at the end of the corridor. "What the hell kind of independent firm picks my fucking ex-girlfriend?"

I clench my fists, stopping a few feet away.

"An independent one," the woman repeats in a warm, husky voice, holding her own against a bully and a thief.

"You have to disqualify her, Zora," Steven seethes.

With a calm demeanor, she says, "There's nothing in the rules saying former girlfriends of the site's editor can't enter."

This guy. I'm not surprised. But there's no way I'm going to let him hurt her ever again. We stayed close to Briar during the cocktail hour, but my senses were on high alert as he glad-handed with advertisers. Now he's showing his true colors. A jack-in-the-box about to spring, Steven steps closer to Zora, lifts a finger.

Not on my watch.

I clear my throat. "Besides, you probably don't want to make a scene here at the event. Or let all your advertisers know that you stole her idea for the contest in the first place," I say pleasantly, laying on the British charm.

He wheels around and bites out, "Who the hell are you?"

One of her great boyfriends. But I don't tell him that. He'll find out soon enough. I don't even know if Briar has the receipts to prove the idea was hers. But I don't care. Sometimes on the ice, you have to fake out the opponent, make them think you have the puck when someone else does.

"A friend. But also an observer. And I can only imagine how terrible it'd look if everyone here knew you wanted to disqualify her after you stole her idea. That'd look a little bit bad," I say it sympathetically, but with zero sympathy.

His eyes turn to slits. Zora seems to fight off a smile.

Steven breathes fire before it dies on an angry, muttered, "Fine." He turns and walks the other way.

"This should be fun," she says when he's gone.

"I can't wait," I say, and after I hit send on the text to my shrink, I return to the ballroom.

When it's Briar's turn to receive the prize, Zora calls her onstage, looking a little like she has an ace up her sleeve. "Congratulations for an enlightening piece on what makes a great boyfriend. The ten-thousand-dollar prize goes to Briar Delaney." She slips a rolled-up sheet of paper from her sleeve. Well, I guess she did have something in her blouse. "And I'd like to invite her to read it to the crowd."

Briar walks to the stage, looking proud, looking deserving.

She takes the podium and surveys the crowd, her eyes finding us quickly. Then, she reads.

69

TOP TEN LIST

Cracking the Case of the Missing *O*—A Guide for the
Great Boyfriend
By Just A Girl

I used to fake it.

Orgasms, that is. I was a gold medalist in curling my toes, grabbing the sheets, and shouting *yes, yes, yes.*

Anything to make the man I was with feel like he'd gotten the job done.

Anything to hide the truth—I couldn't get there with someone else.

I thought there was something wrong with me. Maybe I wasn't trying hard enough. Maybe I wasn't relaxing. Maybe I wasn't good enough.

Then, I met a guy who listened to me. Like, really listened. Who could tell that I wasn't quite there. That I wasn't truly in the moment. And he challenged me, then asked me to show him what felt good.

I was reluctant at first. Saying yes to his offer to teach him made me vulnerable. But I did it anyway.

And I learned what makes a great boyfriend in and out of the bedroom.

1. A great boyfriend listens and shares. He shares his heart with you. His hurt. His vulnerability. He listens, too, when you share yours.

2. A great boyfriend plans a great date. But it's not just the date that he wants. He asks what you like. Whether it's mini golf, playing pool, going shopping, climbing a mountain, walking on the beach, or hanging out on the couch, he wants to know and then deliver it. Sometimes he brings a gift on the date, like a board game. Or maybe a special accessory. Every now and then, he'll bring a friend.

3. A great boyfriend will help you with your career. Sometimes that means listening when you've had a bad day. Sometimes it means holding your phone to shoot a video. Sometimes it means walking you to work.

4. A great boyfriend will take care of you when you're sick. Maybe you have the flu, a cold, or unexpected

motion sickness. He'll carry you home from the Tilt-A-Whirl, he'll pick up meds, he'll make you tea. He'll tuck you in. He'll cover you with a blanket and bring you your dog.

5. He'll walk your dog in the morning.

6. He'll save your cat when your ex tries to steal it.

7. A great boyfriend laughs with you. Often when you're wearing face masks together in a hot tub. Because... why not?

8. A great boyfriend makes a vow. Then, he keeps it.

9. And if he does all those things, he'll do other things too. He'll want to blow your mind in bed. He'll want to overwhelm you with pleasure. He'll want to adore, cherish, and worship you. But he won't assume he can do it. He'll ask you to teach him. To show him what feels good, what doesn't feel good. He'll ask if he has permission to tie you up, if you like to be kissed here, if you don't like to be kissed there, if you want more, less, harder, again.

.   .   .

10. Romance isn't just about what a great boyfriend does for you. You'll want to give to a great boyfriend as well. To plan a night, a special outing, or take him someplace he hasn't been before. You'll want to show him that romance isn't only something that a man needs to do for a woman. Romance is something a woman can do for her man.

Or, as the case may be, her *men*. Because the top ten things I learned from a great boyfriend?

Guess what? I learned them from three men. At the same time. Sometimes a girl needs more than one guy to crack the case of the missing *O*.

And I don't fake a damn thing in my heart, body, or mind with my three boyfriends.

THE BIG BANG

Briar

Later that night, we're at my place, playing Candy Land on my new couch. Dirty Candy Land, to be precise. We don't just take off clothes though. The guys devise a new set of rules. Each location is a place on my body.

When Gavin draws an orange square, entering Peppermint Stick Forest for the first time, he moves his gingerbread pawn, then leans across the coffee table and drops a hard, firm kiss to my lips.

I sigh into his mouth, grabbing his loosened bow tie, trying to pull him closer. But he lets go, sitting back in his chair, making me want more.

Hollis draws a card that sends him toward a mountain pass.

My back.

He shifts me slightly on the couch and slides down

the zipper on my dress, then kisses a hot path up my spine. I shiver.

When Rhys reaches Gumdrop Mountains, he takes over where Hollis left off. In his tux, he kneels in front of me and slips off both straps of the pink dress till the bodice gently tumbles down to my waist, revealing my strapless bra. He unhooks it and draws one hard nipple into his mouth.

I gasp, wriggling against his possessive touch. He moves to the other breast, flicking that nipple too.

When it's my turn, I move my piece to the rainbow trail, and I get to pick the location.

My arm.

An unexpected place where I love to be touched by them. "All of you," I say since it's my turn, my party.

Hollis runs his fingers softly toward my wrist, pressing a kiss there. Rhys drops his lips to the crook of my elbow, lingering for several seconds. Gavin kisses his way down my entire arm.

We go around like that...till someone lands on the Gingerbread Plum Tree.

Thighs.

I stand and they circle me, the three of them skimming my dress off all the way, then roaming their hands down my legs.

Lollipop Woods is next.

"On your stomach," Hollis instructs, and I lie flat on my belly on the couch. Hollis straddles me, then tugs down my panties, exposing my ass.

Three men draw sharp breaths. Three pairs of eyes laser in on my cheeks. Three guys breathe out rough and hard. Hollis drops a kiss to the top of my ass.

A promise.

I flip over, wearing nothing but my heels.

Ice Cream Floats is where they all want to be. Gavin lands there first.

"I'll take this one lying down," he says, then moves me so he can flop onto his back on the couch. He pats his chest.

I climb up him and sit on his face, my silver heels framing his ears. He flicks his tongue down my hot, wet center. In no time, I'm moaning, grabbing the arm of the couch behind him and rocking against his face till it's Hollis's turn.

With a rumble and obvious reluctance, Gavin moves me off him, shifting me to sit on his lap. "Want me to spread her legs for you?" he asks Hollis.

"Yes, nice and wide so I can taste that sweet pussy," Hollis answers, then drops to the floor, his white dress shirt half undone as he slides his palms along my calf muscles.

Gavin reaches for my inner thighs, parting them wider for his teammate.

"So helpful." With a rumble, Hollis buries his face between my thighs, drawing my clit into his mouth, licking, kissing, loving.

I curl my hands into his messy hair, rocking into his face as I rest my neck against Gavin's shoulder, turning to kiss him while Hollis kisses my pussy.

Then it's Rhys's turn.

But he must be done with the couch since he stalks

to me and hauls me up and over his shoulder. As he carries me to the bedroom, he smacks my ass along the way, making me yelp and smile too.

In the doorway, he stops in his tracks. The others are right behind us. "You have an Alaskan king," he remarks, clearly admiring the bed I picked.

"Just friends, huh?" Hollis teases.

"I was manifesting," I say, faux primly.

"Manifest this," Rhys says, then drops me onto the mattress, spreads me out, and settles between my thighs, kissing me till I'm begging, grasping, demanding.

Till Hollis is sucking on my nipples.

Till Gavin sweeps his lips to mine in a rough, bruising kiss that makes me light up everywhere.

Or maybe it's Hollis who makes me shiver.

It could be Rhys.

A delicious pressure builds in my belly, low and intense. Next, sparks zip along my skin, hot and bright. Then they leap as I let go and fall into bliss, crying out as an orgasm crashes over me, unbidden. It's a wave that carries me under, then lifts me up.

When I push to my elbows, there's no question that now is the time. "Put me on my hands and knees. Get me ready."

They know. We've talked about this type of sex. I've told them what I want, how my nightstand filled with toys includes special ones with flared bases. We've all been tested and we're all negative, so we're done with condoms. I'm on birth control too.

Rhys flips me to all fours, slides a hand down my

back while Hollis grabs a vibrator and lubes it up. He stands behind me, pressing his fingers first to my ass, then the vibrator as Gavin strokes my hair, my cheeks, my neck.

Rhys comes to my side, then maneuvers a hand under my belly to my center, using another vibrator to tease my clit. It's like my birthday and Christmas all at once. Hollis opens me up, pressing the toy into my ass while Rhys works me over, stroking my clit.

Gavin's in front of me on the bed, playing with my hair.

They're hitting me everywhere, and I'm shaking and moaning as my three hockey stars in half-opened tuxes prep me.

Soon, I'm dropping my head, arching my hips, and begging. Just begging. "Please fuck me. All of you. *Now*."

Hollis turns off the toy, slips it out. Rhys slows the pressure, stops the vibrator. Gavin cups my cheek. "Say stop if it gets to be too much."

"I will," I assure them, but I'm on edge already, my skin tingling, my body vibrating. "Just get naked."

A minute later, we've tangoed around the big bed. They set a hand towel on the covers with lube next to it. My shoes are off at last. "Lie down, Hollis," I say.

The easygoing man obliges with a dirty smile, offering me his strong body. I straddle him but don't sink over him yet.

"Gavin, behind me," I command.

My broody guy moves into position, standing at the end of the bed, palming my ass. Rhys tosses him the lube. With a click and a drizzle, Gavin's teasing my hole open with his thumb.

It feels so forbidden and so good. A blast of heat roars through my body as he presses into me.

Then Rhys—my possessive and adoring one— kneels by my face, fondling my breasts. "You're so fucking pretty like this, my love. So fucking beautiful, taking all of us," he says, running his fingers along my jawline. "You want all three of us to fuck you now?"

Is this my life? Yes, yes it is. As a hot charge rushes down my spine, I say, "I do, right now."

Rhys's eyes go from passionate to powerful. "Then sit on my friend's dick," he orders, tipping his forehead to Hollis, who's stroking his shaft lazily under me, just taking his time.

Gavin coasts his thumb out of my ass as I move onto Hollis. I'm so wet it's easy to sink down. Hollis curls his big hands around my hips and my breath stutters. Sparks fly through me.

"Ride him for a minute," Rhys tells me. He's the director, and I'm so grateful. "Brush those tits against his chest."

I lie closer to Hollis. He sweeps my hair from my face. "Hi there," he whispers, vulnerable, loving.

"Hey, you."

"You like this? Fucking your men?"

"I love it," I say on a breathless pant.

Hollis grabs my face, kisses me as Gavin does something behind me. Then Gavin says, "You want to lift that ass a little higher, sweetheart?"

I obey, breaking the kiss to watch Gavin push

another finger into me. I clench but breathe through it as he opens me up.

Heat flashes through me, up my chest, along my neck. "I'm ready," I tell him.

Gavin pushes into me. Inch by inch.

"Breathe, love," Rhys tells me, and I listen.

A deep breath, and wow, it goes a long way. I can feel myself relax more. *Accept* Gavin into my body, like I've taken toys.

"Want more?" Gavin asks.

"Yes," I gasp, and he takes his time again, letting me adjust to the new sensations of this kind of sex.

Soon, I'm stretched so full, so deeply, I'm not sure what to do next. I freeze, and it feels like the past, like all the times my body has failed me.

But Rhys reminds me again, saying gently, "Breathe, love."

One deep breath, then two. Then, I rock up and down on Hollis, tilting forward as Gavin eases in and out of my ass.

I can't say all my stretching prepared me for *this* position.

The fullness of it.

This pressure from it.

But in some ways, all those poses have helped. I can move between them. I can brace myself on my palms. And I can arch the hell out of my back as I take my men to the ends of me.

My muscles shake as I turn to Rhys. He's kneeling on the bed next to us, stroking his cock, his eyes dark. "I want your dick," I say.

"You don't have to," he says.

"I want to." I part my lips. He feeds me his cock. My lips stretch and it's sloppy, this blow job. It's artless as I suck Rhys while I'm sandwiched between Hollis and Gavin. I can't move much, but I don't have to, it turns out.

Gavin sets the pace, passionately and with so much care, Hollis's hands grip me hard, holding me tight, and Rhys always, *always* looks out for me.

These are my guys. This is how they take care of me. This is how they love me.

I won't do this every night. Or even every week. But tonight, this is where I want to be—the center of their world as they fill me in every way, making me shiver, making me tremble, making me shudder. I'm like a bottle of soda, all shook up, fireworks shooting inside me. Sensations flying through me.

I'm close—so close I can't hold onto Rhys anymore. I push him out of my mouth, slam back onto Hollis's dick and then shudder. My orgasm is a bolt of lightning, crashing from the sky, bright and strong, lighting me up.

Then, it scrambles all my circuits. Everything's a hot, electrifying blur as I cry out.

When my brain comes back online, Rhys is stroking his cock and I offer my tongue for him, eager to take his release.

With a hard thrust, he comes on my tongue and I swallow his climax. Hollis groans as he pumps into me then stills. Gavin shudders and squeezes my ass, filling me.

And I breathe, taking them.

That was both the hardest thing I've ever done in bed, and the easiest.

It's also definitely the thing that made me the happiest.

Especially when later, I fall into this bed that I manifested for my family.

The three boyfriends who tell me they love me, and the little friends who curl up on my head and by my heart.

EPILOGUE

MY BENDY MEN AND ME

Briar

On Monday, I knock on Nova's door at the Sea Dogs arena. But it's open and she's at her desk, waving me in, twirling a gold pen in her hand. "Did you have a good weekend?" she asks.

It's a normal Monday morning workplace question from a boss and one that's easy enough to answer. "It was great," I say, and that's a perfect segue to *why* I'm here. "And there's something I need to discuss with you."

She sets down her pen, tilting her head. "Sure. What is it?"

There's no easy way to say this, so I opt for direct. "I'm involved with..." I take a beat because what I'm about to say is a lot even in this city. Even with these teams. Even in this hockey world. "With three of the Golden State Foxes."

Her expression is blank for a long beat, then her brow creases. "You...are?"

I rarely see her rattled. She's definitely rattled.

My heart skitters. "Yes. My boyfriends are on the team. Hollis Bouchard, Gavin Worthy, and Rhys Corbyn."

She blinks. "Okay."

I square my shoulders. "And I understand they're rivals and you might want me to resign."

She barks out a laugh. "What?"

"Well, they play for our cross-town rivals."

Another laugh falls from her lips. "What, are you going to give them our yoga playbook?"

It's my turn to laugh. "No. I won't."

But her expression shifts to a deadly serious one. "I mean that, Briar. You have a contract. You're ours. We need you here. Don't share those classes you developed for us with them."

That's what she's worried about? That I'd share stretching secrets? My shoulders relax. "I won't."

"Good. Now let's talk about the stress-relief class."

And that's that.

* * *

A month later, I'm in my regular seat at center ice for a special game, with Trina and Aubrey flanking me as we wait for the start.

"Show me," Trina demands, beckoning with her fingers. "I want to see it in action."

With pride bursting through my chest, I grab my

phone, swipe on the home screen, and click on the photo of me in tree pose. I click on Flow and Flex and the app opens seamlessly.

I give a silent thanks to Griffin's engineering skills.

"Look at you," Aubrey praises as she leans in close, checking out all the videos, tutorials, classes, and series.

I give them a quick tour of the app, showing off years of my work.

"How many videos are here?" Aubrey asks.

"More than four hundred," I say.

Trina whistles. "Damn. That's a lot."

"I've worked hard."

"You sure have," Trina says, then she grabs her phone and waggles it at me, showing that she's downloaded the app already. "There's another subscription for you."

I throw my arms around her, hugging her.

"I've got mine too," Aubrey seconds.

"And so do the book club girls," Trina adds, then stage-whispers, "And we're loving the better sex videos."

I grin, quite pleased. I added that series recently, starting with Sex is a Plank, then adding Men Need to Be Bendy Too, Keep Lower Back Pain from Limiting Your Kama Sutra Options, Stretch Your Girl's Cramp Out and Be Her Hero, and more.

They've been some of the most watched videos during the first week of launch. The downloads for the app are ticking along, thanks in part to the marketing I've been able to do with my prize money.

There's nothing quite like a little sweet revenge in the form of ten thousand dollars.

But the best revenge? Living well, and I've got that down to an art form.

When the Golden State Foxes skate onto the ice I turn all my attention to the game, living my best life as my men take on their cross-town rivals—the Sea Dogs.

When the game ends with a Sea Dogs victory, I wait with Trina and Aubrey in the corridor for my three boyfriends, chatting about book club. Wesley strolls by, stopping to say hello. "I hope you rooted for the good guys tonight, B," he says.

"Of course I did," I say, admitting nothing about my allegiances. I love my job and I love my guys.

"Glad to hear," the outgoing guy says, then checks his watch. "I better get some sleep. I have my charcuterie board class first thing tomorrow."

"You take a charcuterie board class?" Trina asks.

"Mine are top tier," he says with obvious pride, but then his voice trails off at the end as his attention snags on a man and a woman at the end of the corridor.

The guy is Christian, the Sea Dogs team captain. But I don't know who the woman is. Wesley can't seem to take his eyes off her though. She's a pretty brunette with cat-eye glasses and lush hair twisted up in a bun. "Who's the team captain talking to?" he asks, a little mesmerized. He watches her with avid eyes, enrapt from all the way at the end of the hall.

"No idea," I say.

Wesley walks toward them, away from us.

Trina leans in and whispers to me. "That's Josie. Christian's sister."

I arch a brow her way. "The new guy and the captain's sister. That should be interesting."

"Especially since he's made it pretty clear she's off-limits."

And Christian ushers his sister away before Wesley can even meet her.

"Maybe next time he'll have better luck," I laugh.

But whether that's meeting her or resisting her is anyone's guess.

Later, when I head home with my guys, I put Wesley's burgeoning crush, the game, and the app behind us. "I have a surprise for you," I say when we're in the elevator in my building.

"What is it?" Hollis asks, eyes sparking.

"If I tell you it won't be a surprise," I chide.

"Tell us anyway," Rhys says.

Gavin chuckles. "Have some patience, guys."

"Not all of us can be you," Hollis points out.

Once we leash up Donut and take her for a walk, we return to my home—which is nearly theirs—and I tell the dog to go to the couch. Like a good girl, she obeys.

Then, I bring the guys to the bedroom. I tell them to sit on the edge of the bed. I do a little striptease down to my panties.

"Holy fuck," they mutter in unison.

"I'm your superfan," I say, gesturing to the custom-made pair with a fox on them. Just like I promised. "Now, who wants to take them off first?"

Three arms shoot into the air. "I guess you'll just have to share me."

And they do. They share me so well.

* * *

When the season ends with stellar stats for all my men, we hop in Hollis's car and head to Lucky Falls. We rented a certain cottage for the weekend. But first we stop at a café in Petaluma for lunch with my dad.

And his special someone.

Clara.

He's been seeing her for a few months now. We head up the steps of the café, then go inside. The guys straighten their shoulders, smooth out their shirts, neaten their hair. They've had a few meals with my dad. They're scared of him but in a good way. He's a stern, gruff dad after all, who looks out for his daughter.

He was shocked at first when I told him about my boyfriends, but he loves me, and he's come to accept my unconventional romance.

Once we reach the table, Clara beams, smiling at all of us. "Knew it. Called it. I love being right."

My dad rolls his eyes, then pats her hand. I give him a bag of his favorite gummi bears. "Thanks, kiddo," he says as he stands, then brings me in for a hug.

When he lets go, he nods hello to the guys. "Good to see you, Hollis, Rhys, Gavin."

He sits and nods toward Rhys first. "Hear you're sticking around."

My British boyfriend breathes a big sigh of relief. "I am. Signed the contract yesterday."

I grab his arm and squeeze it, still giddy that he's staying put. Amira pulled it off but Rhys did the real work in therapy, learning to manage his expectations and his anxiety. I'm most proud of him for that. "I'm so happy you're staying."

Rhys dusts a quick kiss to my forehead. "Me too."

My dad clears his throat. "If it makes my daughter happy, it makes me happy."

We have lunch, and it doesn't really matter that my dad is my only parent. He loves me as I am. He takes me as I am. He respects my choices. And he makes the effort with my boyfriends.

"Are the twins ready for the college app season coming up?" he asks Hollis.

"They're a little obsessed with it," he says.

"Not a bad thing to be obsessed with," Dad says, then turns to Gavin, "And I hear you took up video editing?"

"Yes, sir," he says. "So I can help Briar."

"Good. That's good."

"And we just invested in a new apartment complex in Darling Springs, not too far away," Rhys says, always somehow knowing what my dad wants to hear. "There's a secure future in real estate for us when we're too old to chase a puck around the ice anymore."

"In a long time from now." I squeeze his leg, but he looks back at me with a smile and worry-free eyes.

When we're done, Clara fixes me with a no-nonsense stare. "You gonna do your review this summer, missy?"

I smile, wide and bright. "Sure am. I'll have company though."

She lifts a brow. "That so?"

"I convinced the guys to learn to fly a balloon."

That summer, we all go up together again and soar over the place where we fell in love.

That's how we do most things. Together. As a family and as friends.

My three real boyfriends and me.

Stay tuned for Wesley and Josie's romance in *The Boyfriend Goal* coming this summer! That spicy, forbidden, roomies-to-lovers romance between the new guy and the team captain's little sister is book one in Love and Hockey — an all-new hockey rom com series I can't wait to launch! The Boyfriend Goal is coming FREE TO KU!

Do you want more from Briar and her men right now? Keep flipping for an extended epilogue of their life together, but first be sure to find out how this series began in Trina's romance with Chase and Ryker in Double Pucked, FREE IN KU! Then binge the series!
Double Pucked

A sexy, outrageous MFM hockey romantic comedy!
Puck Yes
A fake marriage, spicy MFM hockey rom com!
Thoroughly Pucked!
A brother's best friends +runaway bride, spicy MFM
hockey rom com!

* * *

**Click here for the The Well and Truly Pucked Bonus
Epilogue! Or scan the QR code!**

BE A LOVELY

Want to be the first to know of sales, new releases, special deals and giveaways? Sign up for my newsletter today!

Want to be part of a fun, feel-good place to talk about books and romance, and get sneak peeks of covers and advance copies of my books? Be a Lovely!

ACKNOWLEDGMENTS

Thank you to Sharon Abreau, AKA the hockey goddess. Sharon is a life long hockey fan and she has guided me through this whole series.

Thank you to Lo Morales and Rae Douglas for their insight. To Kim Bias, Lauren Clarke, Kara Hildebrand, Sandra Shipman, Claudia Fosca, and Virginia Carey for their eyes and guidance.

Donut's likeness is Clarice, the rescue dachshund of reader Jean Siska. What a model!

Big gratitude to my writer friends Lili Valente, Melanie Harlow, Laurelin Paige, Corinne Michaels, Laura Pavlov, Natasha Madison, K Loraine, CD Reiss, K Bromberg, and Meghan Quinn.

I am indebted to KP Simmon for her tireless support and early reading and feedback. Most of all thank you to my family for their support, to my husband who supported all my wild ideas for this book, and to my dogs for their big, big, big, furry love.

But last and certainly not least, I'm always grateful for YOU. The readers. Thank you.

MORE BOOKS BY LAUREN

I've written more than 100 books! **All of these titles below are FREE in Kindle Unlimited!**

Double Pucked

A sexy, outrageous MFM hockey romantic comedy!

Puck Yes

A fake marriage, spicy MFM hockey rom com!

Thoroughly Pucked!

A brother's best friends +runaway bride, spicy MFM hockey rom com!

Well and Truly Pucked

A friends-to-lovers forced proximity why-choose hockey rom com!

The Virgin Society Series

Meet the Virgin Society – great friends who'd do anything for each other. Indulge in these forbidden, emotionally-charged, and wildly sexy age-gap romances!

The RSVP

The Tryst

The Tease

The Dating Games Series

A fun, sexy romantic comedy series about friends in the city and their dating mishaps!

The Virgin Next Door

Two A Day

The Good Guy Challenge

How To Date Series (New and ongoing)

Friends who are like family. Chances to learn how to date again. Standalone romantic comedies full of love, sex and meet-cute shenanigans.

My So-Called Sex Life

Plays Well With Others

The Almost Romantic

Juliet's And Monroe's Romance (coming in June 2024)

Wilder's and Fable's Romance (November 2024)

A romantic comedy adventure standalone

A Real Good Bad Thing

Boyfriend Material

Four fabulous heroines. Four outrageous proposals. Four chances at love in this sexy rom-com series!

Asking For a Friend

Sex and Other Shiny Objects

One Night Stand-In

Overnight Service

Big Rock Series

My #1 New York Times Bestselling sexy as sin, irreverent, male-POV romantic comedy!

Big Rock

Mister O

Well Hung

Full Package

Joy Ride

Hard Wood

Happy Endings Series

Romance starts with a bang in this series of standalones following a group of friends seeking and avoiding love!

Come Again

Shut Up and Kiss Me

Kismet

My Single-Versary

Ballers And Babes

Sexy sports romance standalones guaranteed to make you hot!

Most Valuable Playboy

Most Likely to Score

A Wild Card Kiss

Rules of Love Series

Athlete, virgins and weddings!

The Virgin Rule Book

The Virgin Game Plan

The Virgin Replay

The Virgin Scorecard

The Extravagant Series

Bodyguards, billionaires and hoteliers in this sexy, high-stakes series of standalones!

One Night Only

One Exquisite Touch

My One-Week Husband

The Guys Who Got Away Series

Friends in New York City and California fall in love in this fun and hot rom-com series!

Birthday Suit

Dear Sexy Ex-Boyfriend

The What If Guy

Thanks for Last Night

The Dream Guy Next Door

Always Satisfied Series

A group of friends in New York City find love and laughter in this series of sexy standalones!

Satisfaction Guaranteed

Never Have I Ever

Instant Gratification

PS It's Always Been You

The Gift Series

An after dark series of standalones! Explore your fantasies!

The Engagement Gift

The Virgin Gift

The Decadent Gift

The Heartbreakers Series

Three brothers. Three rockers. Three standalone sexy romantic comedies.

Once Upon a Real Good Time

Once Upon a Sure Thing

Once Upon a Wild Fling

Sinful Men

A high-stakes, high-octane, sexy-as-sin romantic suspense series!

My Sinful Nights

My Sinful Desire

My Sinful Longing

My Sinful Love

My Sinful Temptation

From Paris With Love

Swoony, sweeping romances set in Paris!

Wanderlust

Part-Time Lover

One Love Series

A group of friends in New York falls in love one by one in this
sexy rom-com series!

The Sexy One

The Hot One

The Knocked Up Plan

Come As You Are

Lucky In Love Series

A small town romance full of heat and blue collar heroes and
sexy heroines!

Best Laid Plans

The Feel Good Factor

Nobody Does It Better

Unzipped

No Regrets

An angsty, sexy, emotional, new adult trilogy about one young
couple fighting to break free of their pasts!

The Start of Us

The Thrill of It

Every Second With You

The Caught Up in Love Series

A group of friends finds love!

The Pretending Plot

The Dating Proposal

The Second Chance Plan

The Private Rehearsal

Seductive Nights Series

A high heat series full of danger and spice!

Night After Night

After This Night

One More Night

A Wildly Seductive Night

Joy Delivered Duet

A high-heat, wickedly sexy series of standalones that will set your sheets on fire!

Nights With Him

Forbidden Nights

Unbreak My Heart

A standalone second chance emotional roller coaster of a romance

The Muse

A magical realism romance set in Paris

Good Love Series of sexy rom-coms co-written with Lili Valente!

I also write MM romance under the name L. Blakely!

Hopelessly Bromantic Duet (MM)

Roomies to lovers to enemies to fake boyfriends

Hopelessly Bromantic

Here Comes My Man

Men of Summer Series (MM)

Two baseball players on the same team fall in love in a forbidden romance spanning five epic years

Scoring With Him

Winning With Him

All In With Him

MM Standalone Novels

A Guy Walks Into My Bar

The Bromance Zone

One Time Only

The Best Men (Co-written with Sarina Bowen)

Winner Takes All Series (MM)

A series of emotionally-charged and irresistibly sexy standalone MM sports romances!

The Boyfriend Comeback

Turn Me On

A Very Filthy Game

Limited Edition Husband

Manhandled

If you want a personalized recommendation, email me at
laurenblakelybooks@gmail.com!